"Come on." Max took hold of Laurel's arm.

She resisted. "Where are we going?"

He indicated the ice cream shop. "Sweet Dreams is my daughters' favorite place. No better way to spend fifteen minutes waiting for the accident to clear."

"I haven't had ice cream in years."

"That's practically illegal," Max said, noting less hesitancy in her step. "A person is required by law to have ice cream no less than once a month."

She stared one last time at the intersection where more first responders were arriving. "Can we sit outside? That way I can watch for when traffic clears."

"We can sit anywhere you want. And, for the record, I'm glad you said yes. I was afraid for a second there I'd be forced to make a citizen's arrest."

They strolled toward Sweet Dreams, Max questioning his judgment. This likely wouldn't—and couldn't—lead anywhere. But he wanted to get to know her better.

Dear Reader,

I'm so excited for the release of *Her Surprise Cowboy Groom*, and also a little sad. This book is my personal favorite in the Wishing Well Springs series. I loved Laurel and Max and his adorable twin daughters right from the start—not to mention their troublesome but loveable dog, Jelly Belly. I had such fun researching fashion designing, particularly wedding dress designing, and glamping campgrounds. Laurel and Max face some difficult obstacles. Getting them to their happily-ever-after was a challenge and very satisfying.

I'm a little sad because this is the last book in the series. I've had a great time creating Wishing Well Springs' wedding venue and Bellissima, Laurel's wedding dress–designing business. While I hate saying goodbye to this charming setting and the characters who inhabit it, I'm excited about the next project.

Warmest wishes,

Cathy McDavid

PS: I love connecting with readers. You can find me at:

CathyMcDavid.com

Facebook.com/CathyMcDavidBooks

Twitter: @CathyMcDavid

TikTok: @CathyMcDavid

HEARTWARMING

Her Surprise Cowboy Groom

—

Cathy McDavid

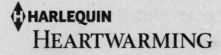

HARLEQUIN®
HEARTWARMING™

ISBN-13: 978-1-335-58494-6

Her Surprise Cowboy Groom

Copyright © 2023 by Cathy McDavid

Recycling programs for this product may not exist in your area.

For questions and comments about the quality of this book, please contact us at CustomerService@Harlequin.com.

Harlequin Enterprises ULC
22 Adelaide St. West, 41st Floor
Toronto, Ontario M5H 4E3, Canada
www.Harlequin.com

Printed in U.S.A.

Since 2006, *New York Times* bestselling author **Cathy McDavid** has been happily penning contemporary Westerns for Harlequin. Every day, she gets to write about handsome cowboys riding the range or busting a bronc. It's a tough job, but she's willing to make the sacrifice. Cathy shares her Arizona home with her own real-life sweetheart and a trio of odd pets. Her grown twins have left to embark on lives of their own, and she couldn't be prouder of their accomplishments.

Books by Cathy McDavid

Harlequin Heartwarming

Wishing Well Springs

The Cowboy's Holiday Bride
How to Marry a Cowboy
A Secret Christmas Wish

The Sweetheart Ranch

A Cowboy's Christmas Proposal
The Cowboy's Perfect Match
The Cowboy's Christmas Baby
Her Cowboy Sweetheart

Visit the Author Profile page
at Harlequin.com for more titles.

To Tina Wheeler, my old friend, my VOS board cohort, my valuable critique partner, my write-in buddy and my new Love Inspired Suspense sister. I'm so glad to have been on this wonderful writing journey with you for all these years. Here's to many more.

CHAPTER ONE

IF WEDDING DRESSES had personalities, this one would be a stubborn toddler in the throes of a power struggle.

Laurel Montgomery released a frustrated groan, stepped away from the current bane of her existence and scrubbed her cheeks with both hands. Despite her unrelenting efforts for the past ten minutes, the strip of delicate lace refused to lie flat and insisted on puckering. Puckering! This was the problem of a first-year fashion student, not a successful wedding dress designer with her own business.

"Might as well surrender," she told the dress. Hands on hips, she glared at the voluminous white gown, looking all harmless and innocent from where it hung on the dress form in what Laurel called the stitch-and-fix section of her shop, Bellissima. "You will not defeat me."

The strip of lace had the audacity to crinkle in the middle.

Laurel sighed. Perhaps a break was in order.

She'd been hard at it since the crack of dawn and would be hard at it until well into the evening.

In a mere two days, June would be upon them. The busiest month of the year for Wishing Well Springs, the wedding barn and miniature Western town Laurel and her brother, Cash, co-owned. As of this morning, thirty-six weddings were on the schedule. Yes, that meant doubling up some days. There were sunrise ceremonies, sunset ceremonies and even a midnight candlelight ceremony. And everything in between.

A few slots remained open for small, intimate weddings with only the couple and their closest acquaintances. Phoebe Montgomery, Wishing Well Springs's wedding coordinator and Laurel's new sister-in-law, would do her best to accommodate every request.

And Laurel would, too. Which explained why she and Phoebe were also best friends since childhood. Both were overachievers.

She studied the long rack of carefully separated garment bags and silently counted. Seventeen—the number of dresses in all shapes, styles and colors Laurel was responsible for, including four matching bridesmaid outfits and one mother of the bride ensemble.

Not to mention the flower girl dresses. Laurel had yet to meet the pair of sisters slated for those. Their mom had ordered their dresses from Laurel's own ready-to-wear line featured on Bellissima's website and scheduled a fitting for next week.

To be honest, that particular wedding occurring at month's end was the least of Laurel's concerns. She had higher priority orders taking precedence.

Besides designing and sewing original creations, she altered, updated and repurposed previously worn gowns. And if she didn't get this stupid strip of lace to lie flat, she'd never accomplish everything on her massive to-do list.

What she needed was a new assistant. Laurel been left high and dry last week when her previous assistant quit with almost no notice. Seemed she'd landed a job in New York City. Yeah, yeah. The very center of the fashion industry.

Laurel had once held the same dream to work in New York. She couldn't be angry with her assistant for accepting the amazing opportunity. Except she'd been left shorthanded, understaffed and with no free time to recruit someone new.

A change of scenery was in order, she decided. With a clear head and lower blood pressure, she'd be able to tame that rebellious piece of lace into submission. Besides, she needed to chat with her brother about their first June wedding on Friday, rumored to have a VIP guest in attendance. The bride and her attendants were being driven to the barn in a carriage—a service provided by Wishing Well Springs at an additional cost for couples wanting the full cowboy and Western experience.

Only they were waiting on the substitute driver to make his appearance—their regular driver was on an extended out-of-the-country trip for, of all things, a wedding.

There were details to discuss with the new driver and a test run from the house to the barn to conduct. A schedule to review. The bride's grand entrance on Friday depended entirely on this stranger Cash had unearthed from who knew where to drive the carriage.

Grabbing her phone and keys off the shelf, Laurel navigated a winding path through Bellissima toward the propped open double doors. She passed the changing rooms and the viewing area with its seating nook for family and friends, and the many dresses on display. Locking the door behind her, she crossed the main lobby separating Bellissima from the business offices. Her sensible yet stylish heels echoed on the converted ranch house's hardwood floors.

"I'm heading over to talk to Cash," she called to Phoebe, visible through the entrance to the business offices. "Be back shortly."

Phoebe waved from her desk, a phone glued to her ear.

At the front door, Laurel paused to consider the merits of a hat. Which was worse, flat hair or windblown hair? She smoothed her chin-length locks. The wind would strip every molecule of styling product she'd meticulously applied this morning and leave her looking like she'd just rolled out of bed. Flat hair would merely require a comb and fluff on her return.

Selecting a floppy straw bonnet off the coatrack by the door, she stuck the ugly old thing on her head and adjusted the chin strap. It was a sight but would serve the purpose. Satisfied, she continued outside to the sprawling porch. At the bottom of the steps, she hopped into one of the two golf carts parked alongside the manicured circular driveway. The barn and miniature Western town, located a quarter mile up the road, were too far to walk to in heels, sensible or not.

Sliding in behind the steering wheel, she started the engine. Electric rather than gas, the golf cart hummed quietly as she traveled the winding dirt road. As frequently happened on her jaunts around the property, bits and pieces of the past tickled the corners of her memory.

Many, many years ago, her grandparents had owned the largest horse ranch in the area, employing both of Laurel's parents. An unexpected economic downturn hit the Montgomerys smack in the piggy bank. Then, her grandmother developed terminal cancer. Neither Laurel's parents nor grandparents had been equipped to handle two back-to-back catastrophes.

At the tender age of fourteen, Laurel's entire life changed when, two years after losing her beloved grandmother, her parents filed for bankruptcy. Not long after that, her father moved out of state when he and Laurel's mom divorced. Acre by acre, her grandfather had sold off the ranch until all that remained was the main house, stables and the barn, which fell into disrepair through years of neglect.

Converting their rundown inheritance into a wedding venue had been Laurel's brainchild. She and her brother, Cash, joined forces, and in three years' time they went from a crazy idea to one of Payson, Arizona's most prominent businesses.

Never again would she and Cash scrape by like when they were teenagers. Never again would they bear the brunt of mean-spirited gossip. Never again would they be helpless victims at the mercy of others. Granted, Laurel was guilty of working too hard. But she was also prepared for the unexpected blows fate regularly dealt.

Approaching the last hill, she pressed down on the pedal and powered the golf cart up the steep incline. Near the top, the wedding barn materialized. She felt a surge of pride and satisfaction at the sight of all she and Cash had achieved. Who wouldn't want to get married in a rustic yet charming barn with a quaint stone well out in front, a venue that was often featured in magazines, newspapers and wedding websites? The miniature Western town could be straight out of an old movie. Except the bank, sheriff's office, jail, livery stable and general store were one-fourth the size of their real-life counterparts.

Located at the end of the miniature town was Cash's architectural office—this one full-scale. Clients loved coming to see him and almost always snapped pictures of themselves in cute or funny poses.

Some days, Cash tethered their pair of old draft horses, Otis and Elvis, to the hitching post in front of the livery stables. Today, however, the only animal tied up outside was a fluffy brown poodle mix that dissolved into a happy frenzy when Laurel parked beside a red extended-cab pickup.

She supposed the dog belonged to the owner of the truck. Shutting off the golf cart, she climbed out and started for Cash's door. The dog yipped enthusiastically and pulled against the leash securing it to the railing.

Laurel frowned. Kind of hot to leave a dog tied up outside, even in the shade and even though the owner had left a pan of water nearby.

"Poor pooch." She tentatively extended a palm as she approached, doubting this bundle of excitement would bite. "How long have you been waiting here?"

The dog, a big puppy, really, flopped down on the wooden boardwalk and rolled over into a please-rub-my-belly pose.

"You're such a silly…" Laurel checked as she bent and gave the dog's stomach a vigorous scratching. "A silly girl."

The dog whined in ecstasy, her tongue lolling out of the side of her mouth and her tail thumping against the wooden planks.

It was then Laurel noticed a piece of paper stuck in the dog's collar.

"What's this?" Curious, she removed the note and read out loud. "My name is Jelly Belly. I'm not hungry, just spoiled. Do not feed me no matter how much I tempt you with my pleading eyes." Laurel laughed and returned the note to the dog's collar. "Methinks you are a con artist, little missy."

Jelly Belly sprang to her feet and, panting loudly, fixed Laurel with the pleading eyes she'd just been warned to ignore.

"Maybe I'll bring you inside with me." Unable to resist, Laurel leaned closer and scrunched Jelly Belly's silky soft ears. The dog took Laurel's actions as an invitation to lick every square inch of her face.

"Enough with the kisses." She uttered the token protest and half-heartedly averted her face.

Laurel loved dogs and missed having one. Maybe eventually, when she wasn't working ridiculous hours and traveling periodically for special projects, she'd adopt a rescue. She loved cats, too, but couldn't risk the damage an errant claw might inflict on her precious creations.

The door to Cash's office banged opened, and Laurel straightened, automatically adjusting her bonnet. Jelly Belly barked excitedly and pulled on the leash.

"That's our dog," a young voice proclaimed.

"Who are you?" a second young voice demanded.

Laurel blinked, thinking for a second she was seeing double. The two freckled-faced little girls were clearly sisters, their resemblance undeniable.

"Hello, there. I was just making friends with Jelly Belly."

"She's a bad dog," the girl with the red T-shirt said in a solemn voice.

"Really?"

"She chews," the girl with the purple T-shirt added. "A lot. And potties inside."

"She pottied in there." Her sister indicated Cash's door.

Ah-ha, thought Laurel. That explained the dog's banishment. "Well, she's just a puppy, and puppies have accidents."

"She's this old." The girl in purple held up four fingers.

Laurel decided she must mean four months. "How old are you and your sister?"

"This many," the girls answered simultaneously.

The cutie pie in red displayed three fingers, the other, four. After verifying with each other, the girl in purple changed her fingers to three.

"So, you're both three?" Laurel smiled, completely smitten.

They nodded vigorously, their crooked ponytails bouncing.

"And you're twins?"

More nodding. The girl in purple sat in front of Jelly Belly and hugged the dog's neck. Jelly Belly's attempts to crawl into her lap produced an eruption of giggles.

Cash's office door again flew open. Laurel fully expected a typical, casually attired, millennial couple to emerge, parents of these girls and Jelly Belly's owner. Or, perhaps, a harried mother who'd stopped in for a quick meeting to go over some detail on her new house design.

Laurel was wrong on both counts. A tall, broad-shouldered cowboy filled the doorway. With his dusty boots, weathered hat, worn work shirt and jeans that had traveled thousands of miles in the saddle, he couldn't possibly be these adorable girls' father.

"Daddy, Daddy!" They rushed over, pulling on his hand and belt loops in a bid for attention.

Jelly Belly yipped and stood on her hind legs, pawing the air.

Okay. Wrong again.

He stepped onto the boardwalk and placed a

hand atop each girl's head. "I'm sorry if these two are bothering you."

"Not at all. They were telling me about Jelly Belly."

He flashed her a thousand-watt smile that lit up his entire face, especially his eyes. Were they green or golden brown? Green, she determined on closer inspection. Definitely. And very compelling.

Suddenly aware of her own appearance, Laurel tugged on the brim of her bonnet. Why had she chosen this wretched old thing? And when had she last applied lip gloss?

"Daddy. Come on. Wanna play in the jail again."

"Yeah. We wanna play."

Jelly Belly barked.

Nothing like two impatient youngsters and a hyperactive puppy to bring reality crashing down.

Laurel straightened and produced her most professional smile. The man standing before her wasn't her type. Sophisticated, well-dressed, neatly groomed professionals appealed to her. Except there was no denying this cowboy's attractiveness and her instant response to it.

Careful, she warned herself and retreated a

step. This was the kind of thing that had gotten her into big trouble once before. She'd allowed herself to become enamored, lost sight of her priorities and then paid the price.

Work and chronic fatigue. There could be no other explanation. Too many hours with her nose to the grindstone had muddled her senses. She'd be fine and back to her old self once she put some distance between her and this not-her-type cowboy who was probably married.

She discreetly checked his left hand. Bare. Not that the absence of a ring meant anything and not that she cared either way.

"Hey." Her brother Cash stepped out from behind the tall cowboy to greet Laurel. "I was just getting ready to take Max and the girls to the house."

"You were?" She tried to mask her surprise.

"He's our temporary carriage driver."

"Oh?" She let that piece of news sink in.

"You said the other day you wanted to meet him and go over what to expect. Maybe tomorrow you can ride with him on the test run with the carriage and horses."

"Test run," she repeated.

Max grinned and studied Laurel with those

absolutely, definitely green eyes of his. "Mornings are better for me. What about you?"

And there went her plan to put some distance between them.

MAX, SHORT FOR MAXWELL—his first name of Leander had never stuck—patted the small head to his right. "This is my daughter Addie, and my daughter Daisy." He patted the head to his left.

"It's very nice to meet all of you," Laurel said.

She manufactured a pleasant smile he'd bet she reserved for customers. Gone was the expression of delight he'd seen when he first walked outside. A shame. She had a nice smile. Nice everything, if he were honest. Even that pitiful excuse for a hat looked cute on her.

"My kids really love this little town you have," he said. "Mind if we let them play while we talk? They've been cooped up most of the day."

"Of course not."

From inside the office, a phone rang. "I need to grab that," Cash said. "You two go on. I'll catch up later."

And then Max and Laurel were alone. If he didn't count his kids and the pain-in-the-neck puppy they'd adopted during a weak moment when his ex-wife had canceled yet another visit.

"After you." He gestured, and Laurel stepped off the boardwalk. The girls were already skipping ahead and paying no attention.

"Addie. Daisy. Did you forget something?" he called after them.

They stopped and stared back at him in confusion.

"Your dog?"

"Sorry, Daddy."

"Yeah, sorry."

The girls scrambled toward him, each trying to gain on the other. It was always like that. A constant competition. What would they be like as teenagers? As young women? He hoped to survive that long.

Leaning down, he untied Jelly Belly with a quick flick of his wrist and handed the leash to Daisy, who'd beaten her sister by a scant second. She snatched the leash away when Addie tried grabbing it.

"Mine!"

"Girls," Max issued the warning in what he referred to as his level one voice.

"Your daughters sure do love that dog," Laurel observed when they began walking.

He grumbled, "Jelly has her good points,

I suppose. She keeps the girls entertained. Doesn't shed. Not sure Addie and Daisy have fully grasped the responsibility aspect of pet ownership."

"They're three. They'll get better."

He slowed, keeping pace with Laurel and maintaining a watchful eye on the girls. "The note on Jelly's collar is as much a reminder for them as to warn strangers. They're always sneaking her food, and I'm tired of scrubbing up dog vomit. Sorry about the visual."

Laurel laughed, and Max found himself intrigued despite his resolve. He'd gleaned not only from her brother, Cash, but also around town that she was smart, talented and driven to make a name for herself. Not that there was anything wrong with ambition to the exclusion of all else. It was fine for other people, but not for Max.

He'd been there and done that with his ex-wife, Charlene. Like Laurel, Charlene had made a name for herself. But their marriage and the girls had suffered as a result. Max had no intention of repeating history.

"Do the girls often go with you to work?" Laurel asked.

"Don't worry. I won't be bringing them tomorrow or to the weddings."

"I wasn't... I didn't mean to imply..."

She paused to regroup, her cheeks coloring. "Okay. That came out wrong."

"My neighbor Mrs. Applewood babysits for me," he said, letting Laurel off the hook.

She blinked. "Mrs. Applewood, the retired teacher?"

"You know her?"

"I had her in second grade, if she's the same Mrs. Applewood."

"How many second-grade teachers by that name can there be in town?"

Laurel laughed again, and the genuine smile he'd spotted earlier bloomed on her face. Max couldn't look away.

Addie and Daisy ducked into the jail with Jelly. Max stopped at the hitching post outside the livery, the spot providing him a clear view of the jail's interior. Laurel stopped, too, and rested an arm on the railing. The contrast between her impeccable business attire and the Old West backdrop made a fetching sight.

He found himself wondering how she'd look without the hat, only to remind himself not to go there. Classy women like Laurel Montgomery didn't give scruffy cowboys a second glance. Especially scruffy cowboys who came with two young kids.

Suddenly, he wanted her to see him as something more. Which made no sense. This spark of attraction wasn't one he intended to pursue.

"Your brother and I are trading services. I'm filling in for your regular carriage driver and Cash is helping me with some construction work."

"You have a ranch?"

"I'm the owner of Happy Trails Glampsite."

"I've heard of that!" Laurel's blue eyes widened with surprise and, he wanted to believe, admiration. "You're the owner?"

"Guilty as charged."

"Good for you. Glamping is very popular these days. Aren't you opening soon?"

"July first. Which doesn't give me much time. Cash is sending his crew out to finish the main firepit, the tent floors and the bathhouses."

"Bathhouses as in…"

"Showers and lavatories. Gotta have those. They're the main thing that makes the experience glamping instead of plain old camping."

She scrunched her mouth in thought. "Do I remember hearing you have a team penning facility?"

"Had. I sold it a couple years ago, after my divorce."

"Oh. That must have been difficult."

What always sounded like an empty platitude from other people came across as a heartfelt sentiment from Laurel.

Max shrugged. "It is what it is. I'd had my fill of ten-hour workdays and decided I wanted a job that would allow me more time for Addie and Daisy. What with their mom living in Phoenix."

"You have full custody?" Laurel grimaced and held up a hand. "Apologies. That was a personal question you absolutely do not have to answer. My clients tend to share the most private details of their lives while buying a wedding dress, and I obviously have no respect for boundaries."

He chuckled. "No worries. I'm an open book." His glance cut to his daughters attempting to put Jelly behind bars. "Technically, Charlene and I have joint custody. Though, truth is, she only visits the girls every few months for a couple hours, or an entire day if we're lucky."

Laurel nodded, her lower lip trapped between her teeth. He could see she had a lot of questions she was stopping herself from asking. He had no problem telling the whole story. She, however, might not be comfortable hearing it.

That was something he'd discovered about being divorced. People were naturally curious, but the details made them squeamish, as if his misfortune was contagious.

My plan is," he said, "once Happy Trails is fully up and running, I'll only need to work half days. Except for grounds keeping and maintenance, a lot of the campsite will be self-sufficient. I figure the girls can ride along with me when I'm cleaning tents and hauling trash."

"I'm sure they'll love that."

"Until they grow sick and tired of their old man."

"Which won't ever happen."

As if in response, Addie and Daisy came barreling out of the jail, Jelly on their heels. Of course, Daisy had dropped the leash, and it dragged in the dirt behind the dog.

"Daddy, Daddy."

They quickly surrounded Max.

"We wanna go home," Addie whined.

"She punched me," Daisy complained.

"What have I told you two about fighting?"

"She started it," they said simultaneously and pointed accusing fingers at each other.

"All right. We'll go. As soon as I'm done talking with Ms. Montgomery."

"Mizz Montgummy," Addie said, mangling the name.

"You can call me Laurel." She bent and tweaked each girl's chin.

Interesting. She liked kids. Max filed that bit of information away.

"Is ten o'clock tomorrow morning okay with you?" Max asked, getting back to the reason for their meeting. "That's when Mrs. Applewood is available. And I'll need time to ready your carriage and harness the horses."

"Um…" Laurel pulled her phone from her skirt pocket and opened a calendar app. "I can do nine thirty. I have an appointment at eleven, another at noon and two more in the afternoon."

"Nine thirty it is. I'll throw myself on Mrs. Applewood's mercy." He ruffled Addie's hair. "Grab the dog, honey, and let's go."

"I'm off, too," Laurel said. "There's a dress with a stubborn piece of lace waiting to determine which one of us will be victorious."

"Having met you, the dress doesn't stand a chance."

She smiled, this time shyly. "See you tomorrow."

"See you tomorrow," Daisy echoed.

"No, you won't," Max corrected her. "But you will see her next week."

"You bringing these little cuties by again?" Laurel asked.

"For the dress fitting. Addie and Daisy are in their aunt's wedding. My former sister-in-law."

Realization dawned on Laurels face. "You're my two flower girls with the ready-made dresses. I had no idea."

"I'm gonna be a bride," Addie sung out.

"Me, too," Daisy joined in.

"They're confused about what exactly a flower girl is," Max said.

"Maybe I can explain during the fitting. Will their mom be there, too?"

"Nah. But I'll let you know if that changes."

Max wasn't even sure Charlene would be there for the wedding, much less dress fittings.

"Sounds good. Tomorrow at nine thirty, then." Laurel turned to leave.

He watched her walk across the dirt road toward where she'd parked the golf cart, impressed she didn't trip in those shoes. Before starting the golf cart, she checked her phone again and made a quick call.

In that one way, she reminded Max of his ex-wife: rarely taking a break, her job always on her mind. This was probably the most sunshine Laurel had seen in a week.

He'd learned the hard way that life was too short to spend it working from dawn to dusk and, as a result, had readjusted his priorities. The next woman he dated would share his attitude, and she obviously wasn't Laurel Montgomery.

He herded his girls and Jelly toward the truck. "Who wants to stop for ice cream on the way home?"

CHAPTER TWO

"Morning, sleepyhead."

Laurel looked up and pinned her BFF/sister-in-law/business partner Phoebe with a grumpy look. The shower she'd taken should have revived her. It hadn't. "Coffee first. Then talk."

"How late were you up working last night?"

"Ten."

"Ten fifty-nine, I'd wager. What time did you finally go to bed?"

"A little later." *Much later.* Laurel had been too tired to sleep, if that made sense.

She added creamer and low-cal sweetener to her coffee, then walked her mug over to the table where she sat across from Phoebe. The simple movement triggered a twinge of nostalgia.

Once, her family had enjoyed delicious Sunday dinners in this spacious country kitchen. Laurel and Cash had sat at this same knotty-pine table and done their homework or played board games. They'd been sitting here when they'd received the terrible news about their grandmother's terminal illness.

Now, the kitchen served as a break room and where Laurel, Cash and Phoebe held their morning meetings. They also kept a supply of beverages and gourmet snacks in the fridge— something for clients to sip and sample while trying on dresses or finalizing wedding details.

Laurel fixed her meals here, too, such as they were. Her creative talents didn't extend to cooking. Mostly, she heated microwave entrées that she then took with her to Bellissima or upstairs.

While one half of the first floor had been renovated into her glamorous showroom and the other half into the Wishing Well Springs business office, Laurel alone occupied the entire second floor. The primary suite had been converted into a spacious workroom with four different sewing machines. Bolts of fabric, spools of trim and lace, boxes of beads and sequins, thread organizers, trunks of accessories and file cabinets containing hundreds of patterns filled the small bedroom next door. Cash had knocked down a wall separating the two middle bedrooms, creating a combo sleeping and sitting area with a TV Laurel rarely watched.

"You're pushing yourself too hard," Phoebe scolded.

Laurel plucked a cranberry muffin from the plate Phoebe had set out. "Tomorrow is June first. Without an assistant, I'll be pushing myself too hard every night this month."

"The fact it's June and your assistant quitting have nothing to do with your insane schedule." Phoebe reached across the table and laid a hand on Laurel's. "If I didn't know better, I'd say you're running away from something or *someone*."

"Seriously?" Laurel pulled back. "Are you really going there?"

Despite her business and personal residence being located literally on top of each other, and the absurd number of hours she'd been putting in, she wasn't running away. No, no, no. Her motivation was entirely selfish. She loved seeing a glowing bride wearing one of her creations as she glided down the aisle to join her future spouse at the altar. It made every painstaking, backbreaking, nerve-fraying, head-pounding moment spent on the gown worth it.

"I happen to enjoy my job," she said.

"You aren't going to lose Bellissima."

Laurel felt a sudden painful stab at the reminder. "No, I'm not. I've learned my lesson."

"You were in love."

"I was stupid. I let myself get carried away and look what happened."

"He hurt you," Phoebe said softly. "You were devoted to him, and he betrayed you."

"That was three years ago." Laurel really hated the direction their conversation had taken. "Why on earth are we talking about him?"

"Because you haven't moved on. Your walls are still sky-high."

She started to object only to reconsider. Falling madly in love and ignoring everything in her life save Jordan had been a grievous error in judgment, and she'd paid the price when her fledgling wedding dress company nearly went under. It was during her darkest hour she'd come up with the idea for Wishing Well Springs, saving both her emotional well-being and Bellissima.

Okay. Maybe she had a few teensy-weensy walls. Who could blame her? The old Laurel had been vulnerable and trusting. Current Laurel was wiser and tougher, someone who refused to be blinded by good looks and charm. Whether those looks and charm came in the form of a polished professional or a ruggedly handsome cowboy she was meeting later this morning.

She expelled a tired sigh. "Can we dissect my failed love life later when I'm not up to my ears in work and exhausted?"

"Aw, hon. I'm sorry. Cash and I just want you to be happy."

"I am. Designing wedding dresses and making a name for myself is my dream, and I'm living it."

"What did you think of Max?" Phoebe asked, abruptly changing the subject.

"Ah-ha! I see the reason for this conversation. What'd Cash say to you?"

"He might have mentioned you lit up like a fireworks display when you met Max."

Laurel feigned indignation. "That's absurd." Not a fireworks display. Maybe a sparkler. "Quit playing matchmaker. I have no desire to date, much less a cowboy. You of all people know that."

"Expand your horizons."

"Fine. I'll take up a hobby." She broke off a piece of muffin and popped it in her mouth. "Join a book club or stream travel shows. That'll expand my horizons."

"Some people work excessive hours to combat loneliness."

Her friend's remark came too close to the truth for Laurel's comfort. "I'm not lonely. How could I be with you and Cash constantly hovering over me and butting into my affairs?"

"When do I butt into your affairs?"

"Ha! Funny."

Cash breezed into the kitchen, bringing the fresh scent of the outdoors with him. He must have just come from feeding Otis and Elvis. Laurel's grandparents had purchased the pair of ancient draft horses back when they still had the ranch, and the horses were barely green broke to drive. These days, Otis and Elvis were well into their twenties and doted on by Laurel as much as Cash.

Like her grandmother's old sewing machine on display in Bellissima and the rooster weather vane atop the stables, the horses were a reminder of those carefree days before their world imploded. Sometimes, the reminders were a comfort, like putting on a favorite pair of slippers. Other times, they opened old wounds, the same way it felt when Phoebe brought up Jordan.

"I was just asking your sister what she thought of Max," Phoebe said.

Laurel pinned her with another grumpy look.

"And what does she think?" Cash kissed his bride on the top of her head before dropping into the empty chair beside her. Grabbing a muffin for himself, he slathered the top with butter. This was a typical start to their morning meetings, chitchat over coffee and breakfast. Except Laurel wasn't usually the topic of conversation.

"Nothing," Laurel interjected before Phoebe could respond. "I just met him. He seems experienced. Guess I'll find out this morning." Sipping her coffee, she added. "His daughters are adorable. Turns out I have a dress fitting with them next week. Did you know they're flower girls in our June thirtieth wedding?"

"Yep. He's devoted to those two. Compensating for their absent mom, I suppose."

"He did mention she rarely visits."

Laurel struggled to understand the arrangement. Phoenix was two hours away, not in another state. The girls' mother could easily come up every weekend if she chose. Or Max could take the girls down there.

"Are she and Max at odds? Is that why she stays away?"

"She has no interest in the girls," Cash said.

"Are you sure? She's the one who ordered the dresses off my website. She must have some interest."

He shrugged. "Max was light on the details. Most of what I know I heard from PBP members. He recently joined."

Cash was active in Payson Business Professionals, a local networking organization. He swore the contacts he made benefitted their business. Laurel had attended a handful of PBP luncheons and was bored to tears.

"What else did the members say about Max?" she asked, trying not to appear riveted when, in reality, she was on the edge of her seat.

"Something about the twins being unexpected and his wife having to leave her high-powered job."

"She resents the girls?"

"I can't say."

"That sounds extreme," Phoebe countered. "Resenting your children. She's probably just career motivated."

Laurel hoped so for the girls' sake.

Cash plucked a second muffin off the plate. "You heard she was on that reality TV show *Pitch Me* and won?"

"No." Laurel shook her head. "What's *Pitch Me*?"

"Contestants present their product and attempt to win financial backing from a panel of celebrity investors."

"What was her product?"

"Organic shampoos. Before winning *Pitch Me*, she was making and bottling the shampoos herself and distributing them out of their house."

"She must be smart and have a good product to win financial backing," Laurel said. "Did Max not support her?"

"The exact opposite. He knew how much she missed her former job. To hire a nanny and give Charlene more time for her new business, he poured himself into the team penning facility."

"Not everyone is cut out to be a stay-at-home mom." Laurel preferred that explanation over Max's ex-wife resenting their daughters. "I doubt I am."

"True," Phoebe concurred, "but you didn't walk out on your husband and children."

"No." Nor would she. Ever. But the business owner side of her had a different perspective. "Look, I'm not defending Max's wife, and I don't agree with what she did. However, appearing on a national TV show and winning is kind of cool. It takes courage and smarts. Plus, talent to create a marketable product."

"She is smart and talented." Cash pushed his empty plate away. "Max said within a year of appearing on the show, her annual revenue was nearing a million. That's when her celebrity investor suggested she move her business to Phoenix in order to expand. Rumor is she's quadrupled her revenue since then and hired a dozen new employees."

"That's impressive."

"She filed for divorce shortly after she moved."

"Oh." Laurel sat back, her admiration for the woman waning. "How awful for Max and the girls."

She recalled his darling daughters. If they were hers, she'd cut off her right arm rather than be separated from them for months at a time. She still wondered how her dad had so easily walked away after her parents' divorce. Maybe one of these days she'd find the courage to reach out to him and ask.

"Max had a successful team penning operation and was one of the top instructors in Arizona," Cash said. "He gave everything up to spend more time with his daughters."

"That speaks very highly of him," Laurel said and meant it. "He's a good dad to make them his priority. And, I imagine he'll do well with Happy Trails. There's nothing like it around here."

"He will do well. Don't let his good-old-boy appearance fool you. Max is one savvy guy. He figured out how to turn twenty acres of empty land into a money-making glampsite with all the amenities."

Phoebe leaned sideways and bumped shoulders with Cash. "Having met him, I can see why Laurel's smitten."

"I'm not smitten," Laurel protested much too vehemently. "Honestly. Will you give it a rest?"

"Just as well," Cash said. "You're probably not the gal for him."

Laurel frowned. It was one thing for her to reject Max, but Cash rejecting her on Max's behalf? "I'll have you know I'm a catch."

"You'll get no argument from me. But, Max has a lot of irons in the fire, raising those two girls and launching a brand-new business. He may not be available for a serious relationship, and I wouldn't want to see you get hurt."

Again, Laurel silently added. *Pinning her hopes on a guy who ultimately dumped her.* "I can take care of myself, big brother," she insisted.

"It's a little more complicated than that. Max was burned by a wife who put her career ahead of everything else and isn't taking any chances. Sound familiar?"

"I don't put my career ahead of *everything* else."

"You kind of do," Phoebe countered. "It's like I was saying earlier. You're afraid of losing Bellissima so you overcompensate."

"I'd hate for him to get hurt, too," Cash added. "He's been through a lot already."

Laurel had no reason to feel annoyed. Yet, her hackles rose. "Appears Max and I have a lot in common. We're two people completely wrong for each other for a bunch of reasons. Now, with that established, can we please drop the subject and talk weddings instead?"

Phoebe picked up her tablet from beside her plate and opened a calendar app. "Any chance you can squeeze in another alteration? Our June twenty-fifth bride left me a voice message late last night. The dressmaker she hired canceled on her, and she's in tears. No pressure, Laurel, but she's the daughter of the Cardinals' defensive coach."

"How extensive is the alteration?" Laurel asked, already knowing she'd say yes.

This wedding, with its prominent father of the bride, would be a huge boost for Wishing Well Springs. Not to mention the potential referrals. Laurel would just have to shift a few things around and skip her regular lunch date with her mom who, Laurel was sure, would understand.

As Phoebe continued reading from her

notes, her and Cash's words replayed in Laurel's mind. It was hard to argue that she didn't put her career ahead of everything else when, deep down, it was true. Not only because she feared losing Bellissima. Laurel dreaded another heartbreak even more and would go to any length to avoid repeating past mistakes.

MAX STOOD IN the filtered sunlight of Wishing Well Springs's stable and ripped off the plastic tarp like a magician revealing a trick.

"Would you look at that?" he said to Jelly Belly, taking in the elegant white carriage. "Pretty darn fancy."

The dog continued to stare intently at a hole in the stable wall. From the sound of her low whines and digging claws, Max assumed she'd located a mouse or a lizard. He wasn't worried. The creature was safe. Jelly's hunting skills were pathetic at best.

"Let's see. Where to start…"

Max removed the wooden blocks from behind the spoked wheels and released the brake. He then lifted the tongue and dragged the carriage outside. It squeaked and creaked as he executed a series of maneuvers, eventually bringing it to a stop directly behind Otis and Elvis.

He'd already harnessed the two old draft

horses and tied them side by side to the hitching rail. They knew the routine, having done this a thousand times, and allowed Max to walk them backward into place. That accomplished, he attached the numerous straps and ran the double set of reins through the rings to the carriage. With the harnessing complete, Max used a damp rag to wipe down the carriage. He made a mental note to give it a more thorough cleaning tomorrow.

"Jelly." He whistled, and the dog came bounding out from the stable. "Good girl." Depositing her in the driver's seat, he told her, "Stay," and then, gathering the reins in one hand, climbed up into the carriage beside her.

She tried to jump into his lap.

"No." He repositioned her beside him. "Sit."

He'd left Addie and Daisy with Mrs. Applewood, and she usually watched Jelly, too. The Applewoods' huge backyard was perfect for kids and a dog. But today the retired teacher's husband had an appointment for some extensive dental work. Addie and Daisy could go with them and Mrs. Applewood would keep the girls busy in the waiting room, but leaving Jelly alone for three hours wasn't an option. So Max had brought the dog with him. When they first got Jelly, he'd tried crating her. She'd scratched at the crate door until she tore off two toenails, resulting in a vet visit and hefty bill. Max hadn't had the heart to try again and was counting on Laurel being okay with Jelly tagging along. She'd seemed to like the dog yesterday.

"You behave," he warned Jelly and tied her leash to the seat handle to prevent her from jumping out of the carriage.

She immediately started chewing on the leash.

Max threaded the reins between his gloved fingers and clucked to the horses. "All right, boys. Walk out."

Otis and Elvis started forward, their big hooves stirring up dust as they plodded along. At their age, they had one speed: slow. Perfect for transporting a bride and her wedding party from the house to the barn. No runaways. No jackpots. Piece of cake.

Jelly barked at a flock of birds flying overhead.

"Why didn't we get a heeler or a border collie?" Max bemoaned. "A respectable ranch dog. Instead, we're stuck with you."

She plopped down and rested her head on his knee.

"Save it. I have a heart of stone."

Sighing, Jelly closed her eyes. Being cute had apparently tuckered her out.

A few minutes later, they reached the house. Max checked his watch. Two minutes behind schedule. He'd do better tomorrow.

He was contemplating calling the office number so whoever answered could let Laurel know he was waiting when the front door flew open. Laurel emerged, attired in a wedding dress complete with veil and bouquet.

Max's throat went dry, and he couldn't quit staring. A crazy notion he didn't dare put into words formed before he shoved it far, far away.

"A wedding dress?" he asked when she approached.

"This is a test run. We're going for realism."

At the side of the carriage, she gathered the many folds of the dress.

"Need help getting in?" he asked, not sure he should leave the horses standing untethered.

"Coming," Phoebe Montgomery called from the porch and then jogged toward them.

Jelly yipped enthusiastically and attempted to crawl over the seat to greet the new people.

"You brought your dog," Laurel said.

He detected the barest trace of annoyance in her voice. Fair enough. This was work. No place for a rambunctious and noisy pup. "It's a long story. I'm leaving Jelly at home from now on. I promise."

"Sorry." Phoebe circled the carriage. Reaching the side, she opened the door for Laurel. "I was in the middle of an online order."

"After today," Laurel said to Max as she accepted Phoebe's outstretched hand, "I'll be the one assisting the bride into the carriage, so I'll ride along with you to the barn. Phoebe's filling in to give you the full experience."

"Will I ever need to get out of the carriage?"

"Probably not. Unless something goes wrong."

Was that a warning? He glanced at Jelly, imagining her barks spooking the horses and causing a mishap. In hindsight, he should have let Laurel know ahead of time about bringing Jelly today.

After she sat and arranged her dress, Phoebe shut the carriage door. It closed with a solid click. "Have fun, you two." She retreated a good ten feet. "Pretend I'm taking pictures. Click, click, click." She moved her hands as if holding an invisible camera.

"You ready?" Max asked.

"Yes." Laurel crossed her feet at the ankles. "And I'm glad you asked. Always check with the bride and whoever else may be with her before starting the ride. We don't want anyone falling off their seat or, worse, out of the carriage."

This wasn't his first time taking passengers in a horse-drawn vehicle. Cash wouldn't have agreed to their arrangement if Max wasn't experienced. Laurel had to know that, but he figured she was simply doing her job. He'd been the same when instructing his team penning students. If in doubt, speak up. That way, there was never a misunderstanding or someone claiming, "You didn't tell me."

Laurel explained his duties in detail as they traveled the dirt road to the barn. Max listened, enjoying the warm sunshine on his face and the relaxing rhythm of the horses' hooves as they trudged up the first hill.

"You'll be driving the bride and her four bridesmaids tomorrow. The photographer and videographer will travel ahead of you in the golf cart, taking pictures and filming the trip. You may be asked to stop along the way for a particular shot. We leave that up to the bride."

Laurel talked fast. Did she ever stop to draw a breath? Max tilted his head to listen but didn't hear any intake of air.

"What will you be wearing?" she abruptly asked.

Her question caught Max off guard, and he straightened, needing a second to respond. "What *should* I wear?" Obviously not his nice jeans and a decent shirt like today.

"You have a Western suit?"

"Ah…no."

"Any suit?"

Just the one he'd worn when he and Charlene married, and he wasn't putting that on again. "Nope. I have a blue shirt, if that's better than this one. And a newer hat."

"Yes to the hat."

He glanced over his shoulder at Laurel. She perched stiffly in the middle of the seat, looking around but not really seeing. Perhaps the stunning view was same old, same old to her. More likely, the whirling wheels in her mind required her entire focus.

"I have a suede vest in the shop you can use," she said. "And a green Western dress shirt that should fit you and matches the wedding colors. Oh, and a bolo tie. I'll have to find it later. Can you arrive early tomorrow to make sure the clothes fit?"

"Mrs. Applewood isn't available until three. I'm already dropping the girls off as early as possible."

"Not a problem. I have a client fitting in the morning not far from Happy Trails. If you're going to be there, I can swing by with the clothes afterward."

Max distinctly heard her inhale at last over the horses' hooves. So, she did stop to breathe.

"Should I have my hat there for you to check out?"

"Great idea!"

He'd been joking. That'd teach him.

Ms. Laurel Montgomery was clearly a perfectionist. He supposed it came with the territory. She wanted to make her clients' wedding day special.

Another time, under different circumstances, he might be amused by her. Intrigued, even. She wasn't as similar to his ex-wife as he'd originally thought. True, they were both driven to succeed. But whereas Charlene was self-absorbed and prickly when things didn't go her way, Laurel was outgoing and friendly, when not instructing him, and willing to be bend when necessary to get the job done.

He chuckled to himself, remembering Laurel's reaction to seeing Jelly earlier. She could be prickly, too, he supposed, when taken by surprise. But then she quickly got over it.

The wedding barn came into sight. Laurel told Max where to pull up to let the bride out.

"Phoebe will be in the golf cart with the photographer and videographer. She'll clear the way ahead of your arrival. Don't proceed without a signal from her."

"Wait for the signal. Got it." Max reined the horses to a stop and engaged the brake. "You want me to help you down? For practice."

"No. That's okay. Tomorrow, after I help the bride down, you wait until all the photos are taken and the bride is inside. Then, you return to the stable."

"Will you be riding with me?"

"Usually, I stay in case there's a last-second dress emergency. I'll catch a ride back with Phoebe in the golf cart after the wedding. Sometimes, the bride and groom request post-ceremony photos with the carriage in the miniature town. Those times, you'll tie up in front of the livery and wait until the wedding party joins you. We have one wedding later this month where the couple have requested a video of them riding off in the carriage. Again, you'll hang around until the ceremony's over."

"Okay. I think I can handle that."

Laurel continued discussing the ins and outs of what Max could expect. Since the horses were content to stand there, and Jelly hadn't woken from her nap, Max cranked himself around in the seat to face Laurel.

He wasn't one to study women in wedding dresses, but given the situation, he did. The dress fit as if made for her. Had it been? Cash mentioned something about his sister being single. Max had assumed Laurel had never married. In hindsight, he might have jumped to a wrong conclusion.

Hard to believe someone as pretty and vivacious as her didn't have a parade of men knocking on her door. Then again, with her habit of working long hours and dedication to her business, she may not answer.

"I said, are you ready to head back?" she asked.

He needed to stop getting distracted around her. "Right." He swung forward, released the brake and gave the reins a shake. "Walk out, boys."

The carriage jerked, waking Jelly. She sprang up as if doused with cold water and started barking at nothing.

"Jelly. Quiet girl. You'll make the boss mad."

"I couldn't stay mad at her for long," Laurel said. "She's too cute."

"Wait until she plants her muddy feet on your nice white dress."

Laurel laughed and, for once, seemed to

quietly enjoy the ride and her surroundings. It lasted an entirety of three minutes. From beneath the layers of her dress, her phone rang. She plucked it out and answered in a pleasant, professional voice.

"Gillian, hello. Yes, of course. Delighted to. The ivory satin? An excellent choice with that style."

The conversation continued for the remainder of the drive. Max learned more about trims and lace and hemlines and beading than he ever imagined. The part about different types of stitching left him completely lost.

"Are you understanding any of this?" he asked Jelly.

The dog ignored him. There, he supposed, was his answer.

Laurel ended the call just as they arrived at the house. She returned her phone to its mysterious hiding place in her dress and rose as if to exit the carriage.

"Hold on a minute." Max wrapped the reins around the brake handle. The horses weren't going anywhere, but he wasn't taking chances. "I'll give you a hand."

"No need."

"You'll slip and fall."

He swung a leg over the side of the carriage and jumped down. He was at her door and opening it before Laurel had finished gathering the dress into a bunch at her side.

"Miss." He grinned and offered his hand.

She hesitated a moment, her glance meeting his and lingering for several beats before she placed her fingers in his. "Thank you."

A sparkly silver sandal peeked out from beneath the dress. She placed it on the footrest, paused as she readjusted the dress and veil, and grabbed the bouquet off the seat. She then carefully exited the carriage—not gracefully. She'd either misjudged the distance to the ground or couldn't see because the dress blocked her view.

"Whoa, there." Max caught her by the waist when she bobbled precariously. "You all right?"

"Y-yes."

"Sure?"

She extracted herself from his hold. "Thanks."

Their brief embrace had been accidental and purely innocent. Nonetheless, he felt weightless and disoriented, like when he was sailing through the air after being thrown by a horse. It had been a long while since a woman had affected him like that.

He wasn't ready for Laurel to leave…which made no sense. "How'd I do? Am I hired?"

A small smile played at the corners of her mouth. "You're not fired."

"Good."

Only a natural disaster could have dragged him away. That, and his dog's annoying, relentless barking.

"See you in the morning at Happy Trails," Laurel said. "With the clothes. About ten?"

"Ten it is."

And then she floated away toward the house, reminding Max of the running bride in those weird perfume commercials that played during the holidays.

Maybe that summed up Laurel, he mused as he drove the horses the short distance to the stable. The wedding dress designer who fled from marriage.

Certainly a contradiction, and Max had always found contradictions intriguing.

CHAPTER THREE

LAUREL'S GLANCE BOUNCED from her minivan's digital clock to the stack of clothes for Max on the passenger seat to the pickup on her right, stopped at the four-way intersection. What was taking them so long? Go already.

She was running late, of course. She'd texted Max before leaving her client's home, letting him know her ETA and confirming he'd be at Happy Trails. She'd tried convincing herself what he wore to drive the brides didn't matter. But he'd appear in a lot of pictures and videos that would find their way to countless social media accounts and websites. As a representative of Wishing Well Springs, he needed to make the right impression.

For the twentieth time at least, her mind returned to the moment yesterday when he'd helped her down from the carriage. She kept telling herself her slight unsteadiness had been because she'd misjudged her step down. Not because of the way his lingering gaze had seemed to drink her in.

Giving her horn a light tap, Laurel motioned the pickup to proceed and then drove through the intersection. Before long, she left Payson behind and cruised down the highway. Pine trees on both sides of the road stretched too tall for her to see their tops without craning her neck. All at once, the dense woods opened to reveal a stunning view of the green valley below.

Laurel didn't slow to appreciate the sight. She was late and pushing the speed limit to the max. In hindsight, she shouldn't have told Max she'd bring the clothes to him. He seemed to have a way of disrupting her thought processes.

She also hated leaving Bellissima unstaffed. Her next appointment wasn't until noon, and then the wedding was at four. But a potential client might drop in. Phoebe was keeping an eye on the shop from her desk across the main entranceway. And Laurel had her phone with her for calls.

Grrr. Once again, she lamented her assistant's abrupt departure.

A mile later, Laurel exited the highway onto Red Canyon Road. A sign for Happy Trails appeared with the words Straight Ahead and an arrow pointing the way. The *a*'s in both

Happy and *Trails* had been replaced with tents used to form the letter.

"Clever," Laurel murmured to herself. Had that been Max's idea?

The curving dirt road was both familiar and different—she'd been here before, but the last time was ages ago. Eleven years, to be precise, during an outdoor survival course she'd taken her senior year of high school. Laurel had been more interested in sketching landscape-inspired fashion designs than learning how to construct a lean-to.

Another sign appeared, and she followed the arrow. To her left, set back from the road, she spotted a house with a red barn. That must be where Max and the girls lived.

Ahead, two large wagon wheels flanked the main gate leading to Happy Trails. A sign with the same tents for *a*'s in *Happy* and *Trails* hung from a squared arch above the gate, this one with the added word, Welcome.

Laurel's minivan bumped along. She'd never seen herself as a mom-vehicle kind of person, but the minivan came with a huge cargo area necessary for her line of work. Wedding dresses took up a lot of space.

Past a stand of trees, a small village of white canvas tents materialized.

"Wow! Look at that."

Near the front and to one side stood a trio of tents with peaked tops and straight sides. Laurel aimed the van in that direction.

Her instincts proved right. A sign above the entrance of the middle tent proclaimed Office. Any doubts vanished when Laurel spotted a compact white pickup with the same Happy Trails and distinctive *a*'s painted on the side. Rakes, shovels, an axe, a step ladder and various other equipment filled the truck's bed.

Max was probably inside this office tent. She pulled up in front and parked.

Climbing out of her van, the clothes in one arm, she approached the tent. Large flaps had been tied back to create an opening, and she called out a hello.

When no one answered, she entered, surprised there was ample room to stand up straight. Expecting to be stopped in her tracks by a musty smell, dirt floor and inky darkness, she was surprised yet again to discover a spacious and well-lit interior, a raised wooden floor swept clean and fresh air thanks to a cross breeze between the front opening and a smaller one in the back.

She turned, surveying her surroundings.

Definitely not like any tent she'd ever seen. "Guess no one's home."

Unless Max was hiding beneath the desk— complete with a state-of-the-art laptop—Laurel was alone.

"I've seen studio apartments smaller than this." And not as beautifully decorated.

Striped saddle blankets lay over the backs of three visitor chairs. Murals depicting Old West scenes had been painted on the canvas walls. In the corner behind the desk sat a small refrigerator. A table by the opposite wall held a display of brochures and maps and a placard with the message Fishing Equipment Available for Rent. Beside the table was an old-fashioned potbelly stove, its chimney extending through a hole in the tent's ceiling. Laurel suspected the stove was more for looks than function but maybe heated the tent in colder weather.

"I'm blown away."

"Yeah? With what?"

Laurel spun to see Max entering.

"Oh. There you are." Flustered at having been caught talking to herself, she hugged the stack of clothes to her chest. "I was just about to call you."

"We were chopping wood behind the bath-houses."

"We as in—"

Jelly Belly zoomed into the tent and ran between Max's legs like a trained performance dog.

The twins tumbled in behind her. "Jelly, come back," one of them yelled.

Laurel was going to have to learn to tell the girls apart. There were slight differences, she noticed. One had a small scar on her chin, the other a cowlick on top of her head that caused her hair to kink.

"Daddy, Jelly has my shoe."

Indeed, the dog carried a pink slip-on sneaker in her mouth. When the girls tried to approach her, she darted to the other side of the tent, bowed down and playfully growled.

"Stay there, Addie," Max instructed and took a step toward Jelly. "I'll get your shoe."

Laurel made a mental note. Addie was the twin with the cowlick.

Max and Jelly squared off. Max won, reaching in and snatching the sneaker. "How did she get your shoe?" he asked, handing it to Addie.

"Um…it fell off."

The furrows in Max's brow telegraphed his suspicions, which Daisy confirmed.

"Addie was barefoot," she said.

"What have I told you? No going barefoot. You might step on something sharp or get bit by an animal. Remember the splinter in your heel?"

"Sorry, Daddy." Addie heaved an overly dramatic sigh.

Laurel couldn't help smiling. "You certainly have your hands full."

Max returned her smile, and she thought his expression held something more than humor.

Granted, it had been a while, but Laurel recognized attraction. The part of her that was attracted in return wanted to respond. The wiser part of her took charge and resisted.

The next instant, Max's smile dimmed, causing Laurel to wonder if she'd been mistaken. He tugged Addie to his side and squeezed her shoulders.

"Don't take your shoes off when you're outside, honey."

She stared up at him with remorseful eyes. "I forgot."

"Hmm. Likely story."

The scolding held no reproach. Max was obviously a pushover where his daughters were concerned. Not that she blamed him.

The girls were darling, and their mom was mostly absent.

He indicated the clothes still tucked in the crook of Laurel's arm. "Are those for me?"

"Yes." Feeling suddenly silly, she held the neat stack out to him. "Take them home and try them on. If there's a problem or they don't fit, call me. We'll figure out something else."

"All right." He set the clothes on the desk, pausing a moment. "Nice bolo tie."

"It was my grandfather's."

"Really? Are you sure you trust me with it? Looks old. And valuable."

"Sentimental value." A memory of her grandfather wearing the bolo tie to church on Christmases and Easter Sundays tugged at her heartstrings. "I think he'd be glad someone was making good use of it."

Max turned back around. "Thanks for stopping by and saving me a trip to town."

"Like I said, I was in the area for a dress fitting."

"How'd that go?"

"Good. Normally, clients come to the shop, but the bride's legally blind. Her mom took a close-up video with her phone during the fitting and then cast the video to a large-screen TV. The bride was able to watch the video and get an impression of herself in the dress."

"That must have felt good." His voice held a note of admiration.

"It did." Laurel thought again of the bride and her mom sobbing with happiness, and the lump forming in her own throat while watching them. The trip had been worth it just for that.

"Well." She glanced around the tent, once again admiring it. "I should probably hit the road."

"Would you like a tour before you go?"

The unexpected offer took her aback. She opened her mouth to decline, say she didn't have the time. She'd planned on spending the hour and a half before her next appointment laying out the patterns for a trio of bridesmaid dresses.

Instead, she said, "I'd love a tour."

At Max's pleased expression, a small thrill wound through her.

He turned to Addie and Daisy. "Come on, kiddos. We're taking Laurel on a tour. Don't forget your dog."

Outside, he pointed toward the two large tents thirty yards away. "Those are the bathhouses. Want a look inside?"

"Absolutely."

They entered the women's bathhouse. Like the office, the tent had a raised wooden floor.

The first thing Laurel noticed was a wall that ran down the middle, dividing the showers from the lavatories. The shower side contained four wooden stalls with shiny brass showerheads suspended overhead and operated by a pull chain.

"Hot water takes a couple minutes to reach the shower," Max said. "It's stored in a tank behind the tent and heated with solar panels."

"Eco-friendly glamping."

"That's one of my goals." After a peek at the other side, they left the bathhouse. "I considered private bathrooms for each tent," he continued, "but, besides being cost prohibitive, it was an engineering nightmare."

"Trust me, as someone who's camped outside in far more rustic conditions, this is luxury at its finest."

They strolled in the direction of the firepit, which on closer inspection was no more than a large hole in the ground.

"Your brother's construction crew will be here on Monday to finish with this and the remaining tents," Max said.

"I like your seating." Laurel walked over and admired the benches constructed from halved pine logs. A half dozen surrounded the firepit in a circle.

"Thanks. Built them myself."

"I bet that was a project."

"We helped Daddy," Daisy chimed in.

"They did." He winked at the girls. "They picked which logs from the pile I should use and then tested out the benches."

"I hammered," Addie insisted.

"Me, too," Daisy added.

Laurel gasped. "You did? All by your-selves?"

"With a little help," Max admitted, ruffling Addie's hair.

"Show me which nails you hammered," Laurel said.

The girls scurried from one bench to the next, pointing and saying, "This one and this one," over and over. Jelly joined in on the fun.

"I'm going to have nightly entertainment around the fire," Max explained. "I've already hired a folk singer and guitarist, a storyteller and a cowboy poet. Working on more."

"I love it!"

"The PBP has been a great resource."

Next, they wandered along the wide path to the nearest glamping tent, also constructed on a wooden platform.

"Each tent has its own barbecue grill and picnic table."

"All the conveniences of home," Laurel said.

"I try." He untied the flaps and held them open for Laurel and the girls.

"Daddy, it's dark in here."

Max entered, his arm briefly brushing Laurel's as he passed. The sensation was both exciting and a little disconcerting.

Seriously, what was wrong with her?

He moved to the side of the opening and turned the knob on a lantern dangling from a hook. Instantly, the battery-operated device emitted a bright glow.

Laurel's mouth fell open. "This is gorgeous."

A large bed dominated the center of the tent, its headboard resting against the far wall. She saw that the wooden frames, also pine, could be pushed together to create one bed or separated into two single beds.

"Did you also make the bed frames?" she asked.

"Yep. For all eight tents. And the nightstands. I purchased the chairs." Max tapped the rocker, sending it into motion. "And your brother's crew built the tent floors. I wouldn't be opening until next spring if everything were left to me."

"This is nice, Max. I mean, really nice."

"Eventually, if all goes as planned, I'll add more tents. I may also have daily wagon rides.

But even without that there's plenty else to do. Hiking. Mountain biking. Fishing."

"I saw the sign in the office for renting fishing equipment."

"I make a buck where I can." He grinned. "I'm considering renting out gold panning equipment. We'll see."

"And you're opening on July first," Laurel said at they headed outside.

"A soft opening." Max refastened the opening, securing it tightly. "Half the tents are ready. The remaining half will take another few weeks."

Only when they reached the office did Laurel think to check her phone. Finding her pockets empty, she patted them again. "What?"

To her shock, she remembered she'd left her phone in her van. How was that possible? She never went anywhere without her phone.

"I'd better run," she said.

"See you later today. Say goodbye, girls."

They did and waved. Jelly barked. Laurel waved back and hurried to her van.

At the gate to Happy Trails, she stopped to check her phone, noting the two voice mail messages, three text messages and seven new emails.

After a quick scan, she set down her phone and continued driving. Her mind wasn't on business. It kept returning to Happy Trails and, okay, Max. The place was incredible. A sure success.

It seemed she'd underestimated him. He did indeed have a good head on his shoulders when it came to business and a solid plan to provide for his daughters.

What other intriguing qualities was he hiding behind his country charm and rugged good looks? Laurel wanted to find out.

SAME AS YESTERDAY MORNING, Max waited with the carriage and horses in front of the main house. The bride was running late. This according to Phoebe, who sat in the golf cart with the videographer and photographer. She checked her phone every few minutes while the man and woman in the cart with her chatted or fiddled with their cameras.

Max supposed delays were commonplace at weddings. The three in the golf cart were probably used to waiting. Otis and Elvis, too. The horses stood with their heads lowered, eyes closed and tails lazily swishing at flies.

Truth be told, Max didn't mind waiting, either. Gave him more time to enjoy the beautiful afternoon and contemplate Happy Trails. Barring any problems, his soft opening should happen on schedule.

Glancing down at his dress jeans, he brushed at a speck of dust. He then readjusted the bolo tie Laurel had lent him.

Would he pass muster? Not for the first time, he recalled Laurel's visit to Happy Trails earlier today. He was pleased with his accomplishments and had enjoyed giving her a tour. Seeing the glint of admiration in her eyes, he'd experienced a surge of pride. Her opinion shouldn't matter more than anyone else's, but it did. He wanted her to think well of him.

The front door to the house abruptly opened. All heads turned at once. Only instead of the bride, Cash sauntered out and down the steps.

"Not long now," he called.

"Is everything okay?" Phoebe asked.

"A hair and makeup crisis. Laurel said to tell you five more minutes."

"Which translates to ten or fifteen." Phoebe took out her phone again. "I'm calling the groom and letting him know about the delay."

Cash came over to stand beside Max, who sat in the carriage driver's seat, his boot propped on the footboard.

"You need a break?" Cash asked. "I can take over the horses."

"Nah." Max leaned back and rolled his

shoulders to loosen a knotted muscle. "I'm fine."

"Sorry about this."

"Hey. Stuff happens. Getting frustrated or angry won't change anything. And the gal wants to look nice. What's another five or ten minutes?"

"I heard from my foreman." Cash leaned an arm on the side of the carriage. "He and the crew will be at your place around six tomorrow morning to start on the firepit. They're picking up the fieldstones this afternoon from the landscape center."

"I'll make sure the gate's open."

Max would need to get Addie and Daisy up and dressed early. They'd complain, but they'd get a kick out of watching the fieldstone delivery. His two kiddos were as much tomboys as they were dainty little princesses.

"How's the opening coming?" Cash asked.

"Should happen on time, thanks to you and your crew."

Cash meandered over to Otis and freed a clump of the horse's tail that had gotten caught in a buckle. He then patted Otis's large hind end. Max knew his friend babied the old horses, who'd once belonged to his grandfather. The affection reminded him of the way Laurel had tenderly handled the bolo tie.

Must be nice to have cherished family memories and possessions passed down from one generation to the next. Max had left home young—home being Fort Worth—and returned only every few years for a funeral or holiday visit. He got along with his parents and older brother well enough. The Maxwells simply weren't close. Habit, he supposed.

Maybe he could change that. Take up a new habit. His mom adored the girls. Max decided to invite his parents to Arizona for the soft opening. Short notice, but they might come.

"I'm the one who appreciates your help," Cash said, returning to stand beside the carriage. "We were in a bind when Rusty requested the month off. Didn't know if I could find someone capable of covering for him. We have a record number of brides requesting carriage rides. Then again, we're having a record number of weddings."

"Anytime, pal. I'm bound to need more construction work down the road."

"Thanks, too, for putting up with Laurel. I love her, but she can be a little bossy."

"She has a lot of demands on her and wants everything to be just right. I can relate."

"Because of Charlene?"

The unexpected question took Max aback.

He hadn't been thinking at all of his ex-wife. "I was talking about Happy Trails."

Cash nodded. "You do have a lot in common in that regard. You're launching a business, and she's attempting to grow hers."

Max wasn't sure where his friend was heading with this conversation. He opted for a wait-and-see approach.

"Laurel wasn't always so ambitious," Cash said. "She changed a few years ago. After she and her old boyfriend broke up."

Max hadn't heard this particular story about Laurel and tried to hide his interest.

"They dated a while," Cash continued. "Pretty seriously. Then he blew her off with no warning when he got a job offer in another state. It affected her in a big way. She nearly lost Bellissima."

"Because of him?"

"She was so focused on their relationship and planning a future together, she let her work slide."

"That doesn't sound like her."

"It wasn't. Then when he left, she… I don't know, Phoebe called it a funk. She spent weeks moping around the house. Bingeing on junk food. Avoiding people. Avoiding work and her clients. Phoebe and I both tried to help. She wasn't interested. I guess she had to deal with the grief of the breakup in her own way."

Max heard the care and concern in Cash's voice. He wanted to protect her from more pain.

"Long story short," Cash said, "when she recovered from this funk, or whatever it was, her business was in a shambles."

"You wouldn't know it today. She's very successful."

"She rebounded all right," Cash agreed. "When she got back to work, it was with a vengeance. She doesn't want to find herself in that position again."

And Cash didn't want to see her there again, either. He was issuing a subtle warning for Max to take care with his sister's heart. Max would do the same in Cash's shoes.

As if she knew they were talking about her, Laurel opened the front door and stepped onto the porch. Outfitted in dark slacks, a pale blue blouse and a thick band pulling her short hair back, her fresh-faced, unassuming beauty stole all the air from Max's lungs.

Cash had made a good point. There was a lot at stake for her. For Max, too. He had his own priorities—his daughters and Happy Trails. This may not be the best time for him and Laurel to act on their attraction. But that didn't mean ignoring it would be easy.

The bride came next, clad in a huge peach gown. She was beautiful and all eyes would be glued to her. Except for Max's. His remained on Laurel.

"It's showtime," Cash said and opened the carriage door. "Good luck."

Five women streamed out after Laurel and the bride. Her bridesmaids and mother, was Max's guess. Hugs were exchanged. While Laurel escorted the bride down the steps, the women scurried to an SUV parked beside the house.

"Meet you at the barn," one of them called.

"You're gorgeous," said another.

"Love you all." The bride blew them air kisses, and the SUV made a quick exit.

Laurel and the bride arrived at the carriage with Laurel holding the bottom of the dress well off the ground. "Hi, Cash," she said, then raised her gaze to Max. "Hello. Again."

"Hey."

"Nice bolo tie."

He gave the tie a slight tug. "It is."

Laurel climbed into the carriage first. Cash offered his arm to the bride on the way up, and Laurel helped her in, mindful of her veil and bouquet.

"Oooh." The bride beamed as she pushed the dress this way and that before sitting. "This is so pretty. Are the seats velvet?"

The videographer and photographer had come to life. Both had jumped out of the golf cart to capture the moment. The bride responded to their presence by smiling wide and posing. Max straightened, conscious of his posture. He'd appear in the video and photographs and shouldn't be slouching.

"Good luck and best wishes." Cash raised a hand in farewell and jogged up the walkway to the house.

Once the bride was settled in and her dress arranged, Laurel climbed out of the carriage and then into the driver's seat, this time dropping down next to Max. He'd been expecting this. Laurel had given him the rundown yesterday.

Still, his mood lifted, as if someone he'd been hoping to run into suddenly appeared.

The videographer and photographer piled back into the golf cart. Phoebe gave Max a thumbs-up.

Max shifted in his seat to address the bride. "What do you say we get you hitched?"

"Oh, yes. Please." She laughed gaily.

When he glanced at Laurel, she was smiling at him. For a moment, he forgot where he was and what he was doing. He might have even forgotten his name.

Probably not the best response right on the heels of Cash's warning.

CHAPTER FOUR

LAUREL GLANCED BACK at the bride, who beamed at the videographer and photographer and gave one of those little parade waves. Phoebe drove the golf cart. She'd speed up, slow down, get in front of the carriage and even behind at various intervals, all in order to capture this important trip from as many angles as possible.

So far, so good, thought Laurel. The bride was thrilled. Filming and photography were going well. Horses were behaving, like always. They were old pros, after all. And Max, ruggedly handsome in his cowboy hat, was—

Nope. Stop. Not what she'd meant to say. Max was competently driving the carriage. He took care to see that the bride was comfortable and her needs met. He was conscious of the route and avoiding ruts in the road. He also… The bolo tie did suit him. Laurel had always thought her grandfather looked distinguished when he'd worn it. It suited Max, too.

"You okay?" he asked.

"Y-yes." She startled at his scrutiny of her.

Had her expression given her away? "Yes," she repeated more confidently.

"You seem nervous."

"Me? No. This is the bride's big day. I'm just excited for her. Months and months of preparation, and it's finally here."

"Nice dress. You did good."

Laurel had heard and basked in far more lavish praise than that, and delivered with tear-jerking emotion, in her career as a wedding dress designer. But Max's simple words, spoken without flourish, elated her. He'd noticed the effort she'd put into the dress. A lot of guys couldn't be bothered.

Perhaps because he had a creative side, though he might not admit it. He'd clearly poured himself into Happy Trails, including the aesthetics, design and amenities. That required a sharp eye and a fair amount of talent.

The bride, no doubt nervous, pestered Laurel with one trivial question after the other for the entire drive to the barn—which Laurel patiently answered.

Cheers and applause erupted from the large group of people gathered outside the barn as they came into view. One of the many reasons Laurel loved summer weddings, and June in particular, was because of the outfits guests wore. Colors abounded. Many of the women had donned floppy hats in bright pastels to go with their floral print ensembles. The men in suits had chosen shades of pale gray, khaki, rose, blue and even white.

The bride wore a nontraditional wedding dress, which Laurel loved. While the strapless fitted bodice and full skirt were typical, she'd selected a peach taffeta fabric covered in silk roses. The effect was stunning, if Laurel did say so herself.

"Wait here," she instructed, and Max reined the horses to a stop.

Phoebe pulled ahead in the golf cart and let out the videographer and photographer in front of the bar. They immediately got into position and raised their cameras. Phoebe then parked the golf cart out of sight. When she returned on foot, she made sure the guests were standing far enough away before signaling to Max.

He jiggled the reins and clucked. "Step lively, boys. This is our big moment."

Laurel watched as Max expertly maneuvered the carriage into position in front of the barn and the waiting crowd. When the carriage came to a complete stop, the father of the bride stepped forward at Phoebe's nod. Laurel hastily clambered down from her seat and met up with the bride's father to oversee him assisting his daughter out. Laurel rearranged the dress and the long train once the bride was on the ground. Then she stepped away.

This moment belonged to the bride, the groom—who waited at the entrance to the barn—their families and the wedding party. Music played from the outdoor speakers, and, as if on cue, the guests parted to create a pathway. The father escorted the bride past the wishing well, where they paused for a quick photo op, and then to the barn entrance where the groom took over.

Together, the couple walked down the aisle to the altar. A little different than usual, yes, but as Laurel had learned over the years, to each their own. Many adhered to custom and just as many made their wedding a unique experience.

A moment later, the bride and groom disappeared inside the barn. The wedding party went next, followed by the immediate family and, lastly, the guests. Laurel peeked in, making sure there hadn't been a dress disaster.

Whew! None, thank goodness. As she watched, a familiar pang struck her. Nothing delighted her as much as seeing a glowing bride standing at the altar during the best day of her life. That Laurel's dress contributed to the specialness of the day added to her elation.

For a moment, she became lost in memories. There had been a time when she'd imagined herself as a bride much like this one. What had hurt the most was realizing Jordan hadn't loved her to the degree she'd loved him. Maybe not even at all. What a fool she'd been and vowed once again not to repeat the same mistake.

From behind her came the sound of a horse nickering, and Laurel returned to the present. Max!

Pivoting on her heel, she half jogged to the carriage. "Go on and tie up the horses at the livery next door until the ceremony's over." The couple had requested post-wedding photos with the carriage.

"About when will that be?" he asked.

"This one will run longer than usual. There's a sermon, several readings and a close friend is a cellist performing two pieces. Thirty minutes. Maybe forty."

"Okay." Max smiled. "I'll find a shady spot to get out of the sun."

On impulse, she pointed to the barn. "On second thought, come inside. It's hot. You'll melt."

He shook his head. "I wouldn't feel right."

"You can stand in the corner with me."

"Now that's an invitation I can't refuse." He released the brake on the carriage. "Meet you shortly."

Laurel headed inside, her tummy aflutter. It was the wedding, she told herself. She always got like this. But as she retreated to the corner, the fluttering increased. Soon, she'd be sharing this small space with Max.

He didn't keep her waiting long. Spotting him standing in the entrance, his cowboy hat in his hands, she beckoned him over. He moved quietly behind the last row of pews, though he needn't have worried about creating a distraction. All eyes were on the bride and groom.

Laurel tried not to stare at Max. She'd never seen him without his hat.

Addie and Daisy were the spitting image of him. Okay, not the spitting image. Their sweet, round faces were girlish while Max's strong features reflected a life spent outdoors and rich with experience. Still, there was no denying the girls' paternity.

He caught her gazing at him and smiled. "Nice wedding," he whispered.

"Yes."

"I suppose one day I'll be walking my girls down the aisle."

"Sooner than you expect."

"Sooner than I want." He released a long breath. "I'm struggling with completing pre-school applications and learning how to braid their hair. I'm nowhere near ready for them to start dating and have boyfriends, much less become a father-in-law." He rubbed his chest. "I think I'm having a heart attack."

"You'll do fine. You're a wonderful dad."

His gaze searched her face, and a tenderness softened the edges of his strong features. "Thanks. That means a lot. Sometimes I have my doubts."

Laurel nodded, moved not just by the way he looked at her but his devotion to his daughters. That was nice. Really nice.

They watched the wedding in silence after that. When the officiant announced, "Let us welcome for the very first time as husband and wife, Joseph and Camilla Soutus," Max turned toward the barn door.

"That's my cue to get the carriage." He hurried out.

Laurel also headed outside ahead of the wedding party and guests. Her job was done. The bridesmaids, mom and new mother-in-law would assist the bride with any dress and train arranging for the photos. Laurel could return to the main house if she wanted, though the walk would be grueling in this heat and in her shoes. She should probably track down Phoebe and see if her friend could use any assistance with cleanup.

Except what Laurel did was stand off to the side and wait for Max. Before long, he drew up in the carriage, much to the delight of the growing crowd. They'd seen the carriage during the bride's grand entrance, but now people—adults and youngsters alike—were able to get close and pet the horses. Laurel lost track of the number of pictures and videos taken. One person was livestreaming on social media.

A woman approached Laurel and asked, "Excuse me. Aren't you Laurel Montgomery? You designed Camilla's dress."

"I am."

"It's gorgeous."

"Thank you."

"I'm Stella Rivera. My parents own Nothing Bundt the Best Bakery."

"I love that place! Your cupcakes are incredible."

Stella went on to tell Laurel about her own upcoming wedding a week from tomorrow. She'd decided to wear her grandmother's dress and was hoping to modernize it. "I know it's incredibly last minute, but any chance you can squeeze me in?"

Laurel gave Stella a business card—she was never without them—and set up an appointment with her for Monday to bring the dress by. "I can't commit without seeing the dress first, but I'm happy to look."

As Stella walked away, Laurel questioned her thinking. Another project on top of all the rest? Pure insanity. Except Nothing Bundt the Best had been good to Wishing Well Springs and Bellissima, referring numerous clients. She hated saying no.

After that, it was hard to justify sticking around. Laurel wandered inside the barn to help Phoebe, who was glad for an extra pair of hands. Two weddings were scheduled tomorrow, and they needed to clean and prep the barn before then. With Laurel's help, Phoebe and the crew accomplished their tasks ahead of schedule.

"Seeing as we're done," Laurel said to Phoebe, "you mind if I take off?"

"Not at all. If you wait another ten minutes, I'll drop you off at the house."

"I'm good."

Something about the way Phoebe smiled told Laurel she wasn't fooling anyone.

"Let Max know he did great." She winked.

"If I see him."

Okay, yes. Laurel was going in search of Max. For a ride back to the house. Nothing more.

He was waiting outside in the carriage. For her? With the final photos taken, everyone had left to attend the reception at a nearby country club. The wedding barn was nearly deserted.

"Climb aboard," he said with a grin.

"You should have gone ahead."

He merely lifted a shoulder. Laurel hauled herself up to sit next to him. Once she was seated, they took off, the horses plodding along without requiring any direction from Max.

"Phoebe said to tell you great job. And I concur. The wedding party and guests loved you."

"Otis and Elvis deserve all the credit."

"Wasn't the cellist awesome? And the vows the couple wrote." Laurel placed a hand to her heart. "Really touching and personal. So glad I got to watch." When she caught Max studying her, she asked, "What?"

"I'm enjoying listening to you."

Her cheeks warmed. "What can I say? I love my job. I wake up every morning excited to go to work."

"I feel that way about Happy Trails," Max said, returning his attention to the road. "Can't think of a better place to raise my kids or anywhere else I'd rather be. Everything I want or need is there."

"Everything?"

"Everything," he reiterated.

Laurel considered Max's statement for the remainder of the ride.

What had she expected him to say? That his life would only be complete with a woman to love who loved him and his daughters in return? Even if that was true, Laurel wasn't that woman. She had a demanding business to run, and according to Cash, Max had been down that road before and wasn't interested in traveling it again.

Twilight was falling by the time they arrived at the house.

"Have a good evening, Laurel," Max said when she got down from the carriage.

"You, too."

She didn't glance back at him as she hurried up the walkway, not until she reached the door. By then, he and the horses were trudging along the drive toward the stables.

Laurel continued to replay their conversation for the rest of the evening, which was ridiculous. Applying her full attention to a pale gold A-line gown for three hours made no difference. The mild sense of discontentment lingered.

"WHY DIDN'T I put in my earbuds?" Laurel grumbled to herself as she hunched over her sewing machine. The needle punched neat, small stitches into the fabric as she fed it slowly through.

Not that an inability to hear Cash's distinctive footsteps thumping up the stairs to her workroom would have made a difference. He'd interrupt her regardless.

She reached the end of the seam and lifted her foot from the pedal just as he entered the room.

"Hi. Busy?"

She cranked her head around and fired a round of invisible daggers at him. "Seriously?"

Undaunted, he stepped closer. "Let me rephrase. Got a second?"

"One. And I'm not kidding." She pulled the fabric away from the machine and cut the thread. "My client will be here at four."

This commission was for Stella, the bride Laurel had met at the wedding on Friday who'd wanted her grandmother's dress modernized. She'd stopped by Bellissima yesterday morning as agreed. Laurel had prepared herself to turn the work down. She simply couldn't handle another project this month.

Then, the woman had unwrapped the vintage 1930s dress from its plastic bag. Laurel fell instantly and madly in love with it. She'd visualized how to update the dress while maintaining the charm of the original. How she'd modify the cape, leave the beaded bodice with its scoop neckline intact, and alter the bottom half to flatter the bride's silhouette.

Honestly, how could she say no? As a result, her neck and shoulders screamed and her eyes burned from toiling for hours. The result, however, would be worth a few aches and pains and potentially stooped posture for the rest of her life.

Cash put aside a stack of material on a folding chair and sat, making himself comfortable. "I know you're busy, but I need you to attend the Payson Business Professionals' luncheon today in my place."

"I can't. I'm sorry. If my client was anyone other than Stella Rivera, I'd say yes in a heartbeat." She didn't need to remind Cash what a great relationship they had with the bakery owned by Stella's parents.

"The luncheon's important," Cash said. "Today's the annual election and Channing's running for president. He needs every vote. His opponent is Bud Axlerod, and that man had a lot of support. Either you or I have to go and bring a proxy from the other."

"What about Phoebe? Can't she attend and carry our proxies?"

"She's not a member of PBP."

"True." Laurel stood and carried the dress over to her worktable where she laid it out, her critical eye taking in every detail. Across from the table, three headless dress forms stood, draped in outfits in various stages of completion and resembling spectators at a parade. "Why can't you go? And please don't tell me you have a meeting."

"I have to take Mom to the doctor."

"What! Is she okay?" Laurel dropped the tape measure she'd been holding onto the table. "What happened?"

"She fell two days ago and twisted her ankle. And you know her. She put some ice on it, took a few ibuprofens and assumed she'd be fine. Apparently, she can hardly walk today, and her ankle's the size of a softball."

"Good grief. Poor Mom."

"I insisted she call her doctor. Luckily, they can fit her in. She's probably going to need an X-ray. Since it's her right foot, she can't drive, so I'm taking her. Plus, I think one of us should go with her."

"Why in heaven's name didn't you lead with that?" Guilt ate at Laurel. She'd postponed her regular get-together with her mom on the same day her mom had fallen. Not that the two events were related, but now her mom needed help, and Laurel might have been there to prevent the fall. "You stay here and go to the business luncheon. I'll take Mom to the doctor."

"She wants me to fix her leaky bathroom faucet while I'm there. The dripping is keeping her awake at night. And clean out the leaves stuck in her hot tub filter." He sent Laurel an amused grin. "Unless you care to tackle her repair list."

"No." Laurel's skill set didn't include plumbing and hot tub maintenance. "But I feel bad. What if Mom broke her ankle?"

"My guess is she has a bad sprain. In any case, let's wait and see what the doctor says before we panic."

He was right.

Cash continued, "Worst case, she can always have groceries delivered and call a ride service whenever she has somewhere to go."

"I suppose."

He shifted in the folding chair, which was

too small for his large frame. "The luncheon starts at eleven thirty. It's at the Red Rock Grill."

Laurel liked that place. They had a nice selection of entrées. But her schedule…

"Okay." She carried the dress to a nearby rack and carefully hung it on a padded hanger. "But I'm only staying for an hour, two tops. Just until the voting is over. Not a second longer." She did have to eat.

Cash pushed to his feet and came over to give her an affectionate squeeze. "Thanks. This means a lot. To me and Channing."

"Going to cost you."

"I assumed as much. What this time?"

It was a give-and-take she and Cash had engaged in since they were children. Whenever one did the other a favor, another favor was required in return.

"You give Phoebe a couple hours off this week to help me look for a new assistant."

"She's slammed. You know how many weddings we have scheduled this month."

"Come on, Cash. If I can give up a couple of hours of my time with my hectic workload, she can, too."

"All right," he grumbled, albeit good-naturedly. "Fair is fair."

"Thanks." She felt a tiny weight lift from

her even though she didn't actually have any help yet.

"Let me know how the election goes," Cash said on the way out.

"And you call me as soon as you have an update on Mom's ankle."

"Will do."

Laurel tidied her workstation, then changed into something more professional than the jean shorts and top she'd been working in. A hasty touch-up to her hair, a dab of mascara and lipstick, and she was on her way.

The Red Rock Grill wasn't too far from Wishing Well Springs. Located in Payson's older district, it was a popular eatery with both locals and tourists. A spacious outdoor patio boasted a misting system which reduced the hot summer temperature to a tolerable level and offered a stunning view of the nearby mountains. The business luncheons, however, took place in the private dining room inside.

Laurel was contemplating how she might revitalize the trim on the vintage wedding dress when she walked into the restaurant. A sign announced the business luncheon and directed her to the private dining room. She entered and was greeted by Channing's wife, Kenna, who was acting as hostess and maybe trying to sway a few undecided votes in his direction. The two hugged.

"Hi! You came."

"Cash had to take our mom to the doctor," Laurel said. "She twisted her ankle and can't drive."

Kenna's expression filled with concern. "I hope she's okay."

"Me, too." Laurel glanced around the half-filled dining room. "Sit wherever?"

"As usual." Kenna's attention drifted to a group of three entering behind Laurel. "Welcome. Come on in."

Laurel left Kenna to her hostess duties and chose a table close to the door for an easy escape later on. Only one seat was occupied. She sat opposite the kindly-faced senior gentleman and smiled.

"Hello."

"Your name tag," he said.

"I beg your pardon?"

He tapped a white sticker on his shirt pocket. "You forgot your name tag."

"I did, didn't I?" Laurel rose, searched and spotted a table pushed against the wall laden with flyers and business cards, as well as name tags, she should have noticed when she entered. "Be right back. Can you save my seat for me?"

He saluted in response, which Laurel took as a yes. "Thanks."

The black marker she chose to write her name dried up halfway through. She found another one and started over fresh. With that task accomplished, she evaluated her blouse for the best location. Affixing the name tag on a spot just beneath her collar, she turned— only to come face-to-face with Max.

He grinned. "Well, hello. I thought that might be you. I was expecting Cash."

"He, um…" Rattled, Laurel gave herself a moment before continuing. "He had to take our mom to the doctor. I'm not staying long. I just came to cast our votes for Channing. I…" She faltered again. "I'd forgotten you were a member of PBP."

"I joined a few months ago, once I had an opening date for Happy Trails. Figured the contacts might come in handy. And they have, actually."

Of course. If she'd attended meetings more than once or twice a year, she might have known that.

"You need a name tag." She indicated hers and stepped back from the table to give him room.

He grabbed the black marker she'd been using and printed his name in bold strokes.

By then, more people were waiting in line for their name tags. Laurel retreated even further. She supposed she should return to her table. Had Max already chosen a seat somewhere?

Her question was answered when he appeared at her side and asked one of his own. "Where are you sitting?"

"Over there."

He touched her elbow and guided her through the growing throng of attendees. Laurel smiled and said hello to the few faces she recognized. Max smiled and said hello to a lot more people. He'd clearly made more friends than her in the months he'd belonged.

At the table, there were now only two empty chairs. Laurel's and the one beside it.

Max acknowledged their tablemates with a nod and a, "Howdy. I'm Max. This is Laurel."

"I saved your seat," the senior gentleman said.

Laurel smiled at him. "I see. Thank you."

Max held out the chair for her before sitting beside her.

"And I saved one for your young man," the senior gentleman added and winked.

"Ah…we're not…" Laurel faltered yet again. What was wrong with her? Why didn't she immediately correct him?

"Appreciate that, sir," Max said and handed

Laurel a menu from the pile in the center of the table, which she automatically accepted.

The next moment, their server appeared.

"Can I start you off with something to drink? Our specialty is peach iced tea."

There went any opportunity to correct the misunderstanding as people placed their orders.

Fantastic, Laurel thought. Now everyone at their table, and possibly the entire membership of Payson Business Professionals, was going to think she and Max were dating.

She waited for a surge of teeth-grinding annoyance. Except it didn't happen. She supposed there were worse things than being linked with Max.

CHAPTER FIVE

"I GIVE YOU a lot of credit, Max Maxwell."

Max set his iced tea down to give Laurel his full attention. "How's that?"

"Joining Payson Business Professionals," she said. "Don't take this wrong, but I never imagined you as the type to get involved in a local networking group."

He hadn't anticipated running into her at the luncheon. He usually sat with Cash and Channing—which was how he'd learned that Wishing Well Springs needed a carriage driver for the month of June.

"I'm not the type," he admitted. "I wouldn't have joined back when I had the team penning facility. I prefer to muck around in the dirt when I work, not attend fancy business events. But I've learned a lot since joining. I wouldn't have known what a soft opening was before someone here told me or that I should have one."

"That's what I'm saying. Kudos to you for

doing what you need to do in order to ensure your business is a success."

"Thanks." There was that surge of pride again. She really brought it out in him. Later, he might have to expend a little effort determining why she, and no other people, had that effect on him. "So, are you a burger and fries or salad person?"

She set down the menu she'd been perusing. "Think I'm going with the turkey and Swiss on sourdough."

"Lettuce? Tomatoes? Mayo?"

"Of course."

"Ah. A gal after my own heart. Not afraid of a messy sandwich."

She pursed her mouth in thought. "Now that you mention it, maybe I should go with the chicken Caesar wrap."

"Yeah?"

"No." She shook her head.

They both laughed. Max noticed she appeared more relaxed than when he'd discovered her at the name tag table. Good. Better still that he and their jovial conversation might be the reason for her change in mood.

"Tell me," Laurel said, "what pearls of wisdom have you gleaned since you started coming to meetings?"

"Business cards," Harry, the older man across the table, offered. "He didn't have any."

Laurel looked at Max as if he'd confessed to committing a grievous crime. "No business cards?"

Max gave a guilty-as-charged shrug. Truth was, he'd had business cards. Plain, uninteresting, basic cards similar to the ones he'd used in his team penning days. Those had been crumpled and the corners bent from being shoved in his pocket.

"Our speaker a few months ago gave a program on branding. I learned a lot. That's when I came up with the idea of using tents for the letter *a* on my signs and in all my advertising."

"That's an awesome idea," Laurel concurred. "Kind of like we use the wishing well in front of the barn for all our promotions."

"You have to give folks a relatable image that's easy to remember," Harry interjected.

"What do you do?" Laurel asked him.

"I own Pamper Your Pet Grooming."

"I love your logo. The little dog sitting under the hair dryer and getting its nails painted. Really cute."

"See?" Harry sent Max a pointed look. "What'd I tell you? An easy to remember image."

The young server returned for their food orders. After that, the candidates for the various board positions were each allotted ten minutes to present their goals for the upcoming year and take questions before the vote. Max liked Bud. The veteran board member running for president had an appealing personality and thought outside the box. But he also agreed with Cash. Channing would bring a fresh perspective and enthusiasm to the position, along with new ideas. Max felt Bud had been in the position too long and, no doubt unconsciously, had assumed ownership of it.

"Is there a speaker today, besides the election?" Laurel asked after their food arrived.

"Expanding Your Client Base on a Budget."

"I can use that for Bellissima."

"Do you have brochures?"

"I have postcards," she said around a delicate bite of her sandwich—which, while potentially messy, she managed not to spill a crumb of.

"Give me a stack the next time I'm at Wishing Well Springs. I'll put them on the table in my office."

"Really?"

"Not sure how many potential wedding

dress clients will come to Happy Trails, but it can't hurt and costs nothing."

"I'll put out a stack of your flyers in my boutique." Her green eyes danced with glee. "In fact, we should agree to a standing referral exchange with Wishing Well Springs and Happy Trails. We send couples looking for a unique honeymoon experience to you, and you send honeymooning couples booking a stay with you to Wishing Well Springs for their nuptials."

"Cash and I are already doing that."

"I should have guessed as much." She flashed him a smile. "Cash is the brains of our partnership. I'm merely the creative one."

"I think you're pretty smart." Max was remembering what Cash had told him about Laurel rebuilding her business after her breakup. That required more than luck and more than talent.

"You know what you should think about doing?" she asked and didn't wait for him to respond. "Offer a honeymoon special. For an added price, naturally. You can include some special touches like rose petals on the comforter. A bucket of chilled champagne and chocolate-covered strawberries. Vase of flowers on the nightstand. A heart-shaped rug and heart-shaped pillows for the bed. Fairy lights on the outside of the tent. Oh, and candles."

Max drew back to study her. "I'm mad at myself for not thinking of that."

"And it isn't hard to do, either. I can help with the rug and pillows. There's a darling boutique on the east side of town. I go there all the time."

"Really? You'd help? I'm pretty sure I can handle the flowers and champagne and strawberries but picking out rugs and pillows? Way beyond my pay grade."

"Glad to."

"Thanks, Laurel."

"You should come to these luncheons more," Harry said to Laurel from across the table.

Max agreed.

Once lunch was finished, ballots were filled out and collected. Laurel produced the paper proxy allowing her to vote for Cash. Three members tallied the votes while the current president, Bud, started the business portion of the luncheon. Max paid more attention to Laurel, studying the nuances of her myriad expressions as she listened and chuckled softly at a joke Bud made.

Max liked her. More than that, he realized, he thoroughly enjoyed her company, even when she was being bossy and intense. It had been a while since he'd felt that way about a woman. Not that he'd been keeping company with many women these past two years.

He silently cursed his bad luck. He'd finally met someone who checked a lot of the boxes. Liked his girls. Had a soft spot for Jelly. Was smart. Warm. Friendly. Funny. Talented enough for two people. Too bad the two most important boxes went unchecked: emotionally available and not intensely career driven.

From what Cash told Max, Laurel hadn't fully moved on after her last relationship, and that presented a problem. Max came with enough of his own challenges to deal with. Two rambunctious daughters. An unreliable ex-wife who continued to play a role in their lives. A business to run that would require him to be available 24/7, twelve months a year.

If a woman he was interested in couldn't deal with all that, well, the two of them didn't have a chance.

Bummer. He liked Laurel's laugh. Another box checked.

Bud finished with the final agenda item, and the three members who'd counted the ballots came to the front of the room.

"We have the election results," the man on

the left said and read from the paper in his hands. "For president, Channing Pearce."

Applause broke out. Kenna gave Channing an enormous hug. The man beside him clapped him on the back. Bud strode over and shook Channing's hand, congratulating him. If there were any hard feelings, the other man didn't let them show.

The rest of the election results were read, and a short break was announced. The speaker would then present his program.

"This is my cue to leave." Laurel pushed her chair back from the table.

"You sure you don't want to stay for the program?"

"I can't. I have an important client arriving at four. She can give Bellissima and Wishing Well Springs a nice boost. This dress has to be exactly right."

"How's it coming?"

"Good. I like what I've done, and I think she will, too."

"What's another hour, then?" he asked, well aware he was nudging, if not out-and-out arm-twisting.

"I can't." She reached for her purse. "It was nice to meet everyone." Her gaze encompassed the entire table.

Harry gave her a salute. "See you at the next meeting."

Max got to his feet. "I'll walk you to your car."

"You'll miss the program," she protested.

"I'll borrow Channing's notes."

Outside, traffic at the nearby intersection had come to a complete standstill due to a three-vehicle accident. In the distance, a siren wailed.

"Oh, no!" Laurel's hand flew to her mouth. "I hope no one's hurt."

Several people, two disabled cars and one pickup truck sitting crookedly were in the middle of the intersection. They completely blocked traffic in all directions, as well as the entrance to the Red Rock Grill.

"Everyone seems okay," Max observed. "Can't say the same for their vehicles."

Laurel surveyed the parking lot. "Is there another exit?"

"Not unless you want to jump the curb."

"What am I going to do?"

"Not much you can do until the intersection's cleared. You want to go back inside?"

She glanced at the restaurant and then at the street. "There has to be another way. I can't be late and disappoint this client."

He put a hand on her arm "This is out of

your control, Laurel. Call the client and explain the circumstances. She'll understand."

"Maybe we can walk over and ask the cops how long they think it'll be."

"I guarantee you it'll be a while." Even as Max spoke, another siren pierced the air. "That's probably the fire department."

Ambulances and tow trucks would be next. A moment later, chaos erupted when cars tried to get around the disabled vehicles and then had to reverse. Two police officers attempted to detour traffic and create room for the fire truck while two more spoke to the drivers. Some people took pictures with their phones. Others made calls. Witnesses had pulled their cars to the side and gotten out, adding to the confusion. One woman sat on the curb and cradled her head in her hands, either in pain or distress.

"What about a ride service?" Laurel mused. "I could meet them up the road a ways. Past the accident."

"They'll be delayed. Traffic's already backed up a quarter of a mile. And you'd have to return later for your car."

"You're right." She began to fidget. "Maybe I *should* call my client and postpone the fitting. I'm sorry this happened and those poor people but…" She increased her fidgeting.

"Come on." Max placed a hand on her arm and tried to usher her across the parking lot.

She resisted. "Where are we going?"

He indicated the ice cream shop a few doors down. "Sweet Dreams is my daughters' favorite place."

"Ice cream? No."

"No better way to spend fifteen minutes waiting for the accident to clear. Chocolate chip is my favorite."

"I haven't had ice cream in years."

"That's practically illegal," Max said, noting less hesitancy in her step. "A person is required by law to have ice cream no less than once a month."

She stared one last time at the intersection where more first responders were arriving. "Can we sit outside? That way I can watch for when traffic clears."

"We can sit anywhere you want. And, for the record, I'm glad you said yes. I was afraid for a second there I'd be forced to make a citizen's arrest."

That earned him a laugh. "Okay. You win. But only a small dish."

"You drive a hard bargain."

They strolled side by side toward Sweet Dreams, Max questioning his good judgment. This likely wouldn't—and *couldn't*—lead anywhere. But he wanted to get to know her better, seeing as they were working together at Wishing Well Springs, and he wasn't ready to end their time together.

At least, that was his story, and he was sticking to it.

LAUREL STUDIED THE array of ice cream behind the glass cabinet, unable to decide on a flavor. Her brain seemed incapable of completing even this one small undertaking, hampered by the dozens of questions and concerns rattling around inside her head.

Why in heaven's name had she agreed to have ice cream with Max? What about the vintage dress waiting in her workshop? She was already running behind. Would Max assume she was interested in him? *Was* she interested in him?

She did find him intriguing, which was completely different and not the reason she was here. They were going to discuss his honeymoon tent and swapping brochures. Which would make this a business meeting. Certainly not a date.

"I'll have a scoop of cookie dough," she finally told the teenage clerk behind the display and straightened.

"Any toppings?" he asked with the bored tone of someone who disdained their job.

"No, thanks."

"Two scoops are a better deal." The clerk quoted the price.

"Go on," Max urged from behind her. "Live a little."

She turned to face him. "Are you getting two?"

He grinned and indicated the clerk. "You heard him. It's a better deal."

Laurel rolled her eyes. "You're a bad influence."

"I try." His grin widened.

And that, thought Laurel, was why she'd agreed when he'd suggested coming here. His charm was difficult to resist.

She wisely stopped her thoughts from going any further and told the clerk, "Okay. Two scoops. But no toppings."

Laurel grabbed several napkins from the counter before they left to sit outside.

Situated along the side of the building was an enclosed area with several tables shaded by large purple umbrellas. Max guided Laurel to one in the corner, doubly shaded by the building.

"How's this?" he asked.

"Perfect." She set her purse on one of the

empty chairs before sitting and, once Max joined her, dug in. "This is good." She closed her eyes.

"See what you're missing?"

"I feel guilty. I should be working." She took another bite and sighed, letting the delicious ice cream melt in her mouth.

"You're taking a well-deserved break," Max said. "A temporary mental vacation. When you do return to work, you'll be refreshed and reenergized."

"You sound like a commercial."

"I'm advocating a lifestyle. One I recently adopted."

"Now you *really* sound like a commercial."

"Hey, I'm in the recreation and relaxation business. My goal is to get people to take time off work. And, if I can make a casual observation, you work too much."

"Maybe. Probably." She peered at him over her spoon. "Okay, I do. Cash and Phoebe think I use work to avoid getting hurt again."

Why had she said that? She rarely talked about herself to strangers. Not that Max was a stranger exactly. But their acquaintance was new, and this sounded a bit like a second or third date conversation.

"Are you?" He returned her gaze over his spoon. "Avoiding getting hurt?"

She supposed she'd opened the door with her comment. She couldn't fault him for walking through it.

"I…" She paused, debating how much to tell him. "I almost lost Bellissima a few years ago. Mismanagement issues, which resulted from having the wrong priorities."

"That says a lot without saying anything."

Precisely what she'd intended, and she'd hoped to leave it at that. Max surprised her by saying nothing. *Nada.* She waited two full minutes for him to pester her for more info. He didn't. Next thing, she was spilling the whole dreadful story.

"I was seeing someone, and I let my attention shift from Bellissima to him. All my attention."

"Isn't that normal for people in a relationship? You like them and want to be with them as much as possible."

"Yes," Laurel concurred. "Not, however, to the point you blow off clients, disregard responsibilities and leave on spontaneous trips for long weekends."

"I can't imagine you blowing off clients."

"I did." She glanced at the traffic, which had yet to clear. "Many times. If Jordan's associates and their spouses wanted to go to dinner or play a round of golf or try their luck at the casino, I went. If there was a company function, I attended it. If his family decided to barbecue hamburgers on Sunday afternoon or threw a birthday party for one of his nephews, I was there. If he wanted me to go to the grocery store with him to help pick out produce, I did."

"You were inseparable."

"I was at his beck and call." She let a bitter note creep into her voice, remembering. "Within six months, I'd flushed years of hard work down the toilet. It was stupid and shortsighted and…" She groaned. "I was living in a fantasy world."

"You were in love."

"More like I got carried away. One day, I was building Bellissima, gaining new clients, honing my skills and getting my name out there. The next day, I'd stopped caring about anything other than pleasing Jordan."

"Everyone gets carried away at some point in their life."

"We weren't engaged. We'd discussed getting married, or I should say, I discussed getting married. Then, out of the blue, he got offered a job in Seattle, and that was that. No 'let's try long distance.' No 'maybe you can come with me and relocate Bellissima.' No 'I love you more than life itself and am turning down the offer.' Just goodbye. It was great while it lasted."

"Wow. That had to be rough. I'm really sorry, Laurel."

She was surprised by the genuine sympathy shining in his eyes. She hadn't expected a guy to feel bad for her making a fool of herself over a man who didn't love her.

"Up until the day he left," she continued, "I half believed he'd change his mind. When he didn't, I wallowed in my misery for weeks. Skipped work. Didn't return phone calls. Avoided friends. Watched sappy movies on TV and cried myself to sleep. I was a mess."

"He broke your heart."

"He did. And to be honest, I let him. There were signs long before he left that I either didn't see or refused to acknowledge. Instead of making clients' dresses, I was designing my own and planning the ceremony with Phoebe."

Max's only response was a nod of understanding. He listened, really listened, and she found herself opening up even more.

"I've often wondered how and why I let myself get into the situation with Jordan. I suppose it had to do with my family and what happened."

He waited for her to continue.

"Good grief, I'm going to sound like a cliché." She attempted a weak smile.

"I doubt that," he said.

"My life started spiraling out of control, when I was twelve, and my grandma developed pancreatic cancer. Her and Grandpa's quarter horse ranch used to be the largest in the county. Apparently having a good eye for horse flesh, as Grandpa used to say, doesn't equate to being good with money. He never bought any health insurance or put anything away for a rainy day. Within two years, Grandma had died, and Grandpa sold off most of the ranch, save the house and barn and surrounding acreage."

"Cash mentioned that."

"Then you know what happened next. My parents, who'd worked in the family business, filed for bankruptcy. The strain was too much. They divorced and my dad split."

"Pretty serious stuff for a teenager to handle."

He reached across the table and briefly squeezed her fingers. Not long, just enough to again let her know he'd truly heard her story and wasn't merely being polite.

"I had some difficult years," she admitted. "I might have developed a few insecurities.

Fear of being hurt. Abandonment issues." She groaned. "Now I sound worse than a cliché."

His expression turned tender. "You're a remarkable person. Look at all you've accomplished.

That touched her deep in her heart. Laurel caught herself staring at Max for several moments before looking away. He had nice features. Strong and compelling. Each time they were together, she noticed something new and fascinating about them…and about him.

"I'm not that remarkable," she said, returning to her story. "While I was dating Jordan, my assistant at the time stole money from me. I wasn't there to supervise her, and she developed sticky fingers."

"Ah. Not good."

"My clients deserted me, as well they should have, and my reputation wasn't worth a flying fig. Bellissima was barely breathing when I shook off my doldrums and returned to work. When I did, I was in shock. I'd nearly lost the company I'd struggled to build, all for a guy who tossed me aside like a pile of fabric scraps. I swore then and there nothing and no one would ever derail me again."

"Do you blame yourself?" he asked, scraping his bowl clean.

"Who else? Think where I'd be now if I hadn't ignored Bellissima."

"Not that. Do you blame yourself for Jordan leaving?"

"What? I—" She bit her tongue and hesitated, not wanting to resurrect old insecurities she'd long buried. "I was a good girlfriend to him. The best."

"I don't doubt that. It's just, I speak from experience. I blamed myself when Charlene left. The only reason she moved to Phoenix had to be because I'd been a lousy husband. And I wasn't altogether wrong. But I realized it takes two to make a relationship and two to break it. Blame is shared."

"I think I made myself too available. I tried too hard. He lost interest."

"Laurel, the man was shy a few marbles if he lost interest in you. You're the most interesting woman I've met in a long time."

A pleasant tingle swept through her at the compliment, and she glanced down at her ice cream before he could notice anything amiss.

"He didn't deserve your love and devotion."

"No." She sat up straight. "He didn't. And Charlene didn't deserve yours."

"I don't agree."

From the seriousness of his tone, Laurel

was convinced she'd overstepped. "I'm sorry. I was out of line."

"I missed the signs with Charlene, too," he clarified. "She isn't a bad person. She was simply miserable, and that affected every aspect of our lives together. I think she would have been happier if we'd waited to get married until she was further along in her career and had achieved more of her goals. She definitely would have been happier if we'd waited longer to start a family. Don't get me wrong. She loves the girls. More than anything. They were just a surprise. Charlene believed she'd be satisfied staying at home with them and running her business out of the house. But, it wasn't enough, and eventually she felt trapped. It didn't help that I was spending ten hours a day at the team penning facility, six, sometimes seven, days a week."

Laurel tried not to judge Charlene. She wasn't a mother, wasn't married and hadn't felt obligated to give up her career to stay home and raise her children. Granted, she'd ignored her business, only that was different. The only person Laurel had hurt was herself.

"You must have burned out, keeping those kinds of hours," she said.

"I did. I hardly saw the girls their first year. I missed a lot. First smiles. First steps. First words. I promised myself that wouldn't happen again. About the time I sold the team penning facility, Charlene went on the TV show *Pitch Me*."

"Cash told me about that."

"Who'd have guessed she'd actually win and walk away with an investor? Before long, she was living in Phoenix, and we were divorced. I wouldn't change anything," he added, sounding like he was trying to convince himself more than Laurel. "Well, that's wrong. I would change one thing. I wish she'd spend more time with the girls. They miss her. They need her. Charlene swears she'll visit more often, except she doesn't."

Again, Laurel tried not to judge Charlene. "The girls will see her soon. In a few days at the dress fitting. And then again at her sister's wedding at the end of the month."

"That's both good and bad. Addie and Daisy love seeing their mom. Then, they're miserable when Charlene leaves and misbehave for days afterward."

"They can't help themselves."

"No, they can't," Max concurred. "They're hurting inside and don't know how to express that hurt in a positive way. Yeah," he said with a chagrinned smile, "I'm quoting a self-help book. I can admit being a good dad didn't come naturally. I needed some professional advice."

Laurel was impressed with his candidness. So very different from Jordan, who'd loathed admitting he needed help or was wrong. Did that account for her attraction to Max? Him being the polar opposite of Jordan?

"I decided work and rebuilding Bellissima would be my therapy," Laurel said. And, in a way, her penance.

"I did the same thing. Then I realized by working such long hours, I was avoiding my problems rather than dealing with them. And not doing the girls or myself any favors."

Was Laurel doing that, as well? Avoiding her problems by pouring herself into Bellissima? Phoebe would have a field day if she heard Max talking like this.

"Sometimes we're our own worst enemy." Max nodded.

Laurel crumpled her napkin and tossed it in her empty cardboard bowl. When she looked up, she caught sight of the intersection and let out a small gasp.

"The traffic's cleared. Cars are moving." She jumped to her feet and grabbed her purse. "What time is it?" Pulling out her phone, she glanced at the display and felt her stomach drop. "We've been here over thirty minutes! How could I have lost track of time like that?"

"It's okay." Max also stood, with far less urgency. "A few extra minutes won't hurt anything."

"The dress! I have to get home. Now." She considered calling her client and postponing, then decided against it. Looking bad was never a good start. She'd learned that lesson the hard way. No, she'd race home instead. With luck, she could make up the lost time. "I've got to go."

"I'll walk you."

She practically jogged to the restaurant parking lot, Max keeping stride.

"Thanks for the ice cream." She wrenched open the driver's side door. "See you tomorrow."

They had another carriage ride scheduled. Though, maybe she wouldn't see him. She hadn't made that one bride's dress.

"Drive careful. The traffic's—"

She closed her door and didn't hear the rest of what he said. With a wave, she fastened her seatbelt, reversed out of the parking space and headed toward the street.

Rude, yes. She'd apologize later. Right now, she was on a mission.

Why had she agreed to ice cream instead

of standing in front of the restaurant or waiting in her car? Laurel didn't make these kinds of mistakes. Not since Jordan.

CHAPTER SIX

WITH TRAFFIC NARROWED to one lane, Laurel had to wait and wait *and wait* until someone let her in.

Naturally, she hit every stoplight on the drive to Wishing Well Springs. Cash called, and Laurel answered on her Bluetooth.

"How's Mom?"

"Good news. Just a sprain." He summarized the care their mom would require for the next several weeks, including wrapping the ankle, icing it and keeping weight off it. "Did Channing win the election?" he asked when he finished.

"Yes." Laurel filled him in on the meeting as she changed lanes, sliding the minivan into an opening.

"You sound rushed."

"In a hurry to get home. I'm really behind on the vintage dress."

"Sorry I stole you away."

"Not your fault. I've been hitting one delay after another all day long." Literally and figuratively, she thought, recalling the traffic jam outside the restaurant and dallying with Max over ice cream. "I have to hire a new assistant. Soon."

"I'll talk to Phoebe about it when I get home."

"Thanks."

They disconnected, and Laurel made a mental note to call her mom that evening.

By the time she reached her upstairs workshop, a film of perspiration coated her brow, her hair had abandoned all effort to hold its shape and her clothes stuck to her skin. Stress sweat, her mom called it.

Laurel couldn't argue with that. She was certainly stressed and sweating up a storm. She set the air conditioning several degrees cooler and, kicking off her shoes, got straight to work on the dress. Hopefully, she'd be able to change before the client arrived.

Unfortunately, nothing went right. The stitching refused to hold in some places, the fabric weak from age, and she wound up having to improvise. She dropped the tin of beads, and they scattered all over the floor. Among the many amateur blunders she committed were sewing the wrong sides of the fabric together, forgetting to change the settings on the sewing machine, inadvertently leaving a small cut along the hem that she would have to creatively repair in order to hide and incorrect measurements.

One interruption after the other didn't help the situation. Laurel's phone rang practically every fifteen minutes. Could she reschedule a fitting? Any chance the evening gown would be ready by Wednesday? A sizing question about one of Laurel's ready-to-wear dresses on the website. A vendor soliciting her business. With each hang up, she gnashed her teeth and asked herself why she'd agreed to attend the PBP luncheon. Her entire day had gone off the rails, and probably the next several days, as well.

Thirty minutes before Laurel's client was due to arrive, she'd reached a state of extreme panic. When her phone pinged, she jumped and then read the text.

"No!" She squeezed her eyes shut. "No, no, no."

Stella Rivera was giving Laurel a heads-up that she'd be early. Laurel quickly hung the vintage dress and cape on the dress form. She was kneeling in front of it, hurrying to hide the inadvertent cut, when Phoebe called to let Laurel know Stella was waiting in the front entranceway.

"Can you show her to the viewing area and

tell her I'll be right down? Offer her a sparkling water, please. And can you bring an extra one for me, too?"

"You got it."

"Thanks."

Laurel blinked back tears. Now wasn't the time to succumb to the pressure.

She climbed to her feet, weary from emotional as well as physical exhaustion. Reaching for a padded hanger, she slipped the dress into a garment bag. Across the hall in her bedroom, she changed into a clean blouse before ducking into the bathroom where she applied lipstick and brushed her hair. A poor attempt, but it would have to suffice.

Holding the garment bag high, she padded downstairs, crossed the entryway and plastered a bright smile on her face as she strode into Bellissima. Stella Rivera perched on the edge of the couch, waiting for her. Thank goodness a second unopened bottle of sparkling water sat on the side table. Laurel was so thirsty she could drain the entire contents in one swallow.

"Hi, Stella. How are you doing?"

"Good. Excited." The woman grinned widely. She must have come straight from work, for she wore a pair of pale pink nurse's scrubs, and her long black hair was caught in a high ponytail. "I can't wait to see the dress. I loved your ideas."

"I'll be honest with you." Laurel swallowed, hating to make this confession but determined to tell the truth. "I'm not as far along as I'd hoped to be. I ran into a few problems. Entirely my fault," she conceded.

At the disappointment on Stella's face, her stomach tensed.

"How far along are you?" Stella asked, stringing out the words. "Will I be able to try on the dress?"

Laurel unzipped the garment bag. "Yes. Absolutely. It's just the little details still remaining. Let me show you and then you can head to the changing room." She removed the dress from the bag and hung it on a rack in the corner of the viewing area. "We'll see how the dress fits and make any adjustments."

"The cape is amazing," Stella gushed and ran her hand along the sheer fabric. "Oh, the hem's not done. Or the beading."

"No. I had an unavoidable business meeting earlier today, after which I was held up by traffic." Only partially true. "I'm so, so sorry."

The words were hard to push out. Laurel sipped her water, trying not to guzzle it. She should have been finished with the dress except for the final fitting. This was an important client.

"But the dress will be done in time?" Stella reiterated.

"Yes. I guarantee it. If you want, you can stop by again tomorrow."

"I may do that, if you don't mind. Is seven too late?"

"Perfect."

"Great. That way, I can bring my mother."

Laurel showed Stella to the changing room, thinking seven wasn't perfect at all. She'd have to juggle her schedule to make time for Stella and her mom. But juggle she would. Anything to satisfy the client.

"It fits great," Stella called from behind the closed changing room door. "Like a glove."

Thank goodness. At least something had gone in Laurel's favor today. When Stella opened the door and emerged, Laurel had to admit, the dress not only fit well, it flattered her figure and looked Hollywood Golden Age glamorous.

"Come." She motioned. "Let's go to the stitch and fix area."

She had Stella stand on the platform in front of the triple mirrors in order to view the dress from different angles. Stella beamed at her reflection and took selfies while Laurel plucked at the neckline, evaluated the hem length, pinned the cape and experimented with a different petticoat.

Eventually Stella left, grinning ear to ear. "See you tomorrow. With Mama."

"Tomorrow." Laurel walked her out, thankful she'd dodged a bullet. Despite the dress not being complete, the client was satisfied. If she needed to work until midnight to finish the dress, she would.

Returning to Bellissima, she plopped down on the couch, closed her eyes, laid her head back and let out a long sigh. She'd sat there for only a few minutes when Phoebe walked in, rousing her.

"Hey, are you free to go over qualifications for your assistant? Whoops. I didn't mean to disturb you."

Laurel sat up straight and then hauled herself to her feet. "No. I'm glad you did. I need to get upstairs." Laurel carefully removed the dress from the rack and returned it to the garment bag. "I have three more besides this one to finish by tomorrow." A moan escaped.

"You're killing yourself with the hours you're keeping," Phoebe scolded.

"I don't have a choice. I screwed up today. Nearly screwed up. I managed to pull a rabbit out of my hat at the last second."

"What happened?"

She recounted her day, starting with covering for Cash at the luncheon, then the three-car accident, losing track of time while having ice cream with Max and, lastly, the problems with the vintage dress. "I can't imagine what was going through my mind when I let Max convince me to go to Sweet Dreams with him. I should have waited at my car for traffic to clear."

"I think it's nice that you got away for a little while, especially with Max."

"No matchmaking," Laurel warned. Grabbing the dress, she left with Phoebe, locking the door to Bellissima behind them.

At the bottom of the stairs, they paused.

"I'm not matchmaking," Phoebe insisted. "Spending time with a nice man sitting outside on a lovely day and talking over a dish of ice cream sounds fantastic. You needed the break."

"I forgot about work," Laurel lamented.

"That was the point."

She felt the muscles in her shoulders and neck constrict into tight ropes of pain. "I screwed up before when I allowed Jordan to consume my life and forgot about Bellissima. I've promised myself that won't happen again."

"This isn't the same thing. A thirty-minute

break is hardly allowing someone to consume your life."

"But it is *exactly* how my downhill slide with Jordan started. A few minutes here. A couple hours there. Next thing I knew, my every day revolved around him and him alone."

"He took advantage of you."

"I know," Laurel said with more vehemence than she'd intended. "And I will never again be that insecure and vulnerable person who needs a guy to make her feel worthy. I may be a product of my lousy childhood, but I will not be a victim of it."

"Laurel," Phoebe started.

"I know you mean well." Laurel patted her friend's arm before starting up the stairs. "And I appreciate your help in finding me a new assistant. No changes in the qualifications from last time, by the way. But I know myself. I can get lost in a guy's attention if I'm not careful."

"You think Max is that much of a distraction?"

"He's not," Laurel said and started up the stairs. "And he won't be."

Especially after today, she silently added.

"I WANT MOMMY," Addie complained.

"I want Mommy, too," Daisy echoed.

"I wish she was here." Max had just loaded the girls into their car seats, given them books and toys to keep them amused and settled Jelly between them. He shut the rear door on his pickup and climbed into the driver's seat. "She said she's sorry she can't make it."

Addie kicked Max's seat with the toe of her sneaker. He felt a bump in the small of his back. Not hard, but enough to irritate him. Though, he couldn't be irritated with Addie. Charlene had canceled yet another visit. This time, for the flower girl dress fitting at Bellissima. Frankly, Max had expected as much, if he were honest with himself.

Still, he was annoyed. Charlene's sudden conflict, as she'd described her reason for canceling, was apparently more important that her daughters and her sister's wedding.

"Don't kick the seat, Addie," he said. "We've talked about that."

She kicked Daisy instead, who squealed, though Max doubted the kick had hurt. Too much distance separated the twins.

"Come on, girls. What have I told you?" He fought to keep the irritation from his voice. "No fighting when Dad's driving. It's dangerous."

He remembered the accident in front of the restaurant the other day. Fortunately, there'd been only minor injuries, but it could have been much worse. According to the small news article Max had read online, the driver at fault claimed to have taken her eyes off the road for only a moment. Bickering siblings could cause Max to take his eyes off the road.

"Mommy promised," Daisy whined.

How was Max supposed to respond? Say what he truly felt—that, yes, Mommy had made a promise and then failed to keep it? Lie? Defend Charlene, which wasn't what he felt inclined to do? It would, however, maintain a united parental front. That was important to him.

"She really wanted to come," Max said. "She had an important meeting."

"You said *we're* 'portant."

"You are. Very."

In his imagination, he gave Charlene a large piece of his mind. She hadn't just hurt their daughters, she'd left Max to deal with the fallout. His understanding of her sudden conflict only extended so far. She didn't have two disgruntled, unhappy children on her hands. She wasn't stuck dealing with the bickering and the moodiness. She got to say a few soothing words on the phone to the girls, hang up and then go about her business.

Max silently counted to ten, not wanting

the girls to sense his anger at Charlene. That wouldn't help the situation.

"Daddy!" Addie shrieked just as Max exited the gate at Happy Trails. "Jelly's chewing Bongo Bear."

A sharp pain throbbed in his left temple. "You're supposed to keep your toys in your lap."

"I dropped him," she wailed.

For all Max knew, Addie had thrown the stuffed toy on purpose. The more Charlene ignored the girls, the more attention they craved from him and the greater lengths they'd go in order to get it.

"Hold on." He pulled off to the side of the dirt road, unbuckled his seatbelt and rescued Bongo Bear from Jelly's clutches. He gave the dog a baleful look. "Not you, too?" he grouched and passed the toy to Addie. "Don't let go of him, okay, honey?"

"Thanks, Daddy." She hugged the toy to her chest as if Max had rescued it from the jaws of a full-grown grizzly.

"We want ice cream," Daisy chirped.

"Yeah. Ice cream." Addie waved Bongo Bear in the air, risking another disaster with Jelly.

"We'll see," Max hedged. "If you behave."

His thoughts drifted to the other day when

he'd gotten ice cream with Laurel. He hoped she'd finished the vintage dress and that her client wasn't mad. There'd been no chance to ask Laurel. He hadn't seen her on Wednesday when he'd driven the carriage for a wedding.

Phoebe mentioned that since Laurel hadn't designed the bride's dress, there was no reason for her to be at the wedding. Max hadn't gone in search of her. They didn't have the kind of relationship where they casually dropped in on each other. Besides, he'd needed to pick up the girls at the Applewoods'.

He'd *wanted* to go in search of Laurel, make no mistake. Strictly as a friend. He'd enjoyed getting to know her better and had frequently replayed their conversation at Sweet Dreams.

Fortunately for his mood, the girls behaved, and the rest of the drive to Bellissima went without incident. Maybe he'd call Charlene tonight after Addie and Daisy were asleep and talk to her about standing them up again.

Promising a visit and then canceling was worse than not visiting at all. Not that Max wished for Charlene to stay away. The exact opposite. The girls needed their mother.

Addie and Daisy wriggled with excitement as Max drove up the drive to Wishing Well Springs.

"Wanna see the little town."

"Me, too, me, too. Let's put Addie in jail." Daisy giggled mischievously.

Even Jelly barked.

"When we're done," Max said. "If you behave." Man, he sounded like a broken record. "First, the dresses."

"I don't wanna wear a dress."

Daisy was being much more tomboy lately than princess.

"It's for Aunt Sarah's wedding," he reminded her.

She sniffed. "I don't care."

In Daisy's defense, she hadn't seen Charlene's sister in well over a year. That was a long time for a three-year-old. She may not remember Sarah.

Max experienced another stab of annoyance. Because Charlene kept the girls low on her priority list, they also had little contact with their mother's side of the family. He tried to recall when they'd last seen their maternal grandparents.

Then again, who was he to talk? He hadn't seen his folks and older brother in ages.

But that was about to change. He'd phoned them a couple evenings ago, inviting them to Happy Trails' soft opening. His brother, a sergeant in the army, wasn't able to get away on such short notice. His folks, on the other hand, were coming for a few days.

After agreeing on the details, Max had put the girls on the phone for a video chat. They were always shy at first with their grandparents. In response to his mom's gentle coaxing, they'd soon warmed up. Max was now looking forward to Happy Trails' opening more than ever. It would double as a mini family reunion.

He parked alongside the main house and helped the girls out of their car seats. Jelly came next. She barely contained herself and pulled hard on the leash, panting and wheezing.

"Let's take Jelly over there." Max pointed to a patch of grass. "She needs to go potty."

"I have to go potty, too, Daddy," Addie announced.

"When we get inside. First Jelly, then you."

A short time later, they climbed the porch steps.

"Hold tight," Max instructed Daisy, when she insisted on holding the leash. "Don't let Jelly near anything."

Good luck with that, he thought.

The bell hanging above the door jingled when they entered. Cash's wife, Phoebe, emerged from the Wishing Well Springs office to greet them.

"Cash will be right out." Reaching them, she bent and put herself on the girls' level. "Who are these two little angels?"

"Addie and Daisy." Max patted each one on the shoulder to identify them.

Daisy stared. "I like your hair."

Phoebe flipped a long blond strand over her shoulder. "Thanks. I like yours." She tugged gently on one of Daisy's pigtails.

Jelly, displeased at being ignored, yipped loudly and tried to jump up on Phoebe.

Unperturbed, Phoebe gave the dog's ears a scratch. "And what's your name?"

"That's Jelly Belly," Daisy said. "She went potty outside."

"Oh. Well, that's good."

"I have to go potty, too," Addy chirped.

"Down the hall, on the left," Phoebe told Max. "How about I watch the dog for you?"

"Appreciate that."

The dog danced with excitement at being left with her new friend, her front paws tippy-tapping.

Cash was waiting in the entryway with Phoebe and Jelly when they returned.

"You have your hands full, my friend," Cash said.

"I shouldn't have brought Jelly, but she isn't trustworthy at home alone. Is there by chance somewhere I can put her? The kitchen? An empty room? Laurel doesn't need a trouble-making puppy in her shop."

"We can puppysit in the office," Phoebe volunteered before Cash could answer. "Right, sweetie?"

He smiled in amusement. "Why not?"

"I owe you. Again." Max removed his hat and propelled his daughters toward Bellissima. "All right, kiddos. Let's go," he said as they entered. "Remember, no touching. Keep your hands to yourself."

"Oooh!"

"Ahhh!"

Addie and Daisy came to a stop and stared open-mouthed.

"Pretty!" Addie exclaimed.

Max felt overwhelmed and acutely out of place. Not only because of his dusty cowboy boots and jeans, but also because he was too big and rough and ungainly for a delicate, frilly shop like Bellissima.

"Okay, let's find Miss Laurel," he said, gathering himself.

From out of nowhere, Jelly burst into the shop, barking at the top of her lungs. She stopped in front of them, her toenails catching on the carpet, an expression of pure joy on her puppy face.

"Jelly, get over here," Max said sharply and started toward her.

Startled, the dog backed up and continued backing up…straight into a dress hanging from a rack.

After that, everything happened in a fast-moving blur. Addie ran toward Jelly, arms outstretched and calling the dog's name—which only scared and confused Jelly even more.

"Honey, no!" Sensing disaster, Max tried to snatch her back but was too late. His fingers merely grazed the back of her hair.

The next second, both Jelly and his four-minutes-younger daughter slammed into a headless mannequin wearing the biggest, puffiest wedding dress Max had ever seen. They were instantly lost among the dress's huge folds. Before Max could quite register it, the mannequin wobbled unsteadily before toppling over, taking Addie and Jelly with it. Dress, mannequin, little girl and dog hit the floor with a series of thuds.

Daisy screeched. Addie wailed from somewhere beneath the dress. Jelly barked and thrashed.

Max hurried toward them, silently berating himself. Could things get any worse? Once again, he'd thought he had the situation under control, and once again he'd messed up. He should have left Jelly at home and let her chew the coffee table leg. Anything would be better than this.

Phoebe suddenly appeared, her breath coming in shallow spurts. "Oh, my gosh! I'm so sorry. She got away from me."

At the same moment Max was attempting to uncover Addie and Jelly, Laurel emerged from the rear of the shop. She drew up short, took in the scene and then fixed her gaze on Max, her expression one of horror.

He'd been wrong. Things could definitely get worse.

CHAPTER SEVEN

LAUREL INSPECTED THE dress as she rehung it on the rack, her eyes and fingers not missing a single inch. Fortunately, Addie and Jelly hadn't caused any damage. No rips or tears, no streaks of dirt or paw prints, no missing buttons and no chewed trim. Even more fortunate, the dress was one of her own ready-to-wears for sale and not a custom design waiting for a client to take home.

She turned back around to face her visitors. While she'd been busy going over the dress, Max had stood the girls side by side. Phoebe had carried a resistant Jelly away to the office where, hopefully, she'd stay out of trouble.

"Addie." Max nudged his daughter forward. "What do you say to Miss Laurel?"

"I'm sorry."

The miserable little girl hung her head. Daisy did, too, though, as far as Laurel could tell, she'd done nothing wrong.

"Thank you for apologizing," Laurel said.

"I'm sorry, too," Max added. And while he

didn't hang his head, he might as well have. "I should have left Jelly home or rescheduled when Mrs. Applewood could have puppysat."

He'd already explained. Twice. Phoebe, too. She'd assumed the blame, claiming she'd only looked away for a second when the dog escaped.

Laurel wasn't an ungracious person, but she needed a bit longer to let go of her annoyance. Mistakes happened. Phoebe had meant well. Addie, too. And Max had been in a bind, something Laurel understood. Still…

Putting on a smile, she mentally counted to ten and then did it again. The dress had survived the assault. No harm, no foul.

"You were just trying to catch Jelly. None of this is your fault." She reached out and smoothed Addie's hair, the gesture calming her frazzled nerves as much as Addie's. "Would you and your sister like to see the shop?"

Both girls nodded shyly.

Max sent her a grateful look.

Maybe if Laurel let them handle a few of the ready-to-wear dresses, hold a bouquet of silk flowers and try on a veil, they'd expend some of their pent-up energy and not fidget when it came time for their fitting—sometimes challenging with very young girls. Laurel had tried this trick before with success.

"Come on, Dad," she said to Max.

"Sure you want me tagging along?"

Laurel wasn't sure in the least, and it had nothing to do with the calamity she'd encountered when she first came around the corner.

Since Tuesday, when her attention wasn't focused on work, she'd been contemplating her near disaster with Stella's vintage wedding dress. She still couldn't believe she'd gotten so caught up chatting with Max that she'd forgotten about her client. She knew better.

After Stella had left, Laurel toiled late into the night and, by some miracle, finished the dress before Stella and her mother arrived the following day. They'd been overjoyed with the modernization. Stella's mother had cried, and Stella had crushed Laurel to her in a fierce hug. Wishing Well Springs' relationship with Nothing Bundt the Best had been saved, and maybe even improved.

Weak with relief, Laurel had rededicated herself to putting Bellissima first. Some people were good at compartmentalizing their lives. Laurel evidently was not. Like whenever Max gazed at her as if they shared a special connection.

"Come on," she said to him. "I think an extra pair of eyes on the girls wouldn't hurt."

"You're right about that."

Laurel started with the ready-to-wear racks, pulling out several dresses for the girls to touch and gawk at—all the while maintaining a secure hold on the hangers. From across the entryway came the sound of barking.

"Pretty," Daisy cooed, skimming her tiny hand along a satin sash.

"I wanna be a bride," Addie announced.

"You will," Laurel said. "One day."

"One very far-off day," Max grumbled.

Laurel pressed her finger to the tip of Addie's nose. "Then you can come here, and I'll make your dress."

"Will you make me a dress?" Daisy asked.

"Of course." Laurel patted her cheek.

"Where's your sewing machine?" Max asked, glancing around.

"My workroom's upstairs. This is just the shop." They ended the tour in the stitch and fix area. "I have an idea. Would you girls like to make your own little bride dolls? I'll help you."

"Yes, yes." Clapping accompanied their exclamations.

"Can we keep them?" Daisy asked.

"You certainly may."

Laurel picked through the supply bins she kept in this part of the shop. She located fabric, scraps of lace and trim, a dozen mismatched beads and buttons, ribbons, a black permanent marker, her glue gun and, most important, a pair of wooden clothespins for the dolls' bodies.

"What are these?" Addie asked when Laurel handed them each a clothespin.

"Your doll."

Both girls made funny faces and giggled.

"Doesn't look like a doll," Daisy commented.

"Not yet," Laurel said. "Just wait."

She had the girls sit on the floor and pulled a stool over for herself. She laid out the material for the girls to sort through.

"What color do you want your dress?" When they had each selected a scrap of fabric, she said, "Now pick out the lace for the veil."

Laurel supervised the scissor work. She drew patterns on the fabric and let the girls do the cutting with a small pair of blunt-tipped safety scissors. When it came to the glue gun, Laurel was in charge. She allowed the girls to glue a few pieces with her assistance. She covered their hands with hers and guided the glue gun for them, controlling the flow of glue and making sure no small fingers were burned.

"Now for the veils." That done, Laurel found a few tiny silk flowers to use for bouquets and glued them to the front of the dolls. "Ready for the faces?"

Addie and Daisy drew their dolls' faces with the colored permanent markers—Daisy neatly and Addie sloppily. They gave their dolls red lips and blue eyes. Daisy added ears.

"Daddy, look!" Addie jumped up and ran to Max, who'd been sitting in the viewing area watching them. At times, watching Laurel. She'd caught him when she was sneaking glances at him.

Daisy chased after her sister. "See my bride!"

While the girls showed off their treasures, Laurel cleaned up the stitch and fix area, joining them when she was done.

Max smiled at her. "Nice."

Her insides went all soft. Darn him. She wasn't sure his compliment referred to the dolls, her interaction with his daughters or both. He had a way of saying a lot while saying very little.

"My grandmother taught me how to make dolls out of clothespins when I was about their age," Laurel said. "I had a collection of over a hundred by the time I was six."

"A fashion designer even then."

"Yes." Leave it to him to make the connection.

"Did she teach you to sew, too?" he asked.

"She did. That's her sewing machine over there." Laurel indicated with a tilt of her head.

"Still use it?" His gaze returned to her.

"These days, it's just for show."

"How's your mom, by the way?"

"Fine. Better. It was just a sprain. She should be back to her old self in another week."

Max hesitated, appearing unsure of his next words. Finally, he spoke in a low voice. "Charlene was supposed to bring the girls today."

"She called this morning and told me you'd be bringing them instead."

His glance cut to Addie and Daisy, who were walking their bride dolls down a makeshift aisle along the couch cushion. "That's why they've been out of sorts. Another canceled visit."

"I'm sorry," Laurel said and meant it. "I'm sure they were looking forward to seeing their mom."

"You're good with my girls. Those dolls, it's just what they needed to cheer them up."

You're good with my *girls*. His comment felt personal, like there was a deeper meaning.

Laurel squared her shoulders. She recognized the move as steeling her defenses against the now familiar discombobulation Max evoked in her whenever he was around.

"We should probably get to the fitting. I have another appointment scheduled after you." With that, she started toward the changing area.

"Is everything okay, Laurel?"

She paused before turning back around. She knew he was really asking if he'd done anything wrong. She'd changed the subject abruptly, but she wasn't ready to talk about how he made her feel. Especially not in front of his daughters. "Everything's great."

"Yeah?" His raised brows said she hadn't convinced him. "You seem distant."

"You and I, we're friends. Strictly friends."

"Okay."

"I don't want you to get the wrong idea after the other day."

"What idea is that? Two *friends* can't have ice cream together?"

It never felt like two friends when they were together. Not for her. "I forgot about the time. Was late. I could have lost my client. That can't happen again. Under any circumstances."

"Gotcha," he said evenly.

Had she hurt him? He didn't appear hurt. He didn't look anything. Whatever Max felt about her dismissal, he did a stellar job of hiding it. Because of the girls. That had to be the reason. Children picked up on their parents' emotions and understood more than adults credited them with, so he must be good at hiding strong emotions from them.

"Who wants to go first?" she asked Addie and Daisy in a bright voice.

"Me, me," they both said.

"Well, come on, then."

Laurel escorted the girls to the pair of changing rooms where earlier she'd hung the flower girl dresses on hooks. Unzipping the garment bags, she removed the dresses, then took them and the girls into the room on the left. Ten minutes later, they emerged.

"Daddy, Daddy!" Addie and Daisy skipped over to where Max stood waiting. "Look at us."

Beaming, they held out the sides of their white taffeta dresses. While from Laurel's ready-to-wear selections, and ordered off the website by their mom, the dresses fit well and would require minimal alterations. A dart here, a tuck there, lengthening the hems by an inch and a half.

Max clasped his daughters' hands, one of theirs in each of his, and twirled them in circles. "Aren't you something special? My two little princesses."

"We're brides," Daisy announced.

"Bride helpers," Laurel added. She'd been charmed by the delight on Max's face in spite of herself.

She gave them a few more minutes and then herded the girls to the stitch and fix section where she pinned the dresses. Afterward, she returned them to the changing room where she helped them out of the dresses and into their clothes.

"Guess it's time for us to hit the road," Max said when Laurel reappeared with the girls. "Thanks for everything."

Again, that even, unemotional voice. She supposed she should be glad. Relieved. Thankful. Not analyzing every nuance of his tone, for pity's sake.

When Laurel and Jordan had dated, he'd occupied every molecule of space in her brain so that there wasn't room for anything else. Since meeting Max, she'd been spending a lot of time thinking about him. Too much time. Before she'd quite realized it, he'd snuck past her carefully constructed walls and touched her heart.

She escorted him, Addie and Daisy to the lobby. Phoebe must have been watching, for she emerged with Jelly. The dog acted as if she hadn't seen her family for the entire day rather than an hour and went wild with excitement.

"Jelly," Daisy admonished, avoiding the dog's abundant kisses. "Down."

Max took the leash from Phoebe, who gave the dog an ear-scrunching goodbye. "If you need any help with the preopening event," she told him, "let me know." With a wave, she turned and headed toward the business office.

"Preopening event?" Laurel asked Max.

"More like an open house. At Happy Trails, a week from Friday. People will be able to try out the different amenities, sit around the campfire and listen to the storyteller, cook on the barbecue grills. I've invited a few friends to spend the night in the tents. That way I can make sure everything goes as planned and remedy any problems before the July first soft opening."

"Good idea." It really was, she thought. "Another PBP meeting idea?"

He shrugged and grinned and then threw her for a giant loop.

"I know you have a lot going on. But don't worry, you only have to stay a couple hours."

"Oh. You're inviting me." She shook her head. "I'm sorry, Max, but I can't come."

"I… Ah, okay." His grinned waned. "My mistake. I assumed you were. Wishing Well Springs and Bellissima are sponsors, and Cash said you both usually attend the events you sponsor."

"We do usually. And I'd love nothing more than to be at Happy Trails' preopening. I just don't have a second to spare this month."

"Hey, look. No worries. Like I said, my mistake." He didn't hide his disappointment.

"I'm sorry, Max."

"I get it."

"Another time?" she asked, hoping to make amends.

"You bet."

"I'm serious."

"Me, too."

Laurel pinched the girls' chins. "Bye, you two. Be good." To Max, she said, "I'll call you when the dresses are ready."

She watched while Max's truck pulled away, recalling the look on his face. Max was becoming a good friend, one who'd agreed to help them out when they were in a tight spot. She should have told him she'd be at the event.

For the first time since breaking up with Jordan, she wondered if sacrificing everything for her business was worth it.

MAX SLIPPED THE bridle over Elvis's massive head. The horse mouthed the bit while Max fastened the buckles and threaded the reins through the metal rings. He'd done the same with Otis a few minutes earlier. With the harnessing complete, he led the pair outside to the hitching rail where he tethered them until he could bring out the carriage.

After four outings, including the initial test run with Laurel, this was becoming old hat for Max. Elvis and Otis must have agreed, for they stood there, waiting patiently.

Max returned to the stables for the carriage—gleaming from an earlier washing. He couldn't help wondering if he'd see Laurel today. She'd called this morning and left a voice mail—he'd been busy getting the girls and Jelly ready for their afternoon at Mrs. Applewood's and hadn't heard his phone ring. The message, delivered with almost no inflection in her voice, had said the flower girl dresses were ready, and Max could pick them up after the wedding this afternoon. He didn't need to return her call unless there was a problem.

There was a problem, all right, but he didn't call Laurel. What would he say? That she shouldn't let one whoops ruin their growing attraction? All right, two whoopses. Both his fault. She'd gotten back late from the PBP luncheon, and Jelly had wreaked havoc in the shop after Max had promised Laurel he'd leave the puppy at home. But weren't those flirty smiles he and Laurel had exchanged while she made dolls with the girls, or just wishful thinking on his part?

But then, there was that remark about them just being friends. And her overly neutral tone when he'd mentioned HappyTrails' preopening that Cash hadn't mentioned to her. She was annoyed at her brother, not Max—that had to be the reason for the tone.

He'd called Cash the day after the flower dress fitting and, without mentioning Laurel being upset, casually suggested only Cash and Phoebe attend as representatives of Wishing Well Springs and to let Laurel off the hook. Except Cash, in a rush and unable to talk, had hastily assured Max everything was fine.

All for the best, he admitted as he lifted the carriage tongue and aligned the wheels. She was going places on the fast track, and Max wasn't looking to repeat history. He had his girls to consider. They really liked Laurel. What if the four of them made plans and Laurel canceled last minute because of a conflict? It wasn't beyond the realm of possibility and too much like what constantly happened to the girls with their mother. Max was determined to protect them from more heartbreak.

While he was hauling the carriage outside, Cash strode into the stables. Talk about timing.

"Need a hand with that?" he asked.

"You bet."

Cash pushed while Max pulled. Once outside, they finished harnessing the horses to the carriage.

"What brings you here?" Max asked, adjusting Otis's girth. He doubted Cash had just happened by.

His friend rubbed the back of his neck as if it ached. "I had to get out of the house."

"Problems?"

"I was in my office when Phoebe called for reinforcements. Our bride today, she's a real…" He paused. "How do I say this? She's not easily pleased and has a long list of complaints. Our tablecloths are linen, not silk. She'd requested gold candlesticks. We only have brass. The decorations aren't the right color. Lavender instead of lilac."

"There's a difference?"

"Apparently a significant one, though I can't tell. Worst of all, we have the wrong version of the song she chose for her walk down the aisle. But according to Phoebe, her sister provided the music."

"What does the sister say?"

"She's denying it. I think she's afraid. We're all a little intimidated by the bride. Consider yourself warned. She hasn't been happy with one thing. I give Laurel credit. She's taken more flack than anyone. The dress is too tight. The bride can't breathe. The buttons are the wrong style. There are no pockets."

"Wedding dresses have pockets?"

"Don't ask me."

"I'm surprised. Laurel seems pretty meticulous about her designs."

Max recalled the flower girl dress fittings for Addie and Daisy. Laurel had paid close attention to every detail. Same even with the clothespin dolls, which his girls treasured and were still playing with five days later.

"She is," Cash said. "I'm told the dress fit perfectly at the final fitting, and the bride was overjoyed with all the arrangements. But that was then, and this is now."

Laurel really did have a lot on her plate.

"Hey, look," Max said. "She doesn't have to come on Friday to the preopening if she's busy."

Cash offered Max a chagrined smile. "I landed in some hot water over that. I shouldn't have committed her without asking first."

"You think?"

"You've been good to us. We owe you. And we'll have an opportunity to promote Wishing Well Springs."

"You've more than repaid any debt," Max insisted. "The firepit is better than I could have hoped for."

"I'll let Laurel know that skipping the event is okay with you."

"Good." Max nodded. A part of him had wanted her there, but it was better she stayed away. No troubles between her and Cash that way or between Max and her.

Cash helped Max close the stable doors and slide the long wooden latch into place. "I heard she got home late from the luncheon. Believe me, I heard."

"That was my doing."

"If it's any consolation, she blamed me first, then the traffic, then you, then herself."

"Everything worked out in the end. At least that's what she told me. The client was happy with the dress."

Cash dallied, which prompted Max to wonder if his friend had another reason for dropping by out of the blue. Finally, he said, "Things are complicated for my sister. Almost losing Bellissima scared her, and I suppose she's overcompensated since then. She can't help herself. Her ex-boyfriend did a real number on her."

"I do that sometimes with the girls—overcompensate for Charlene."

"I was hoping you'd understand. Which is why, and don't take this the wrong way, it might be a good idea if you gave each other some space for a while."

Max made a noncommittal sound.

"She likes you. And you like her, I can tell."

"I have no intentions of starting anything with her, if you're worried."

"I am worried. Laurel puts her whole self into everything she does. Her career, her shop, Wishing Well Springs, family, her friendships." He paused again. "Jordan. I'm no expert, but I suppose it has something to do with our family filing for bankruptcy when we were teenagers and then our dad leaving."

"She mentioned something about that."

"She was already dealing with her share of issues before Jordan came along and messed with head. If you were to hurt her—"

"Hey, I'd never do that."

"Not intentionally." Cash shrugged. "Stuff happens."

"You're not saying anything I haven't told myself already."

"That's good."

Cash was Laurel's big brother. Max considered himself, if not warned exactly, then duly advised. He'd heed Cash's advice for all their sakes.

"Can I give you a lift back to the house?" he asked.

"Nah." Cash chuckled. "I'm going there now on the chance complete chaos has erupted and I'm needed to be the voice of reason."

"I have trouble picturing Laurel angry."

"Oh, she can throw a fit with the best of them. But if anyone has a meltdown, it'll be this bride, not my sister."

Cash untied Otis's lead rope once Max climbed into the carriage and then headed toward the house at a brisk walk. Max followed, the horses clip-clopping along at their usual sedate pace. His nerves hummed. Nerves at seeing Laurel?

He reached the main house and parked. The bride walked—no, marched—toward the carriage while continually barking orders at Laurel and various bridesmaids and mothers.

The one lone man, the photographer, snapped pictures while maintaining a safe distance.

"Hold my train higher," the bride demanded. "Don't let it drag in the dirt. Did you remember my lip gloss? No pictures. Not yet. Stop taking pictures!" She stumbled briefly and instantly righted herself. "Good grief. You should do something about these holes. I nearly lost the heel on my shoe. These are Jimmy Choos."

Laurel appeared unfazed at the barrage. Max gave her credit.

"My strap is slipping," the bride complained. "Did you bring that fabric tape? I think a sequin fell off." When she neared the carriage, she came to a grinding halt as if hitting an invisible wall. "Is that awful stench the horses? OMG. If I wind up stinking…" She held her nose and grimaced.

Laurel came up beside her. Max suspected the others were too afraid. Cash was nowhere to be seen.

"You won't stink," she said. "I promise. And you look beautiful. All everyone will notice is you."

Marginally mollified, the bride climbed into the carriage with the assistance of Laurel and the only one of her six bridesmaids brave enough to venture near. Once she was settled, everyone scattered, making beelines for the vehicles parked by the house.

Max waited until Laurel had settled the bride and climbed into the seat beside him.

"Ready?" he asked the bride with a smile after the vehicles had gone ahead.

"I don't want the breeze to ruin my hair."

"I'll do my best." He managed to keep the humor from his voice and glanced at Laurel. At her nod, he released the brake and clucked to the horses. "Step lively, boys."

The bride complained for the duration of the ride. Not to Max or Laurel, but rather to the person on the other end of her phone call. Whoever they were, Max pitied them. Ahead, Phoebe drove the golf cart with the photographer.

He and Laurel didn't talk much, beyond an initial hello and him saying, "I got your message about the dresses. I'll stop by the shop after I unharness and put the carriage away."

"Sounds good."

After that, silence. Max wanted to let her know that he and Cash had talked, and she wasn't expected at the preopening event. He didn't, and wouldn't, in front of the bride who could be the reason Laurel was quiet. Holding in a scream?

At the barn, more photos were snapped and

videos recorded on countless phones. The bride, for all her previous difficulty, beamed as if she'd swallowed sunlight and made a stunning exit from the carriage.

Max waited for Laurel to climb down. His duties were over for the day, as the bride had only wanted to arrive in the carriage. Nothing else. Max was free to return to the stables. Only Laurel didn't move.

He waited a full minute, expecting her, like before, to head inside the barn should the bride have a dress crisis or to see her creation float down the aisle.

Eventually, she turned to him. "Aren't you returning to the stables?"

"Yeah."

"Mind if I ride back with you?"

He didn't say aloud how very little he minded.

CHAPTER EIGHT

LAUREL HUNG THE flower girl dresses near the front of Bellissima for when Max arrived. She guesstimated he'd be another thirty minutes. Unharnessing the horses and putting away the carriage took time. As it was past five, he'd probably also feed Otis and Elvis after returning them to the stables. He had before, saving Cash the trouble.

Max was helpful like that. And considerate. He'd taken their difficult bride's demands in stride when another person might have grumbled or snapped at her. He was also a good friend to Cash and, yes, Laurel. He hadn't pressured her into talking on the return ride from the barn to the main house. He just let her unwind from the hectic day in peace.

Not for the first or tenth or twenty-fifth time, she wondered if she shouldn't carve out an hour and make an appearance at Happy Trails' preopening event. Her immediate refusal had as much to do with her demanding schedule as it did with her fear of falling into the same pattern she had with Jordan. Okay, maybe more to do with her fear.

For a short time there, sitting with Max outside the ice cream shop, it had felt a lot like her early days with Jordan when she'd been content to simply bask in his company. Only later, as the months passed, had Laurel become...not obsessed or clingy—she really hated those words. Attached was a better description. Yes, very attached. Loyal. Devoted.

Codependent. She winced at that one.

Except Jordan hadn't depended on her at all. He'd led, let her follow and then abandoned her without the least hesitation.

Had she sensed him drifting away from her and refused to admit it? Was that the reason she'd become so intensely focused on him? Laurel hadn't considered that before now. Or how deep her insecurities ran. Two years had changed her perspective, it seemed.

"You are not the same person today as you were then," she told her reflection as she sprayed the changing room mirror with glass cleaner and wiped away the streaks. "You're stronger, smarter and more confident. Less vulnerable."

She stood straighter and smiled at herself, determined to be the has-her-act-together person staring back at her from the mirror.

No reason she and Max couldn't have a nice, pleasant working relationship. Possibly be friends. *Casual* friends, she reminded herself.

He strode into Bellissima just as she was preparing for tomorrow's three appointments. One look at him, changed out of his fancier clothes for the carriage ride and into a long-sleeve blue work shirt, and a small thrill tumbled through her. So much for casual friends.

Laurel steadied herself. "Hi, Max. You're here." Nothing like stating the obvious.

"Am I interrupting?"

"Not at all. Let me get the dresses."

He waited by the seating area while she retrieved the flower girl dresses from where she'd hung them. She straightened the garment bag containing both outfits as she rejoined him.

"If there's any problem when Addie and Daisy try them on, call me."

"Thanks," he said, taking the garment bag from Laurel.

She was glad to see he held it by the hangers and didn't drape it over his arm. She wondered if he'd been paying attention when the girls were here the other day for their fitting.

Even as she entertained the thought, Laurel knew she was wrong. Max had been paying attention to *her*. The same way she'd been paying attention to him. And still was.

She should say goodbye. Tell him she'd see him in a few days at the next wedding. But that wasn't what came out of her mouth as she accompanied him to the shop entrance.

"You handled yourself well and didn't get riled when you easily could have."

"I think I'm getting the knack of it." He smiled. "Though Otis and Elvis are champs and make things easy."

"No. Not the carriage. Well, yes, that, too. But you did well with the bride. She wasn't easy, and you rolled with the punches. I appreciate it. Cash, too. I told him earlier."

"She was something else." Max grinned, his green eyes alight with humor.

Her heart gave a soft flutter, and she longed to touch his arm. She wanted to experience more of the sparks flying between them. The next second, Laurel chided herself. This was exactly what had happened at Sweet Dreams. Fortunately, she didn't have a client waiting for her. Only a few dozen half-finished projects upstairs in her workroom.

"You're being kind," she told Max. "She was what I secretly refer to as a bridezilla. And if you tell anyone I called her that, I will flatly deny it and accuse you of lying."

His grin widened, letting her know he was in on her joke.

"You're the one deserving praise," he said. "No offense to the bride, but you took a lot of guff from her. Undeserved guff. That dress was pretty darn incredible, not that I'm any expert. You outdid yourself, and she didn't offer you a single word of thanks."

"I'd like to say treatment like that means nothing to me. Water off a duck's back. The truth is, it can try the limits of my patience and sometimes hurts. I did pour myself into that dress and I think it was one of my better efforts."

"I'm surprised you don't quit."

"Never. I love designing wedding dresses, and what happened today was the exception, not the rule. Even my worst days are better than being stuck at a job I hate. And I've seen enough brides to know they don't all deal with their nervousness the same."

"You think she was nervous?" Max asked.

"Absolutely. I learn a lot during dress consultations and fittings. Her mom is really nice, and, apparently, a good seamstress herself. She contributed several excellent ideas to the dress. But the bride's new in-laws, especially her mother-in-law, are extremely interfering. They've tried to dictate every aspect of the wedding, to the point of hijacking it from the bride. She was venting to the only people she safely could without repercussions."

"I'm impressed. You take customer service to a new level. I hope I can be half that tolerant and understanding."

"You will be," she assured him. "And you'll learn that a part of our job is to figure out what people need and why. They'll unload on us, tell us their secrets, their hopes, their fears. Stuff they'd never reveal to their family and friends. You're going to find out your guests come to Happy Trails for all kinds of reasons other than a vacation. And if you listen more than you talk, they'll have a wonderful time and recommend you to others."

"You learn that at the PBP luncheons?"

"No." She shook her head in amusement. "The school of hard knocks. I'm sure you had some of the same experiences with your team penning facility."

He scraped a knuckle along his jawline. "Not so much. Chasing calves around an arena and herding them into pens doesn't allow for a whole lot of unloading or secret telling."

"Still, I bet you're a good listener."

"I like getting to know folks. Keeps life interesting. Can't do that if you're yapping instead of listening."

"See. I can already tell you're going to be a success."

"Here's hoping. I've poured a lot into Happy Trails."

Laurel imagined he had. More than time and money. He'd put himself into the venture, not to mention his hopes for the future and that of his daughters.

She surprised herself again with what came out of her mouth next.

"If, um, the invitation is still open, I'd like to stop by on Saturday for the preopening event. I can't stay long. An hour at most. I have a full weekend, including an interview with the local paper on Friday. They're doing a spotlight on Wishing Well Springs and Bellissima. That happens several times a year. We'll probably suggest they use a picture of you driving the carriage from our web page."

"As long as they pick one with my good side."

They both laughed at that. Laurel didn't mention his former sister-in-law was coming in for a fitting on Saturday morning, along with four of her five bridesmaids—Max's ex-wife would miss this wedding obligation, and the chance to visit her daughters, as well.

He most likely already knew, and a reminder would be painful.

"I'll do my best to see they pick a good picture," she said, thinking every side of Max was attractive.

"And you bet the invitation is still open. In fact, you have a standing one to Happy Trails. Come by anytime you have a hankering. The girls will be thrilled to see you. Jelly, too."

"I'll drop by sometime in the afternoon."

"Looking forward to it."

They walked across the lobby to the front door. There, they paused. He was close enough she could make out the dark bristles of his five o'clock shadow and count the tiny lines at the corners of his eyes. Four on each side.

Casual friends, she reminded herself even as her heart gave another soft flutter. She couldn't allow more than that or to let herself repeat past mistakes.

Max, too, for that matter. He had a lot to lose if Laurel disappointed him like Charlene had—something entirely possible.

"Goodbye, Max."

He dipped his head slightly. "Goodbye, Laurel. See you Saturday."

And then he left, taking all those lovely flying sparks with him.

MAX STOOD IN front of the office tent and let his gaze wander the grounds of Happy Trails. Taking in all the chaos, he wished he'd accepted Phoebe's offer to help. He was clearly a dismal failure at organizing large events. Too many things had fallen through the cracks.

Next time—if there was a next time—he'd hire a puppy sitter for Jelly. The sorry excuse for a dog hadn't stopped barking once: in excitement, fear, confusion and warning off the many intruders entering her territory. If Mrs. Applewood and her husband weren't coming today, Max would have paid her double to take Jelly. The girls were only slightly better behaved than the dog. Keeping an eye on them amid the chaos was no easy task and left Max at his wit's end.

Inside the taco truck he'd hired for the pre-opening, the owner and his helpers scrambled to prepare lunch—scheduled for an hour from now. Cash was bent over the firepit, inspecting the work his crew had done. Phoebe was inside the office tent, setting out promo material for Wishing Well Springs. The idea to cross-promote was proving to be a good one. Two of Max's recent reservations were honeymooning couples getting married at the Springs. Phoebe had suggested Happy Trails to them. Max hoped to return the favor today and send a few people her way.

He'd yet to decorate the honeymoon tent, as Laurel had suggested. There hadn't been time. Mostly, he was hoping that Laurel would help him pick out the pillows and rugs. If she came today, maybe he'd mention it. *If* she came.

How, he wondered, did Laurel juggle everything? When he'd owned the penning facility and worked long hours, Max had been busy, but his days had been constant with few surprises. Not like this. It wore him out while Laurel seemed to thrive in this kind of environment.

Could two people with such different approaches to life make a go of it? Maybe. If they could meet in the middle. He'd like to explore the potential.

Next thing he knew, the first guests were arriving. Max strode over to say hello, chat a few minutes and then send them to walk the grounds on their own. He'd wanted to accompany them but wasn't able to get away. Not until he'd found an extra tank of propane for the barbecue grill at tent number four.

"Cash." He'd tracked down his friend who was pushing a wheelbarrow full of logs toward the firepit. "Can I ask a favor? Another one, actually."

"What do you need?"

Max explained about the propane tank. "Can you keep watch for any guests and greet them for me? I'll be back in fifteen minutes tops."

"No problem, buddy."

"Thanks." Max called to his daughters who were playing nearby. "Addie, Daisy. Come with me." Once he corralled them and Jelly, they all headed toward the maintenance tent.

"I have to go," Addie said, and dashed into the bathhouse as they passed. Jelly pranced along beside her, yipping in excitement.

"Me, too," Daisy exclaimed and ran after her sister.

Max didn't worry and continued toward the maintenance tent and the golf cart parked in front. The girls had frequently gone alone to the bathhouse. If they weren't out in five minutes, he'd check on them.

He was loading the propane tank into the golf cart's small rear bed when he heard Jelly furiously barking from the bathhouse. At first, he didn't pay attention. The dog could carry on nonstop. Upon hearing a pair of high-pitched screams, his blood ran cold.

Addie and Daisy! He bolted toward the

bathhouse door and ran inside. "Girls. Where are you?" He followed the barking to one of the toilet stalls, his chest ready to explode. "What's wrong?"

"Daddy!" Daisy shrieked and pointed to where Jelly stood in the far stall, barking incessantly. "In there. Look."

Addie clutched her sister's arm. "It's a snake."

"Get out of here," Max hollered to the girls. "Now."

They inched backward, still clutching at each other.

Bending, he grabbed Jelly around her middle and pulled her out of the way. If a rattlesnake bit the dog, she might not survive. If a rattlesnake bit one of his guests or his precious daughters... Max didn't want to think about that.

Jelly refused to come willingly. She was determined to drive the snake away with the force of her loud bark. She had courage, he'd give her that, if not an abundance of brains.

He pulled again. Harder. Jelly's toenails scratched across the wooden floor as they fought for traction.

"You fool dog. You're going to get bit."

And then Max spotted the snake wound into a loose coil behind the toilet. Worry left him in one long rush, and he chuckled with relief. A harmless gopher snake. And a baby at that, given its size. Not a rattler. No reason to panic.

"All right, Jelly. Good job protecting the girls." He released the dog, who resumed barking, but held on to her leash. "Now, let's get this intruder out of the bathhouse and someplace where it won't cause any trouble."

Addie and Daisy stood by the sinks, watching intently.

"It's okay, kiddos." He ruffled their hair and passed Daisy the leash. "This snake won't hurt you." But since he didn't trust his daughters alone, he said, "Come with me."

"Where are we going?" Addie asked.

Max took them to the maintenance tent where he collected a pair of leather gloves and a bucket. Ten minutes later, Mr. Baby Gopher Snake, as the girls had dubbed him, was living his best life beneath the boulders thirty yards behind the maintenance tent. Not long after that, Max was driving the golf cart with the propane tank aboard to tent number four. Addie, Daisy and Jelly rode with him in the back seat.

Leaving the golf cart in the same spot as before, Max, the girls and Jelly returned to the firepit. He surveyed the area, noting with pleasure that everything appeared ready. The girls were still talking about Mr. Baby Gopher Snake.

Earlier, he'd set up a croquet course along with a beanbag game. He planned on digging sandpits for horseshoes between now and the soft opening on July first. In the meantime, croquet would have to suffice.

Guests had also been encouraged to bring whatever they wanted to contribute to the fun. Frisbees. Mountain bikes. Metal detectors. Binoculars and butterfly nets for nature walks. Sketch pads. Kites. Yoga mats. Even their dogs.

The girls shrieked again, this time in delight. "Mrs. Applewood! Mr. Applewood."

They broke away from Max and ran toward the older woman and her husband, who embraced them fondly. Jelly barked, just as happy to see her caretakers as Addie and Daisy.

Max shook Mr. Applewood's hand. Mrs. Applewood was a hugger, and she drew Max into a fond embrace, reminding him of his mother. He couldn't wait to see her and his dad. They'd been unsure about coming to the soft opening at first. It had required some finagling with getting time off work and finding someone to watch the house. But his mom had called the other day to deliver the good news.

Two weeks wasn't far off, yet now that his parents were coming, it felt like a decade to Max. He couldn't wait to see them again and introduce them to his friends. Cash and Phoebe. Channing and Kenna. The Applewoods.

Laurel.

His mom would love her. She admired creative people. And anyone who adored her granddaughters, as Laurel did, was A-okay in her book.

Was Laurel on her way or too busy with work? She hadn't called to either cancel or confirm. Not that she owed Max an RSVP. The pre-event was more like an open house. Show up if you can, no problem if you can't.

Still, Max hoped she'd be here. He was pleased and proud of what he'd accomplished and wanted her to see it.

To the Applewoods, he said, "Can I show you two around?"

"Don't bother with us." The older woman waved him off. "You have plenty enough on your plate as it is. Addie and Daisy can give us the grand tour." She took the girls by the hands. "Can't you, sweetums?"

"Yes, yes!" Addie and Daisy chorused.

Max wasn't fooled. Mrs. Applewood was taking charge of his daughters and Jelly so that he'd be free to attend to his guests. "I didn't invite you here to babysit," he said.

"We're not babysitting," she protested, her wrinkled face breaking into a wide smile. "We're enjoying ourselves, right?"

"Right," Daisy repeated happily. "We're 'joying ourselves."

"My parents are flying out for the soft opening," Max told the older couple. "I'm hoping you can meet them."

Mrs. Applewood beamed and took the girls' hands in her plump ones. "We'd love nothing more."

"Great," Max said. "We'll decide when and where once I have a better idea of their schedule."

Charlene's sister's wedding was the day before the soft opening. His parents had met Sarah a few times, and he was considering asking her if he could bring his parents to the wedding. Just long enough to see Addie and Daisy perform their flower girl duties.

"Well, where to first?" Mrs. Applewood asked.

"This way," the girls simultaneously said and pulled her along with them.

Mr. Applewood chuckled and followed along.

Max watched them go, grateful for the day an old team penning acquaintance had recommended the older couple to him.

No sooner had they reached the croquet course than Max was swept up in a small tide of arriving guests. Cash and Phoebe stepped in to help—Cash gave directions while Phoebe escorted guests into the office tent where they signed a register and received a brochure that included a list of amenities and a map of Happy Trails and the surrounding area.

He owed his friends big time. Max couldn't have pulled off the preopening without them.

It wasn't until past two that the place quieted down. The guests staying overnight were settling into their tents. Various groups had taken off to engage in one activity or another. Those who just wanted to relax were occupying the log benches surrounding the firepit or reclining in the hammocks.

Max was settling his bill with the taco truck owner when the Applewoods reappeared, Jelly and the girls in the lead. Everyone looked tuckered out.

"We hate to leave, but we have to get going," Mrs. Applewood said. "I have bunco tonight with the girls."

Max thanked them profusely. "See you Tuesday." That was the day of his next wedding at Wishing Well Springs.

By then, Addie and Daisy were desperate for a nap. Max took them into the office tent and made them lie down with pillows and stuffed toys on an air mattress behind the desk. They protested for a full five minutes and then fell sound asleep. Jelly, too. The dog lay in a sloppy pile on the floor beside the girls, snoring softly.

Max busied himself with paperwork, answering emails and stepping outside to say goodbye to departing guests. All expressed having a good time and wished Max well with Happy Trails. This was exactly how he saw himself in the coming days. Working at a job he loved, spending time with his daughters, meeting new people and partaking in life's little pleasures.

He tried not to think about Laurel, who hadn't come after all. He consoled himself with the knowledge he'd see her Tuesday at Wishing Well Springs. She'd set the boundaries between them, he reminded himself. He needed to respect them.

The girls and the dog woke up from their nap forty-five minutes later, full of energy. With everything in order and his overnight guests occupied, Max was free to spend the next few hours until dinner relaxing and recreating with the girls.

"Who wants to go fishing at Bear Creek?" Max asked.

"We do!"

After packing a cooler of snacks and drinks and a jar of salmon eggs for bait, they emerged from the tent. A survey of the grounds assured Max no new visitors had arrived and most of those not staying overnight had left. Just in case, he hung a Gone Fishing sign on the office tent door that included his cell number.

Next, he selected gear from the fishing equipment rack and carried everything to the golf cart.

"Where are we going, Daddy?" Daisy asked as she and Addie crawled into the back seat.

Max set Jelly on the floor between the girls. "How about our special spot?"

"Yay!"

Just as they were pulling out from around the office, a lone, late-arriving guest strolled toward them.

Max stopped the golf cart, his heart rate spiking as he broke out into a grin. The girls squealed and bounced in their seats. Jelly stood on her hind legs and pawed the air.

"Have I totally missed the event?" Laurel asked. "The place is nearly deserted."

"Not at all." Max grinned. "Hop in. We're going fishing."

"Oh." She appeared suddenly flustered. "I can't."

He patted the seat beside him. Here was the chance he'd been hoping for, a way to explore any potential for meeting in the middle.

"Sure, you can. It's the only way you can experience the best Happy Trails has to offer."

CHAPTER NINE

"I'M NOT DRESSED for fishing," Laurel protested as they bumped along in the golf cart. "These aren't the right kind of shoes." She held up her left foot, clad in a chic canvas flat.

Max spared her a brief glance before returning his gaze to the dirt road they traveled. "You're dressed fine. We aren't going on a hike in the woods. There's a nice, easy to get to spot on the bank of Bear Creek about a half-mile up the road."

"I haven't been fishing since I was a kid."

"We're fishing *with* kids. You'll fit right in."

She rolled her eyes, not sure why she'd climbed into the golf cart with him. Clearly, she'd lost her mind. The girls had also influenced her bad decision, begging her to accompany them. "I can only stay an hour," she reiterated.

"Which is about all the fishing Addie and Daisy can tolerate before they lose interest and want to come home."

"Then why go at all?"

"Fishing is relaxing." Max slowed for a curve in the gently winding road. "I need to unwind after my hectic day. I'm betting you do, too."

He had her there. She'd spent the morning putting the finishing touches on his former sister-in-law's wedding dress. Worried that might be a sore subject, she refrained from mentioning it.

They left the main road and veered onto a trail marginally wider than the golf cart. Low-hanging branches slapped the metal canopy roof and grabbed at them with prickly fingers. Laurel instinctively tucked her arms close to her body and scooted toward Max to avoid getting scratched. He grinned down at her.

To ensure he didn't read anything into the situation, she peered over her shoulder to check on the girls, relieved to see they were also keeping their arms and legs inside the golf cart. Even Jelly hunkered down where she rode between them.

"How do you know I need to unwind?" she asked Max when the trail eventually widened, and she could sit up straight.

"You're a workaholic. You're always stressed."

She'd resent that remark if she didn't re-semble it. "Fine."

"And you were late to the preopening event."

"Hmm."

Partially in protest—she didn't like Max being right about her—she removed her phone from her purse and started scrolling through her emails. One caught her attention, and she let out a small, excited squeak as she read it.

"Are you okay, Miss Laurel?" Addie asked, leaning forward from where she sat behind Laurel.

"I am. Very okay. I just got some good news." She scanned the email again just to be sure she wasn't mistaken. The phone jiggled in her hands, making reading difficult.

"Good news you can share?" Max asked.

"I've hired someone."

"That's great!"

"It's the reason I was late today. One of the reasons," she amended. "I was interviewing Helena. She's just a part-time seamstress, not a full-fledged assistant. But at this point, I'll take anything I can get. Plus, her work is ex-cellent. Incredible, really. She brought several samples to the interview for me to look at."

"When does she start?"

"Monday. She couldn't accept the job until she talked to her husband. He's undergoing chemo, and she drives him to the hospital for his treatments and to his doctor appointments. She's just emailed to accept the job and let me know when she's available."

"You must feel good."

"I do." In fact, Laurel felt fifty pounds lighter. She would survive the craziness of June and the next busy wedding season now that she had help. "You won't believe where I found her. She's Emmy Lou's mother. The bride from yesterday's wedding."

"Not the difficult one?"

"Yes! I had no idea her mother was so talented. A good seamstress, yes. But she's really skilled. I'm surprised she didn't make her daughter's dress."

"Maybe they don't get along."

Laurel considered that. "I don't think that's the case. My guess is every bride is different. Some want their family involved in all aspects of their wedding. Others, like this bride, prefer complete control, right down to the color of toothpicks used in the canapés."

"I get that."

Something in his tone made Laurel think his ex-wife had been the latter. Had she snubbed Max's mom? From Laurel's small interaction with Charlene over the flower girl dresses, and what Cash had told her, she suspected Charlene liked things done her way.

Laurel related to a degree. She was certainly a perfectionist when it came to her dresses. However, she'd learned the value of delegating. Sometimes, too much. She'd relied heavily on her last assistant and been left high and dry when the gal abruptly quit. Then, there was the one who'd stolen money from Laurel after her breakup with Jordan.

That wouldn't happen again. Helena struck Laurel as both honest and reliable. Fingers crossed, anyway. She just needed to pay better attention this time. There were always risks in hiring an employee. In Laurel's case, the benefits outweighed the concerns.

"We're here, we're here!" the girls cried out, bouncing in their seat.

Jelly barked. Evidently, she'd been here before, as well.

"This is nice," Laurel said when they came to a stop.

The towering pine trees had opened to a lovely clearing, revealing a wide bend in the creek with large boulders at the water's edge perfect for sitting. The shady trees and cool running water would keep the temperature comfortable. Birds flitted from branch to branch in search of food. Fluffy white clouds drifted by overhead. All in all, Laurel couldn't picture a nicer place to spend an hour relaxing.

Had she actually just thought the word *relaxing*? What had come over her?

Could Max be on to something? This peaceful place had her slowing her gait and breathing more deeply. Kind of like when she and Max were at Sweet Dreams and she'd forgotten about the time.

She watched him help the girls out of the golf cart, all the while instructing them to stay close, keep hold of Jelly's leash and not go in the water under any circumstances. Once the girls and Jelly were all on solid ground, he reached for the fishing equipment in the cart's small rear bed.

"Remember what I said," he called as the girls and Jelly raced toward the creek.

"Can I carry something?" Laurel asked. She'd left her purse on the golf cart's floorboard but pocketed her phone.

"Thanks." Max handed her a soft-sided cooler, scooping up the fishing poles and tackle box.

By the time they reached the creek bank, the girls were already testing the very limits of Max's order to stay out of the water by dipping the toes of their sneakers in. Jelly dug furiously at something beneath the surface, her front paws like a pair of high-speed pistons shooting water everywhere.

"What are we using for bait?" Laurel vaguely remembered that part of fishing from her childhood.

"Salmon eggs. They're in the cooler."

She involuntarily pushed the cooler away from her. "With the snacks and drinks!"

"They're in a jar. They won't contaminate anything."

Hearing a soft chuckle, she asked, "Are you laughing at me?"

He grinned. "Me? No."

She supposed she should be glad they weren't fishing with worms. The thought of one wiggling on the end of a hook caused her to grimace.

"Girls," Max called. "Be careful."

They retreated from the creek bank a whole three inches.

"You have incredible patience," Laurel observed.

"Hard to tell from where you are, but I'm grinding my teeth to nubs."

He laid the fishing equipment on the ground next to a large boulder, sat down and started on the poles—one adult size and two child size emblazoned with Disney characters.

Laurel placed the cooler beside the fishing equipment. She chose the boulder beside his for her makeshift chair and, stretching out her legs, raised her face to the sun's warm rays.

"You can use this one once I add the bait," Max said as he attached a neon orange bobber to the line.

Laurel shook her head. "Oh, I don't want to fish. I'm fine with watching."

"You can't come all this way and not experience the best part."

"I don't know." She resumed her sunbathing. "This part's pretty nice."

"Yeah. It is."

She looked over to find him gazing at her and felt a small tingle of awareness in response. The next second, she worried she'd given herself away, for his mouth, sexy to begin with, quirked up at one corner.

"When was the last time you took a break?" he asked, his voice taking on a lazy quality.

"I take breaks."

"I'll rephrase. When's the last time you had a vacation?"

"It hasn't been that long." She crinkled her brow in thought. "Three years ago, I guess." She and Jordan had taken a trip to the Grand

Canyon. It was during the days when she dropped everything at a moment's notice to be with him. It was also right before he broke up with her.

"Hasn't anyone ever told you time off work is good for your mental health?"

"I like working," Laurel said. And, apparently, as she'd been informed by Phoebe, running away from her past. "Besides, what would I do with time off?"

The other side of his mouth quirked up. "I can think of a dozen things."

"Like fishing?"

"Absolutely. And horseback riding. Lingering over a nice dinner. Long walks."

"Those all sound like dating."

"Do they?" he asked.

She found turning away impossible as the intensity of his gaze anchored her in place. Eventually, her phone buzzed, breaking the spell. She grabbed it, read the message and typed a response. Then, since her phone was out, anyway, she checked her emails and tracked a supply order.

"Do you ever go anywhere without that thing?" he asked when she finished.

"Yes." She put the phone away, trying to remember when she last went anywhere with-

out it. Unable to, she reached for the cooler.
"You're going to need those salmon eggs."

Addie and Daisy had broken another of
Max's rules: they'd let go of Jelly's leash
and were trying to engage her in a game of
fetch. The dog was great at chasing the stick,
only instead of bringing it back, she ran off,
splashing through the water.

"Daddy," Daisy complained, "Jelly's chasing all the fish away."

Addie promptly threw a handful of pebbles
into the creek. If there were any fish left in
the vicinity, Laurel would be very surprised.

Max finished getting the girls' poles ready,
including adding the bright pink salmon eggs,
which weren't that gross.

"Come get your poles," he called, and they
ran the short distance over to him. "And no
more playing in the water. You have to sit and
hold your poles really still."

"What about Jelly?" Daisy asked.

"She has to stay still, too."

Max settled the girls on the boulders next
to him and Laurel, cast their lines into the
water and then handed them the poles. He
managed to grab Jelly's leash, which was
sodden because she'd been dragging it behind her, and tied the end to a strong exposed
root. Jelly's response to being restrained was

to flop onto the ground and rest her head on her paws.

"Good girl." Max patted her head. "You know what this fishing stuff is all about. R and R." He turned to Laurel as he sat and grabbed the other pole. "You ready?"

Laurel drew back. "I'm serious. I don't want to fish."

He ignored her protest and, after baiting the hook, passed her the pole. "You remember how to cast?"

At that exact moment, Laurel's phone rang. Her hand stilled midair as she met Max's gaze. Gone was the smile.

She brushed off a stab of annoyance. What if there was a dress emergency? She should take the call. At least check the number.

"Thirty minutes," Max reached out and touched her arm. "You can leave the outside world behind for that long, can't you?"

She opened her mouth, intent on refusing. Somehow this felt a little too much like her relationship with Jordan. The spontaneity of the fishing trip that required her to drop everything to be with him. The request to leave work behind and focus on the moment.

But Max wasn't Jordan, and his motives weren't selfish. Rather, he was trying to get her to take a break from her insane schedule. Like the other day at Sweet Dreams.

But look what had happened then. She'd almost lost an important client and damaged Wishing Well Springs' relationship with Nothing Bundt the Best.

The refusal was almost out of her mouth when she caught the look in Max's eyes. He was expecting her to say no. He didn't believe her capable of leaving work behind for a measly thirty minutes.

"Fine." She snatched the pole from him, ready to show him she wasn't beholden to her job and up to the challenge.

His grin returned.

Too late, she remembered she didn't know how to cast a line.

MAX WASN'T SURE his day could get any better. Heck, his week. His year. The preopening event at Happy Trails had gone well, he was fishing with his daughters and he had an undistracted Laurel for the next half hour.

"Need help?" he asked when her line landed in the wrong place for the third time.

"I got it." She stood and went to the creek's edge, detangling the hook from a cluster of half-submerged weeds.

Water rushed past, tumbling over rocks

and creating small whirlpools of white froth. The creek was shallow in this particular spot, making it fairly child safe as long as Max kept an eye on his mischievous offspring—which he did, like a hawk.

"Aim to the left," he told Laurel, also keeping an eye on her. "The water's deeper there. More likely to be some fish." If they hadn't scared them all away with their noise and antics.

"Daddy!" Addie shrieked. "I got a bite."

He rushed over to investigate her taut line, pretty certain she was mistaken. And she was. A piece of dark green moss clung to the end of her hook, which had gotten caught on some underwater rocks.

"Ewwww." She and Daisy both made faces at the long, dangling piece of slime.

Max cleaned the hook, added fresh salmon eggs and recast the line. With both girls contentedly fishing and Jelly sleeping soundly beside them, he could concentrate on Laurel. She'd managed to drop her line somewhere in the vicinity of the spot he'd indicated, and the two of them resumed sitting on their side-by-side boulders.

"Do you come here often?" she asked, only to laugh. "That sounds like a tired pickup line."

He laughed along with her. "Whenever we get a chance. Two or three times a month. I admit, I like fishing more than the girls."

"Catch a lot?"

"That's not the point. We have fun. I get to unwind and partake of the great outdoors. The girls aren't sitting in front of a TV. They're learning patience, if nothing else. Me, too."

"Max, I honestly haven't met a more patient man than you."

"I wasn't always."

She moved her pole, drawing an invisible Z in the air with the tip. Her bobber danced in response. "You're joking."

"You didn't know me back in the days when I owned the team penning facility."

"Is that another reason you sold it, besides wanting to spend more time with Addie and Daisy?"

He glanced over at his two little darlings, now reaching their small, cupped hands into the water and splashing each other. "I don't want to be like my dad, hating my job and always in a bad mood when I get home from work."

"Do you see your family much?" Laurel asked. "You haven't mentioned them."

"Not often enough, which is entirely my fault. But my parents are flying out for the soft opening. I'm hoping you can meet them. I invited my brother, but he can't get away on such short notice." Or he wasn't as interested in renewing his relationship with Max. He wasn't ready to give up and would try again.

"I'd very much like to meet your parents." Laurel reached for her phone in her pocket, though she apparently remembered her agreement to leave the rest of the world temporarily behind before she pulled it out. "Are you close? Do you have any other siblings? How did they feel when you moved to Arizona? And why did you move here?"

"You ask a lot of questions."

"I'm…curious, is all. Isn't that what people do when they're fishing? Talk?"

For a moment, he wanted her to say she was curious about him, in the way someone is curious about a person they're attracted to. It seemed that wasn't the case.

"My parents and I…drifted apart, I suppose you could say. Same with my brother. Not like we fought or became estranged. My brother's six years older than me and career army. Joined right after high school. I left home young, too. Set off to find my way in the world." He took in the majestic mountains visible above the pine trees. "I wasn't cut out for academics or the military, and I've always hated being stuck indoors."

"Where's your brother stationed?"

"Fort Hood in Texas."

"Must be hard on your parents, having both their children living far from home."

"It is. And they don't get to see Addie and Daisy much, which is why I invited them out and have made an effort to call more often. They really like video chatting with the girls."

"I'm sure they do." Laurel changed to drawing invisible circles with the tip of the fishing pole. "But how did you arrive in Arizona?"

"Long story short, at twenty I wound up working for a ranch in Montana, which is where I learned about cattle horses and team penning. I was good at it, if I do say so. Won a few competitions."

"More than a few, according to Cash."

Max shrugged. In fact, during his peak, he'd been one of the top five earners in the country. "I started training and selling cutting horses. Did all right at that, too. Then, about five years ago, an opportunity came along to buy the facility here in Payson, and I took advantage of it. My parents weren't thrilled at first. They'd have rather I moved home."

"Do you miss it? Running the facility?"

He checked on the girls for the tenth time

in as many minutes. They'd lost interest in fishing, set down their poles and were now picking wildflowers. Jelly laid stretched out in a patch of sun, snoring. She'd had a big day, too.

"Sometimes," Max mused. "Team penning is an exciting, challenging sport that requires a lot of skill. I miss training horses more than competing. That was satisfying. Nothing beats the feeling of taking a horse with raw potential and turning them into an outstanding performer. I don't miss running the facility. Keeping to a strict schedule. Balancing the books every month. Dealing with personalities. Fielding problems. Late hours."

"You sound like me," Laurel joked.

"I did learn a lot about maintenance and grounds keeping, which has come in handy with Happy Trails."

"Not all bad, then."

"I made some good friends through the years. And the facility is where I met Charlene. She came to take lessons and compete."

"Oh." Laurel raised her brows in surprise. "I didn't realize she rode cutting horses. I… assumed she was in business of some kind."

"She rode cutting horses in her spare time. She sold advertising for a local radio station, but it wasn't her dream. She was more the creative type, which is how she started experimenting with making her own shampoos and lotions. But her experience in advertising did help her prepare for *Pitch Me*."

"Interesting."

"Part of me really does admire her for what she's accomplished," Max admitted. "I just wish, for the girls' sakes, she'd carve out more time in her life for them."

"She may slow down, once her business reaches a certain level of success. The first years are the toughest."

"She may."

Was Laurel speaking from personal experience? Would she eventually slow down?

"What about you?" he asked. "What got you into designing wedding dresses?"

"I told you my grandma taught me to sew. I started making my own clothes in middle school. But it wasn't until I made a friend's dress for the senior prom that I realized how much I wanted to study design. I was lucky enough to win a scholarship to Northern Arizona University and even luckier to hire on with London DeLane after graduating." She said the name with reverence.

"She's someone famous, I take it?"

"Not a person. London DeLane is a top manufacturer of resort wear. Their clothing is highly sought after. If you visit any five-star resort, you'll see guests wearing London DeLane. I spent three years with them."

"Why'd you leave?"

Laurel sighed. "Don't get me wrong, it was a great place to start, and I learned an incredible amount. Made important connections in the industry. But resort wear wasn't my passion, and that's all London DeLane makes. They also refuse to consider anything not specifically their brand. I reached a point where I was miserable."

"Like me."

She returned his smile. "I suppose. Yes."

"See. We have something in common."

"Something else," Laurel said, her tone decidedly flirty.

Max needed a moment to respond, clearing his throat before he spoke. "Don't all famous designers believe their ideas are the best?"

"Not all. Some welcome input from their team members and give them chances to showcase their work. Like Nikolai, for example. He frequently takes young designers under his wing and helps them build their careers."

"He must be pretty famous, if he only has one name."

"He's very famous," Laurel concurred. "*The*

fashion designer to the stars and women who want bragging rights for owning a dress by such a renowned designer. At any red-carpet event, you'll find celebrities decked out in a Nikolai original."

"Is that what you want? To be so famous you only need to go by one name?"

"I'd settle for being the most famous designer in Arizona." Her eyes twinkled. "And to have my gowns appear on the cover of a magazine or two."

"I think you will."

"Maybe." Her expression changed to contemplative. "More likely I'll make a decent living with Bellissima and be known around Payson. And I suppose that's fine."

"I'm sure there are a lot of wannabe fashion designers who'd give their right arm to be you."

She beamed at him in a way that made him think a chance for them might exist. People overcame differences all the time. Surely, he and Laurel could, too. If they both wanted it. He did.

Max felt himself drawn to her by a force impossible to resist. Who was he kidding? A force he didn't even try to resist. Inch by inch, the distance separating them narrowed. He dipped his head.

"Daddy. Daddy. We're bored."

Addie and Daisy came bounding toward Max and Laurel.

Jelly woke up with a start. Springing to her feet on legs flying in all directions, she began barking.

Max retreated from Laurel and straightened. Had she been drawn to him, as well? In hindsight, he couldn't say for sure, and her expression revealed nothing. Then again, she hadn't recoiled. Of that, he was sure.

Max pushed to his feet. "Hey, kids."

Only when they were packing up to leave did he concede the interruption was for the best. He had no idea how his daughters would react if they saw him kissing a woman who wasn't their mother, and no way was he ready for that conversation.

CHAPTER TEN

"I WANNA GO HOME, DADDY," Daisy said, her tone plaintive.

"She pushed me," Addie complained.

The girls' boredom with fishing had increased to the point they were bickering nonstop.

"All right." Max rose with some reluctance. "Miss Laurel's thirty minutes are up, anyway."

"They are?" Laurel retrieved her phone and glanced at the display. "That went fast."

Too fast, as far as he was concerned. He waited, half hoping she wouldn't check her messages. She did. He kept his mouth shut, not complaining. She'd risen to the challenge and then some, lasting an extra five minutes.

Gathering the gear, he carried everything to the golf cart. Laurel brought the cooler and her pole, handing both to him.

"Feeling refreshed?" he asked.

"Yes," she admitted. "But I'll be a wreck by the time I get back to Bellissima, obsessing the entire drive there about everything on my to-do list."

The girls chatted away during the return ride to Happy Trails, filling the companionable silence between Max and Laurel. Her phone rang the moment they arrived, and she answered it without hesitation.

Max waved to a few of the overnight guests enjoying the amenities. He stopped to answer an elderly couple's question and, once he'd parked, a family of four approached. The wife asked Max if the girls wanted to play beanbag toss with their children. At the girls' eager squeals, and the wife's promise to supervise them and Jelly closely, Max agreed.

Laurel spun to face him, disconnecting her call. "I need to leave. I have a minor crisis to resolve."

Her voice had changed. The light and relaxed quality from when they'd been fishing creek side had been replaced with an undercurrent of tension.

"Say goodbye to Miss Laurel," Max called to Addie and Daisy.

While the family patiently waited, the girls ran over to give Laurel a hug, which she returned with exuberance. "Have fun," she told them. "See you soon."

Jelly lavished her with kisses and received a head scratching in return.

Max liked seeing his daughters not only accepting Laurel as someone new in their lives but genuinely liking her. And—who was he kidding?—he envied the attention she gave them and pictured what it might be like to receive one of her hugs.

"I'll walk you to your van," he said after the girls returned to play with their new friends, Jelly racing ahead.

"You don't have to," Laurel insisted.

"Happy Trails' policy. The owner sees off all guests."

"You just made that up."

"I'm the owner. I can make up rules on the spot."

"Hey, how's your honeymoon tent coming along? I forgot to ask earlier."

"I haven't started on it yet," he admitted. "The final construction and preopening kept me too busy."

"I'm planning a trip to that store I was telling you about. Not before your soft opening. Soon, though. The first week in July. I can pick up the rug and pillows for you. That is, if you trust my tastes."

"Or I can come with you." He waited for her reaction, which didn't take long.

"Okay. I was going to combine it with another errand, but I'll reschedule that one for another day."

"I don't want to inconvenience you."

"You're not." She took out her key fob and pressed a button to unlock the minivan doors. "I'm trying to keep the first week of July as open as possible to recover from June."

"Wait. Did you just say you're reducing your workload?"

Laurel laughed. "Not that. Simply keeping my hours to forty a week."

"It's a start."

Max walked with a noticeable spring in his step. Spending time with her, even if it was running a business-related errand, appealed to him. Probably more than it should.

Reaching her vehicle, he opened the door for her. "I'm glad you stopped by today."

"Thanks for inviting me. I had a nice time. Fishing wasn't nearly as bad as I thought it'd be."

He held a cupped hand to his ear. "Are you actually admitting there are benefits to taking a break and relaxing?"

"I wouldn't go that far." Laurel's teasing smile said otherwise. "The conversation was interesting. And enlightening."

The quality of her voice had changed again,

taking on an intimate tone. The pull from earlier returned, stronger than before. He shifted closer. "Say that again."

She laughed, the merry sound reminding him a little of Bear Creek rushing by them as water tumbled over the rocks.

Huh. Where had that come from? Max was hardly a poet.

"It was fun getting to know you better," she said, and also shifted.

An invitation? Granted, it had been a while since Max exchanged subtle messages with a woman. For all he knew, he'd forgotten how to send or read them. And Laurel had made it quite clear that she wasn't looking for a relationship, especially one with him.

"You're intriguing, Max Maxwell. Much more complicated than I initially guessed and with far more layers."

"I can say the same about you."

She lifted her face to his. That had to be an invitation, didn't it? Then, she closed her eyes.

Max felt like he'd lost control of a situation he'd been in complete charge of a minute ago. Laurel, he realized, could do that to him with a movement or a look or a single word.

Enough second guessing, he decided. "Unless you tell me no and that it would be a mistake, I'm going to kiss you, Laurel."

"I'm not going to tell you no."

That was all the encouragement he needed. Max had only to lower his head and his lips found hers, eagerly waiting for him. His arms slid around her waist. Hers circled his neck and rested lightly there. The next moment, he surrendered, falling into the kiss. Or was he flying? It was hard to tell the difference.

Really? More poetry? Max had no idea where all this sappiness sprang from, but, hey, bring it on. As long as she kept kissing him.

Lifting his hand to cradle her face, he traced the line of her jaw with his thumb. The shape was exquisite, like the curve of a seashell.

Okay, this really had to stop. He was a guy. Tough as leather, hard as nails.

One moment melted into two as they lingered. He knew with certainty there would never be another kiss like this one. Ever. Or a woman like Laurel.

From what seemed like a great distance away, he heard Jelly barking and his girls' high-pitched voices. The distraction was enough to jerk them back to reality. Letting his arms drop, Max retreated a step, every fiber of his being resisting. He doubted anyone had seen him and Laurel. The minivan shielded them from view.

For that he was glad. They'd be spared any embarrassing explanations.

"So, we did that," Laurel said, a shy but pleased smile on her face.

"Yeah, we did." Max studied her, noting no signs of regret. Good.

"I have to say, you didn't disappoint."

"Glad to hear. I can say the same about you."

"I… I'm not usually that impulsive. I don't want you to get the wrong idea."

"Should I be flattered?" he asked, feeling precisely that.

His expression must have given him away for she laughed. "Don't let it go to your head."

"So, kissing me was an impulse?"

"Partly. And…" The shy smile returned. "I've been wondering what it would be like."

"I'm game anytime, should your curiosity strike again." He was only half joking. He'd very much like to kiss Laurel again.

She hesitated. He didn't pressure her for more.

"How about this? We leave the prospect of any future impulses up to you," he said with a hint of teasing and a large dose of seriousness.

"My, aren't you confident." She dug her

phone from her pocket and tossed it through the open van door.

"I'm optimistic. But you call the shots. And whatever you decide, I'm okay with that."

She sighed. "I worry about repeating past mistakes. For both of us. What if we start something, and then I disappoint you? Or the other way around. You're launching a new business and you're a full-time dad. I have my obligations, not only to Bellissima but to Wishing Well Springs. Cash and Phoebe depend on me."

"It was just a kiss, Laurel," he said. "No commitments. No promises. No demands on each other. We had a moment. A nice moment we enjoyed. Let's leave it at that for now."

"You're right. I'm getting ahead of myself. I have a tendency to do that."

Neither of them moved. Max might have kissed her again, only he'd just told her she could call the shots.

The next second, her phone rang. Instantly distracted, she practically dived into the car to get it and answered with a breathy, "Hello. Yes. Of course, I remember. How nice to hear from you. No, you didn't interrupt me." She sent Max a glance. "How can I help you?"

He expected her to leave and was surprised that she continued to stand there conversing with her caller. He supposed he should be the one to leave. Yet, he didn't.

Laurel was talking to someone about photographs. That was clear from her side of the conversation. It sounded as if the woman wanted to take pictures of Bellissima. Laurel put her phone on speaker so she could open an app. Max caught sight of a calendar.

"Absolutely," she said, returning the phone to her ear. "I can do the fifth, no problem. Eleven o'clock." After a pause, she added, "I'm looking forward to meeting you, Keisha. Thank you, again, so much. I'm thrilled and honored. Truly. Bye and take care."

She disconnected and typed an entry into the calendar, her face alight.

"More good news?" Max asked.

"The best. That was Keisha Gilmore, feature editor of *Fashion Forward Magazine*."

The name meant nothing to Max, but he nodded as if it did.

"They're going to include one of my designs in an upcoming issue featuring wedding gowns. *Fashion Forward* is out of Phoenix and relatively new. They don't have the largest distribution. But, they're growing and earning a name for themselves. Keisha attended the wedding of one of my clients a few weeks ago and researched me. Researched me!"

"Congratulations, Laurel. This is what you wanted. To be in a magazine."

"Well, I won't be on the cover. Just included in an article."

"It's a step." He squeezed her arm and could feel the excitement running through her. The exposure, even in a fledgling magazine, could give her career a giant boost. "You're really going places."

"I have so much to do to get ready. Keisha asked me to send her pictures of five potential gowns. Oh!" Laurel shoved her fingers through her hair as if to jump-start her brain. "I need to locate a model. Maybe Phoebe can do it. I'll have to alter the gowns, too."

"Can your new employee help?"

"Yes. Thank goodness I have Helena." Laurel's hands fell to her sides. "I may have to postpone our trip to the store for the pillows and rugs."

"This is more important."

"I'm sorry."

"It's okay." Max wouldn't dream of holding her back from an important opportunity. "We can reschedule."

"For sure. I'll call you. This is just…eeee!" She drew Max into a brief, distracted hug. "Wait until Phoebe hears."

With that, Laurel hopped into her minivan

and pulled away. Her rear tires shot small plumes of dust into the air as she sped down the dirt road.

Max watched her go. In her haste, she'd forgotten to say goodbye. Had she forgotten their kiss, too?

Laurel, he'd learned, was capable of putting work aside temporarily and had more than once with him. But he worried that was all it would ever be with her. A moment here, an hour there. And he knew from past experience he wouldn't be satisfied with being someone's afterthought.

LAUREL LEFT HELENA in the workroom, confident in her new seamstress's ability to finish the intricate beadwork on her own. Helena had shown herself to be capable and, though she could only work fifteen hours a week, Laurel had high expectations.

She carried three giant, overstuffed plastic bags down the stairs, carefully watching every step. They weren't heavy, just awkward. At the bottom, she set the bags on the floor next to two rolled and bound rugs leaning against the wall. Satisfied the stack wouldn't topple, she made her way across the entryway, down the hall and to the kitchen.

The clock on the microwave told her it was

twenty past eleven—which explained why hunger had driven her from her workroom and in search of food. Laurel had missed the morning breakfast meeting with Cash and Phoebe again. She'd meant to grab a protein bar and piece of fruit, along with her second cup of coffee, but forgot. As a result, she was ravenous.

After a quick inventory of the fridge, she removed some leftover chickpea salad, a hard-boiled egg and a bag of apple slices. Not a feast, but her growling stomach voiced its appreciation while she set the food out on the table.

Sitting, she sent Max a brief text before stabbing her fork into the chickpea salad and stuffing a bite into her mouth with a satisfied, "Yum."

As she ate, she thought about the last time she'd seen Max, three days ago at Happy Trails' preopening event. They'd gone fishing. Chatted. Kissed. And hadn't spoken since, until now.

Granted, she should have reached out to him sooner. They'd kissed, after all, whether they should have or not. To ignore him seemed, if not rude, then dismissive. In her defense, she'd been so excited by the call from Keisha at *Fashion Forward Magazine* and getting ready for the photo shoot, she'd thought of little else. Add to that, and on top of her regular workload, she'd had ten client appointments this week alone.

She'd remember the kiss at random moments. In the middle of a discussion with Phoebe. While fitting a client or on the phone with a supplier. At night when she couldn't sleep. Never during a good moment to call or text.

And, to be honest, Laurel wasn't sure what to say to Max. *Great kiss. Bad idea. Things are still okay with us, don't worry.*

Ugh! The longer she went without contacting him, the harder it was and, she was convinced, the worse she looked. The items in the bags were an icebreaker. An excuse to talk to him. A segue into a conversation.

Did she need to apologize?

Peeling the egg and salting it, she wondered whether things were okay between them.

To Laurel, it felt like they'd known each other much longer than three weeks, which could be an indication of how well she and Max clicked. Only they shouldn't be clicking. They shouldn't be anything.

Picking up her phone, she viewed the display. No response to her text. Should she have called him instead and left a voice mail? Texting was kind of chicken and impersonal.

Just as she popped the last bite of hard-boiled egg in her mouth, Phoebe breezed into the kitchen.

"You're having an early lunch," she announced and fetched a bottled beverage from the refrigerator.

"I missed breakfast."

"Yeah. We noticed." She sat at the table across from Laurel and, uncapping the bottle, took a sip.

"Any important business?"

"The new misting system arrived yesterday. Cash is overseeing the installation." Phoebe continued for another five minutes, updating Laurel on miscellaneous business at Wishing Well Springs.

She tried to pay attention and not continually sneak glances at her phone.

Phoebe paused and sipped again at her beverage. Only then did Laurel notice the label.

"When did you start drinking vitamin water?" she asked.

"Last week."

Laurel chuckled. "I didn't think you liked that stuff."

"I don't. I'm trying to learn to like it."

"Why?"

Phoebe's cheeks turned a light shade of pink. "Cutting back on caffeine and sugar. I want to, need to, eat healthier."

"You? The queen of junk food and caffe lattes?"

"I know." She avoided Laurel's gaze.

"Hey, what's going on?"

"Nothing."

Laurel studied her best friend and sister-in-law, concern growing. "I don't buy that for one second. Come on, tell me. Is something the matter?"

"No." Phoebe smiled shyly. "Cash and I, we're…"

Realization dawned, almost knocking Laurel off her chair. "No way! Are you guys pregnant?"

"We're trying. Fingers crossed."

"Oh, honey." Laurel reached for Phoebe's hand. "I'm so happy for you. And here's to a short wait."

"Let's hope." Phoebe squeezed Laurel's fingers before letting go.

"Not that it's any of my business." Laurel tread carefully, not wanting to be the interfering in-law. "I thought you and Cash were going to wait a few years. You haven't been married that long."

"We were but my sister had all those problems conceiving. We, I," she emphasized the latter word, "started worrying. What if I have the same problems? Cash and I talked a lot and decided we're in good a place. Wishing Well Springs is making a decent profit, especially since you've grown Bellissima so much. His architectural practice is taking off. And you're here to help if we need time off. We could wait, it's true, but why?"

"Why, indeed?"

Despite her efforts, Laurel's mind traveled a familiar road. If she and Jordan had gotten married like she'd planned, she and Phoebe might be raising their children together.

Was that what she'd genuinely wanted or what she'd believed was expected of her? How would she fit a child in her life now? Motherhood and a career were both very demanding.

She thought about Max's ex-wife. Charlene hadn't been able to accomplish both and chose to make work her first priority. As a result, her daughters got the leftovers. When Laurel had devoted herself to Jordan, Bellissima suffered from neglect.

There had to be people out there who successfully balanced their personal and professional lives. But how did they do it? Until recently, Laurel had been content with only work to fill her hours. But while she wasn't ready for, and perhaps not capable of having, a relationship with Max, he'd shown her that taking small breaks wasn't all that bad. Doing so was, possibly, beneficial.

"I realize I'm jumping way ahead here," Laurel said to Phoebe, "but have you thought about how you're going to manage work and raising a baby?"

"Naturally, we've talked about it. If I had my choice, I'd stay home for three months. Georgia Ann can cover for me."

"Is she qualified? I have nothing but respect for her. She's a great crew leader, and no one can oversee a post-wedding cleanup like her. But she's not a wedding coordinator. She can't creatively solve problems and juggle ten tasks at once. Something you excel at."

"I'd train her and be available to answer questions. I could even come in for a few hours if there was a problem." Phoebe gave a small shrug. "Where there's a will, there's a way."

"I've always wondered how I'd feel going back to work after a maternity leave. I'm not sure I could leave my baby with a sitter or at day care for forty hours a week."

"I'm hoping to work from home two or three mornings a week. Cash can work from home, too, once in a while."

"Can you really get anything done while watching a baby?" Laurel had heard plenty of stories from clients who struggled with holding down a job while simultaneously taking care of their young children. But some people managed it.

"My mom will also help," Phoebe said. "And your mom. Worst case, we hire a nanny."

"Hmm."

"Look at Max. He's figured out how to work and raise children."

"Not everyone can completely rearrange their life like he did. Or find a job that allows them the kind of flexibility he has."

"Of course not." Phoebe paused to study Laurel. "Where are these questions coming from? Are you asking for me or yourself?"

"I'm just curious. You have a demanding job."

"Laurel, you are never *just curious*."

She polished off the last of her chickpea salad and pushed her plate aside. Phoebe was good at reading her. Too good, in fact.

"Max and I kissed the other day at his preopening event. A kiss I may or may not have initiated."

"And you didn't tell me!" Phoebe gasped. "I want details."

"It was an impulse. Nothing more."

"Impulse or not, did you like it? How'd you feel afterward?"

Laurel propped her chin in her hand. Three days later, and her emotions continued to run the gamut from exhilaration to uncertainty to worry. "I liked it, yes," she acknowledged. "That said, we both agreed it was just a kiss and nothing more." Unless she changed her mind. He'd left her that option. "We both have a lot going on. Neither of us is in a good place to start something we may not be able to finish."

"That's what I used to say about me and Cash. I eventually realized I was afraid of rejection. Sound familiar?"

"I'm not afraid," Laurel insisted. "I'm committed to Bellissima and Wishing Well Springs. Max is distracting. *Very* distracting." Had she given in to temptation, she'd have continued kissing him…and kissing him. "The problem is, I can see myself becoming the exact same person with him I was with Jordan. Then, where would I be?"

"Max isn't Jordan. He's nowhere near as demanding as Jordan was. And he has his daughters to consider, plus Happy Trails. He wouldn't insist you make him the center of your universe."

"Jordan wasn't solely to blame for what happened."

"Yes, he was," Phoebe insisted. "He was selfish and needy. Sorry, but it's true."

"I'm the one who thought lavishing attention on him was a form of love. I didn't realize, or refused to realize, he was using me."

"My point exactly. That wouldn't happen with Max. You learned your lesson and won't make the same mistakes."

"We haven't spoken since the kiss," Laurel admitted.

"Did you leave things on a bad note?"

"Maybe. I got that call from the feature editor at *Fashion Forward Magazine* and left right after that." She'd told Phoebe and Cash about the amazing opportunity as soon as she'd returned home, and Phoebe had agreed to be her model.

"Wasn't he happy for you?"

"He was. I think. Honestly, I'm not sure. I hurried out of there. Later, I wondered if I reminded him too much of his former wife."

"Ah."

"You agree, then."

Phoebe shook her head. "I don't know Max well enough to guess what he's thinking. It's possible, though?"

"I just sent him a text." Laurel folded and refolded her napkin, unable to sit still.

"Good. He may feel like you blew him off after the kiss. It might have felt like a rejection."

Laurel grumbled, "I messed up. And I might have messed up even more."

"How?"

"I told him at the PBP luncheon I'd help him decorate the honeymoon tent. Take him to that shop I love so much to buy pillows and a rug. Then, I had to postpone after the call from *Fashion Forward Magazine*."

"Postpone, though. Not cancel."

"Not cancel."

"Okay. Reschedule, then," Phoebe said.

"Well, it's too late for that. I had another errand yesterday near the shop and picked up the items on my own. I have them in bags by the stairs. That's why I texted him. Asked if he wanted to come by." Laurel checked her phone yet again. "He still hasn't answered."

"He could be busy. His soft opening is in less than two weeks. And aren't his parents coming out for a visit?"

"They are." She nodded, remembering Max had mentioned wanting her to meet them. Would he now?

"And his former wife will be here, too, for

her sister's wedding," Phoebe added. "The guy has a lot of irons in the fire. Not to mention driving the carriage for us."

"True." Laurel stood and carried her dishes to the sink where she rinsed them off. "I should have at least texted him the day after our kiss. Now he thinks I'm mad at him or distancing myself. And what if he's upset that I bought the pillows and rug without him after we agreed to go together?"

"For someone who insists she doesn't want a relationship, you're doing an awful lot of overanalyzing."

"I am," Laurel admitted and blew out a long, worrying breath. "This might sound weird."

"What?"

"I've been thinking a lot about my dad lately."

"Yeah?" As usual, Phoebe didn't press and let Laurel continue when she was ready.

"His abandoning us when he and Mom divorced, well, it may have had more of an effect on me than I've realized."

"How so?"

"He could have been the reason I went overboard with Jordon."

"I suppose it's possible,"

"And he could be the reason I'm hesitant to get involved with Max."

Phoebe threw an arm around Laurel's shoulders. "You *are* overanalyzing, *Seriously*."

"But what if there's a connection, and I'm messed up because I have…" She made a face. "Daddy issues?"

"You're not messed up," Phoebe said. "You just picked the wrong guy."

"Maybe." Laurel wasn't convinced.

"Have you ever considered reaching out to your dad? It's been a while since you've talked, right?"

"I have. I wondered if Cash was going to invite him to your wedding. But he didn't." Laurel shrugged.

"Do you know where your dad is?"

"Not exactly. I can probably get ahold of him through my Aunt Corrine."

"Why don't you then?"

Should she? Laurel had to dwell on that for a while. "Maybe one day."

"Talk to Cash. Get his take on the subject."

I might."

Laurel stood and walked to the sink where she loaded her dishes and plastic containers into the dishwasher. She was ready to set the conversation about her dad aside. For now.

As she turned back to Phoebe, her phone pinged and the display lit up. Seeing Max's name, she had to force herself not to fly at the table.

"It's him," she said in the most casual tone she could muster and read the text.

"Well?" Phoebe prodded when Laurel didn't immediately respond.

She smiled, her mood instantly lightening. "He's driving the carriage for a wedding this afternoon. He says he can drop by before then."

"That doesn't sound like he's mad."

"No." Laurel's relief at hearing from Max instantly morphed into anxiety. "Doesn't sound like he's happy, either." She reread the text. "Pretty neutral, actually."

"You'll find out soon enough."

She would. "I'd better run. I have a lot to do this afternoon."

Phoebe pushed back from the table. "Me, too."

The two friends parted. Laurel grabbed the bags and rugs on her way back to Bellissima. For the next hour, she tackled work while mentally rehearsing what she'd say to Max.

CHAPTER ELEVEN

MAX STOOD AT the entrance to the main house and paused. He tugged on the hem of his dress vest, then adjusted his bolo tie before removing his cowboy hat and smoothing his hair.

Who was he kidding? He was stalling.

Laurel's text message earlier had been amiable, though impersonal. Considering their kiss, that either boded well or not well. The neutral wording could be her way of saying they were still friends. Nothing had changed. Or she was establishing boundaries. Keeping things strictly business, if not pushing him away by small degrees.

He'd read the text enough times he had it memorized.

If you're not busy, any chance you can stop by? I have some stuff for the honeymoon tent.

She hadn't elaborated, and Max hadn't asked. She was reaching out to him after a three-day dry spell. At least, he preferred to think she was reaching out to him.

To be fair, he was responsible for their zero contact as much as Laurel, though their reasons were vastly different. He'd been willing to see if their kiss would lead to more, but she seemed to think it had been a mistake. So he'd chosen to let Laurel make the next move. Her text could be an attempt to put out feelers. The question was, what did she hope to discover?

I'll be at WWS at 2 for a wedding. Are you free before then?

He'd retyped his reply multiple times before sending it, attempting to keep it as friendly and neutral as she had hers.

How's 1?

His reply to that had been a thumbs up.

Now, stomping his boots to dislodge the dust, he turned the doorknob and entered the house. The bell jingled, announcing his arrival. His steps slow and deliberate on the hardwood floor, he walked across the lobby toward Bellissima. Inside the shop, he waited, noting the absence of customers. Good. No witnesses should things go south.

"Hey." Laurel's voice floated to him from

behind a rack of colorful dresses. "Be right there."

"No hurry." The carriage and horses were ready to go.

Max noticed several large plastic bags sitting on the left couch in the waiting area. On the floor in front of them were two long cylinder objects he couldn't identify. The stuff for the honeymoon tent?

Was he supposed to sit? Stand? Pace? Max wasn't usually this indecisive. He shifted awkwardly for a full minute until she appeared.

"Thanks for coming by." She smiled.

"Thanks for the...whatever." He pointed toward the far couch.

She approached him, her attractive features apologetic. "I may have overstepped. If what I got isn't to your tastes, please say so. You won't hurt my feelings."

"I'm sure I will. Like what you got, that is," he added.

She nodded at the couch. "Have a seat, and I'll show you."

He put his cowboy hat on the coffee table and sat. As he watched, she untied one of the bags with clumsy fingers. He'd observed Laurel in many different moods. Happy. Anxious.

Relaxed. Irritated. Frustrated. He'd never seen her nervous. Interesting.

At last, she managed to open the bag. Reaching inside, she pulled out a shiny, bright red pillow.

"Hmm." Max wasn't sure what to say.

"You like it?" she asked. "Too much?"

"It's fine." He was no throw pillow connoisseur. At her waning smile, he added, "No, it's terrific. Thanks, Laurel."

"There's more."

The bags contained eight pillows altogether, ranging in shades from dark red to pale pink.

"Those are some pillows," he commented.

"They're satin."

"Okay."

She returned the bags to the couch. "And I have two area rugs." She bent and lifted the closest cylindrical object, which Max could now see was indeed a rug. "If you like them, I can get more. I'm not sure two will be enough." She grabbed a small pair of scissors from the coffee table, snipped the tape and then unfurled a black rug with red hearts. "I thought you could put one on each side of the bed. That way, the couple's bare feet won't have to touch the wooden floor when they get up in the morning. And black will hide the dirt."

"It's fluffy."

"They're shag rugs." She ran her hand over the rug, smoothing the pile.

He cleared his throat. "Thanks, Laurel. I appreciate this. What do I owe you?"

"What? Nothing. Consider them a house-warming gift. For Happy Trails' opening."

"I can't. I'm sure they weren't cheap."

"I'm happy to help." She flushed prettily.

He didn't say what was really on his mind since she'd revealed the first pillow: the two of them weren't going shopping. Not the first week of July or, apparently ever. He considered asking why but didn't. He wasn't sure he wanted to hear the answer.

"Can I come back for them after the wedding?"

"Whenever's convenient for you." Laurel rolled up the area rug and used her foot to push it over to lie beside the other one.

Max started to rise, assuming their conversation had come to an end. She surprised him by sitting beside him.

"If you have a minute, there's something else I wanted to talk to you about."

He tried not to react. His pulse picked up speed. Was she going to bring up their kiss? Say she'd reconsidered and was ready to take a step forward in their relationship? "Sure. What's up?"

"First off, I want to apologize for running off the other day. And for not contacting you the last few days. I hope you didn't think I was ignoring you."

"Hey. I didn't contact you, either."

"I guess we're still feeling a little awkward."

"I don't want to make a wrong move or say the wrong thing. I like you, Laurel," he admitted.

"I like you, too. A lot. If things were different, I'd be pursuing you."

"Same here."

"It won't always be this way for me. At least, I hope it won't always be this way," she added. "I'd like to believe there's a light at the end of the tunnel."

"I'm sure there is."

She leaned a fraction closer. "Whatever this is with us, we need to go slow. One day at a time kind of slow."

"I agree."

"Good. Because there's more than you and me to consider. Addie and Daisy are already missing their mom. They don't need to be missing their dad, too, or feel neglected because he's spending time with someone else."

He liked that she was considering his daughters. Addie and Daisy were sensitive and continued to struggle with their mom's absence. He could see them reacting badly to him being away more than usual and pre-occupied.

How did other single parents handle dating? He had, naively, assumed any outings he and Laurel went on would go much like fishing the other day—the four of them getting along like gangbusters.

"I'd hate for them to start resenting me," she said.

"They like you too much for that to happen."

"And I want them to keep liking me. Not grow to resent me. The fact is, you're a family man with two children."

"Are you ready for that and everything it entails?"

"I don't know. Which is another really good reason to go slow."

"You keep making good points."

"Relationships, even causal ones, come with expectations. I can't help wondering, are we ready for that and not setting ourselves up for failure? Just look at the other day. I disappointed you when I left. I'll disappoint you again. It's inevitable. My job and my life are demanding."

"How about this?" he said, attempting to ease her concerns. "We hang out whenever we're free and the mood strikes. No pressure."

"I like that. But would you be satisfied with whenever we're free?"

"I think so."

"Really?" She gave him a dubious look. "Something tells me you'd want more. Sooner rather than later. And then there would be pressure."

"Or not. We don't know unless we try."

Her worried features melted into a smile. "You're a hard man to resist."

Max resisted sweeping her into his arms. That would be proving her point. "Glad to her it."

"What with PBP and our two businesses cross-promoting, we'll be seeing a lot of each other. I suppose we can see where that leads."

He grinned.

"If things get sticky, however, we can call it quits with no bad feelings."

Was that possible? "Fair enough. Do we shake on it?"

"How about a hug?"

They stood and embraced. She pulled away much too soon.

"I hate to sound like a broken record, but

I need to get back to work. When's Charlene getting in?"

Laurel was changing the subject, and Max went along. He'd agreed to go slow and for her to take the lead.

"She's supposed to arrive the day before the wedding," he said. "Along with the rest of her and her sister's family. Between that and my folks visiting, Addie and Daisy are bouncing off the walls. They'll be spoiled rotten by the time everyone leaves."

"Would you have it any other way?"

"No." He grinned, feeling much better than when he'd arrived. "Charlene's sister, Sarah, invited my parents to the wedding so they could see the girls."

"That was really nice of her. They must be thrilled."

"Yeah. Lucky for me, Mrs. Applewood will watch Jelly for the day. Who knew when I agreed to getting a puppy, I'd have to find regular day care for her, too."

"The girls adore her."

"Unfortunately."

"Oh, come on," Laurel teased. "You love her, too."

"Love is a stretch. I tolerate her," he grumbled.

"Liar."

"Charlene sent a doggy costume," he said.

"I guess to make up for missing the fitting for the flower girl dresses."

"That's cute."

"Problem is, it's way too big. And Jelly just wants to chew it."

"I could alter the costume," Laurel offered. "If you want."

"No." Max shook his head. "You're way too busy. You just said as much."

She dismissed him with a wave. "That's a twenty-minute project."

"Laurel. No. You've already done too much."

"Bring Jelly and the girls by later this week."

"You remember what happened the last time we were here? One of your dresses barely survived the attack."

"I'll meet you in the entranceway. We'll avoid Bellissima altogether."

"I don't know."

"You bring ice cream for everyone from Sweet Dreams. We'll eat in the kitchen. I'll fit Jelly for the costume there, measure her and do the pinning. The girls will have to hold her steady. That should prevent any calamities before they happen."

"I like that idea much better."

"I'll need a couple of days to complete the alterations."

"Thanks, Laurel."

"Is Thursday all right?" She checked the calendar app on her phone. "Around three is good for me."

"We'll be here. Cookie dough ice cream, right?"

"Yes." The pretty blush from earlier returned to color her cheeks.

As much as he wanted to stay, Max had a carriage to drive. "I'd better get going. Otis and Elvis are waiting for me at the stables." He stood, with far more enthusiasm than when he'd first arrived.

"Good luck, though I'm sure everything will go well."

Max retrieved his hat from the table, unsure what to do next. They'd already hugged to seal the deal. Another would be pushing it, but a handshake felt too impersonal.

"See you."

She walked him to the shop entrance where she squeezed his arm. "See you Thursday."

"Bye." He left then, a spring in his step. He and Laurel were getting together again in two days. Not a date. Hanging out, like they'd discussed.

If things were different, I'd be pursuing you.

Laurel's words settled in the vicinity of his heart.

He could be patient and wait for the time when things were different. Very patient.

TWO DAYS LATER, Max and the girls arrived at Wishing Well Springs for Jelly's costume fitting. He'd texted Laurel earlier, letting her know they were on their way.

Holding open the front door to the main house, he motioned for the girls to enter. Addie went first, grappling with a small insulated beverage cooler containing the ice cream.

"Daddy, where's Miss Laurel?"

"In the shop."

Daisy brought up the rear, carrying the bag with the costume and wearing a disgruntled expression. She'd wanted to walk Jelly, but Max was in charge of the troublesome dog. After the disaster last time in Bellissima, he wasn't taking any chances.

"I wanna make another bride doll," Addie announced as they crossed the lobby, not using her inside voice.

"I wanna wear a dress," Daisy countered.

"Not this time, kiddos."

The flower girl dresses were hanging in their closet at home. Max had taken pictures of the girls wearing them, which he'd sent to Charlene. She'd responded that she wished she could have been there for the fitting. Max had resisted being snide, instead replying that the girls were excited to see her soon.

He didn't hate Charlene. Far from it. He hated that she put her career ahead of Addie and Daisy. Mostly, he felt sorry for her. She was missing out on the best parts of parenthood. He considered the pros and cons of talking to her once again about her absence in the girls' lives.

Pros: understanding could bring him peace of mind and potentially eliminate some of the tension between them so that she'd visit the girls often. Cons: the wedding wasn't the best time or place for an important conversation. Charlene would be busy with maid of honor duties and, he hoped, spending every available moment with Addie and Daisy. He also didn't want to risk angering her in case she disinvited his parents. Still, he'd try to find that time and place while she was in Payson. Perhaps the day after the wedding.

Max vowed to keep his cool whenever they did finally talk. He had just over a week to figure out a good approach that wouldn't cause Charlene to shut down like she tended to do.

"Stay right here," he told the girls when

they reached the entrance to Bellissima. "Do not move. Do not fight. Do not blink."

"I wanna go inside," Addie complained.

Did every sentence the girls uttered start with "I want"?

"Not today, honey." He tugged on Jelly's leash and told her, "Sit."

She did on the third attempt, her lolling tongue hanging out of the side of her mouth, her attention wandering.

"Laurel," Max called. "We're here." He called her name again.

From the silence, he concluded she must be upstairs in her workroom. He was about to phone her when she appeared from behind a dress display.

"Sorry I'm late. I got stuck on a Zoom call with the bride and groom and the mothers."

"No worries."

"Hi, Addie. Hi, Daisy." A wide smile appeared on her face, not forced as much as strained. "Don't you two look cute in your denim jumpers." She bent and gave Jelly's head a pat. The dog immediately flopped over onto her back. "You goofball."

"Hi, Miss Laurel," the girls chorused.

"Everything okay?" Max asked.

"I… No." Laurel heaved a frustrated sigh.

"Do you mind if I leave you on your own for a few minutes? I won't be long, I promise."

"Go on. We'll keep ourselves amused. Outside."

"I'm hungry," Addie announced.

"There are some animal crackers in the truck." Max patted her shoulder.

"Ew. Yucky."

"Those taste bad," Daisy added.

"Why don't you wait in the kitchen," Laurel said. "There's a cheese and fruit tray in the fridge and a half gallon of milk."

"Cheese," Addie exclaimed.

"You can put the ice cream in the freezer."

"You sure?" Max took the cooler from Addie, already liking the idea. The farther away from Bellissima, the better.

"Kitchen's that way. You can't miss it." Laurel pointed down the hall. "I'll meet you there when I'm done."

"Sounds good."

Ten minutes later, the girls had polished off a fair amount of cheese, apple slices and grapes and a glass of milk each. Jelly had swallowed three cubes of cheese that accidentally fell—or had been purposely dropped, depending on your point of view. Five minutes after that, Addie and Daisy were growing restless. Jelly, too. She started barking at every little noise. A door banging from up-stairs. People talking outside the window. A honking horn.

"Quiet, Jelly." Max placed a hand on the dog's head.

"I wanna go home," Daisy groused.

"Let's give Miss Laurel another five min-utes, okay? Then we'll leave."

Max was just returning the remaining cheese tray to the fridge when Laurel hur-ried into the kitchen.

"I'm so, so sorry."

"It's okay." Max started to gather the girls, helping them out of their chairs. Now that they'd eaten, he hoped they'd be less cranky and more cooperative. "Come on, kiddos. Why don't we get started? Daisy, where's the costume?"

"No." Laurel wrung her hands. "What I meant to say was, I can't get away. Not yet. My emergency has turned into a catastrophe."

"Your Zoom call?"

"They're happy. This is someone else." She shot a glance at the clock. "I'm going to be a while longer. Twenty minutes, at least." She grimaced apologetically. "We could resched-ule if you're busy."

He did have errands to run for Happy Trails.

Parcels to pick up at the post office and parts he needed at the hardware store.

"Daddy," Addie whined. "What about Jelly's costume?"

"It's okay, sweetie. Miss Laurel has something important to do."

"Like Mommy," Daisy said, pouting.

"Not like Mommy," Max answered more forcefully than he intended. Because of embarrassment at Daisy's remark and because, for a brief second, he'd thought the same thing. "I apologize for Daisy."

"No need." Laurel took several deep breaths and turned toward the girls. "I know it's a lot to ask, but if you can wait, I'll fix the costume for Jelly. I promise."

"You don't have to, Laurel," Max said.

"I want to. I do. This is important. And then we can have ice cream." The smile she offered this time shone with sincerity.

"If you're sure," he said.

"You could take the girls to the miniature town. Let them play and burn off some energy."

The warmth in her voice touched him. She didn't like letting them down and wanted them to wait for her. Max wanted to wait for her, too.

"Would you like that, girls?" he asked the

girls. "Or would you rather pet the horses? We can see Elvis and Otis in the stables."

"Pet horses," Addie cried.

"Can we ride them?" Daisy asked.

"Yes, ride them!"

"Why not?" Max would sit the girls on one of the old boys and lead them around. Both Elvis and Otis were dead broke and lazy to boot. It might be a great way to spend twenty or thirty minutes. Better than being cooped up inside or running errands.

"Okay, good," Laurel said. "I'll text you when I'm done." The stress returned to her face as she darted from the kitchen.

Must be some catastrophe, thought Max as he, the girls and Jelly ambled the short distance to the stables.

Laurel's warning from the other day came back to him. She said she'd disappointed him and would again. And here, less than a week later, she was trying hard to stop her prediction from coming true.

He could have gotten mad and stormed off when she said she had an emergency. Rather, he held his temper. Another lesson learned, this one from his daughters.

Elvis and Otis, gentlemanly as always, allowed the girls to dote on them, kiss their noses and comb small fingers through their long manes. Max didn't bother to put a halter on Otis. He followed Max around the paddock, carrying both Addie and Daisy on his back. Elvis plodded along behind them. Jelly, on the other hand, had gone in search of mice or lizards inside the stables.

"You three appear to be having fun."

Seeing Cash, Max broke into a grin. "Hey, pal."

His friend reached the paddock fence and rested his forearms on the top railing. "Laurel told us this morning she was…what? Making a costume for your dog?"

"Altering one that's too big." Max joined Cash, standing opposite him on the other side of the paddock fence.

Jelly promptly bounded out from the stables. Yipping a hello, she ran straight to Cash, jumped up and planted her dirty paws on his clean jeans.

"Jelly, down," Max said.

The dog ignored him. In her defense, Cash encouraged her by scratching her ears and telling her she was a good girl. Why Max even bothered trying to train the dog, he had no clue. Jelly was a lost cause if ever he saw one and indulged by everyone she met.

Cash gave her one last pet before gently

pushing her down. "So, why are you here and not with Laurel?"

"She had a work emergency. Said she'd be free soon. We came here to kill some time."

The horses stood behind Max while the girls, still sitting atop Otis, played a game of count-the-white-hairs on his back.

Cash reached through the paddock fence to give Elvis's neck a pat. "I bet these old boys have carried a thousand youngsters between them, including me and Laurel. Grandpa used to call them babysitters. Grandma adored them. They were some of the last horses Grandpa bought before Grandma got sick and he started selling off the land."

Max could see by his friend's sorrowful expression that the memory still haunted him. He uttered a silent thanks that his family hadn't experienced tragedy like that. The Maxwells had grown apart, it was true, but Max was committed to bridging the distance between them, starting with his parents' visit.

"Elvis and Otis are good old boys, for sure," Max agreed.

"You know, if you keep hanging around my sister, you'll have to get used to waiting on her."

"We're just friends."

"That's what she says, too." Cash grinned.

"It's kind of fun watching the two of you deny what's obvious to the rest of us."

He debated telling Cash about the kiss, and then thought better of it. "We agreed we both have a lot on our plates right now and shouldn't start anything."

"And how's that working out? The not starting anything?"

"Better some days than others," Max admitted.

Cash turned suddenly somber. "You know I think highly of you, Max."

"Why do I hear a but?"

"Personally, I can't imagine a better choice for my sister. But the thing is, I'm not sure she's the right choice for you."

"Because of what happened after she broke up with that guy?"

"Yeah. And those two little ones over there." Cash hitched his chin at the girls. "All of you could wind up being hurt. Not intentionally—Laurel wouldn't do that. But she has trust issues with herself. As your friend, I have to say I'm worried she may panic and run. If that happens, where will that leave you? And the girls?"

"To be honest, I don't know."

"You should probably think about it."

At that moment, the girls began to squabble. Before someone fell off and broke an arm, Max lifted them down from Otis and set them on the ground. That triggered an eruption of protests and whining.

"We'll come back soon," he told the girls and opened the gate for them to squeeze through. He went next, leaving Otis and Elvis behind.

When his pocket played a Tim McGraw song, he said, "Get Jelly," and retrieved his phone. "It's your sister," he informed Cash and put the phone to his ear. "Hello."

"I'm free now, if you're still here," she said uncertainly.

"We're at the stables."

"I'm surprised you waited."

"We had nowhere else to be." He glanced at Cash, who gave him a you're-hopeless-my-friend look. "We'll be right there."

"You heading to the house?" Max asked Cash when he'd disconnected from Laurel.

"Nah, back to my office. After I get a box of old architectural drawings from the storage room above the stables." He paused. "I hope you don't think I'm interfering."

"You're not."

"Good. See you later." Cash headed toward the stables and disappeared inside.

Jelly tried to follow him, and Max called

her back. For once, she obeyed, and Daisy put the leash on her.

"Hurry, girls. Miss Laurel's ready for us.

They refused to leave without first saying goodbye to the horses. As the three of them returned to the main house—Max walked, Addie and Daisy skipped and Jelly pulled hard on the leash—he considered his conversation with Cash.

What would happen if Max and Laurel were to get involved and, as Cash feared, she panicked and ran? Despite what Max had told his friend, he was falling for Laurel and could see a future with her. But if she didn't see one with him or got scared, maybe Max should get out now while his heart remained intact.

CHAPTER TWELVE

LAUREL RAISED HER head as Max, his daughters and Jelly entered the kitchen. She'd already opened the package containing the dog costume—a neon pink and green dinosaur, complete with scales down the back and horns on the cap—and laid out the various pieces.

"I went ahead and got started," she said, smiling.

She'd brought her travel sewing basket with her that held the basics: scissors, pins, a tape measure, needles and thread and a few extras. She'd perform any sewing needed for the costume later on her machine.

"Mind if we give Jelly a drink?" Max asked. "She's tuckered out."

The dog panted loudly, her sides heaving and her tongue hanging out.

"Poor puppy." Laurel went to the cupboard and retrieved a plastic bowl, which she filled with water and set on the floor. Jelly lapped thirstily, spilling everywhere. Laurel grabbed some paper towels off the roll.

Max reached for them. "Let me do that."

She relented, giving him the paper towels and then showing him the trash bin beneath the sink.

"I'm thirsty, too, Daddy," Addie said.

"I have just the ticket." Laurel removed a pitcher of lemonade from the refrigerator and poured four glasses.

"This isn't a ticket," Daisy exclaimed, staring at the glass Laurel placed on the table in front of her.

"You're right, sweetie. That's just a saying for having the perfect solution."

"Thanks," Max said and took a long drink. "This really is perfect."

"What about the ice cream?" Addie asked.

"Later, after we're done with Jelly's costume."

"Sorry I made you wait," Laurel said, sitting beside Daisy.

Max dropped into the chair across from her. "Is your catastrophe under control?"

"Mostly. Tensions can run high during wedding preparations, and the dress triggers all sorts of emotions. Add in family dynamics and…" She shook her head and sighed. "In this particular case, the bride and groom and both families are splitting the cost of the wedding. The groom's mother feels entitled to a say in the dress. A significant say."

"Should she?"

"I don't play referee." Laurel sipped at her lemonade. "While I personally believe the bride has the final vote, I let the family work out any disagreements on their own."

"Wise move."

"I suggest compromises that favor the bride but consider everyone else's wishes. It doesn't always succeed. Today, it did. Eventually." Looking fondly at Jelly who'd collapsed onto the cool tile floor by the water dish, she asked, "Shall we get started?"

"What first?" Max asked.

Following Laurel's instructions, he and the girls put Jelly in the dinosaur costume. The young dog didn't cooperate and attempted to chew the sleeves and tail. She repeatedly shook her head, knocking the cap askew.

"Jelly, be good," Daisy admonished.

Fat chance, thought Laurel, but laughed, anyway. They were all cute. Dog. Twins. And, okay, Max. She loved watching him doing his dad thing.

Was it possible Charlene felt confident leaving the girls in his care because he was such a good parent? Laurel hadn't considered that before. Still no reason for Charlene to neglect her daughters, but he made it easy to say, "Max, you handle that."

"Hold her still," Laurel instructed, and the girls somewhat managed to restrain Jelly while Laurel pinned the costume. She was careful not to stick the dog. "You know, you have another choice," she said to Max.

"What's that?"

"You can wait until Jelly grows into the costume."

"That won't be for months."

"We want Mommy to see it," Addie insisted.

Max exchanged glances with Laurel, and she saw his dilemma. He'd been put in a tough spot. Charlene hadn't checked with him about Jelly's size before buying the costume, and three-year-olds failed to grasp the concept of waiting.

"All right." Laurel continued pinning while Jelly alternately licked and nibbled her fingers. "I'll leave a little room so she can wear it for a few months at least. It might still fit at Halloween. Then you can take her trick-or-treating with you."

Both girls got excited at that prospect.

Laurel finished soon after and carefully

removed the costume. She folded it and returned it to the package for safekeeping.

"I really appreciate you doing this," Max said.

"I can't tell you when exactly I'll have it finished, but it'll be soon. You have carriage rides next week, don't you?"

"On Monday and Friday."

"I'll shoot for Friday," she said.

Max scooted back in his chair. "Well, kids. Time to hit the road."

"What about our ice cream?" Laurel asked.

He flashed the grin that always made her feel a little giddy. "I hate to take up more of your time."

"I have a few minutes for a bowl of ice cream." Really? Was that Laurel talking?

A twinkle appeared in his eyes, mirroring his grin. "Ten minutes for ice cream. I must be wearing off on you."

"I wouldn't say that." Except, he *was* wearing off on her. More than she would have thought possible.

After her stress-filled afternoon with the bride's difficult mother-in-law, the time with Max and his daughters was a pleasant reprieve. Laurel found she wasn't eager to return to the grindstone.

Stop right there! These thoughts and feelings of hers were too similar to those she'd had with Jordan and gave her pause.

While she spooned ice cream into bowls, and Max occupied the girls, she embarked on an emotional deep dive. Today didn't feel exactly the same as with Jordan. She wasn't focusing the entirety of her attention on Max. Rather, she'd allowed herself a short, pleasant interlude after a difficult day. That was good mental health practice. No different than going on a short walk or meditating. And fine as long as she didn't lose track of time like that day at Sweet Dreams.

Okay, she decided. This was new and reminded her of the person she was before she met Jordan. Someone who fell somewhere between blowing off work entirely and obsessed with it to the point of running herself ragged. A *normal* person.

She let the realization sink in. If she was using work as an excuse to shield herself from hurt, did taking this mentally healthy break with Max mean she was, if not fully recovered, at least on the road?

Laurel smiled to herself as she served the ice cream. While eating, they discussed Max's parents' impending visit and what they planned to do together. When they'd finished, Laurel carried the dishes to the sink.

"I'll walk you outside," she said.

The girls took Jelly and ran straight for the golf cart parked in its usual place beside the porch steps.

"Addie, Daisy," Max hollered. "Come back."

"It's all right," Laurel said. "Let them play. The key's inside the house. The golf cart isn't going anywhere."

Addie "drove" while Daisy sat beside her in the passenger seat with Jelly between them.

Laurel strolled over to the porch railing and braced her palms against it. Max came, too. Seemed she wasn't quite ready to end her break and return to the grind.

"You're really have a way with kids," he observed, maintaining a friendly distance between them.

"Your girls are precious."

"Not always. They can be little tyrants."

"You're exaggerating."

"You wouldn't say that after spending a full day with them."

Was he dropping a hint? Possibly. "All kids test boundaries. I see it often in my line of work. Hasn't changed my mind about having them one day. My own or stepchildren. Maybe adopting. There are no rules to what comprises a family. I've seen my share of that, too."

He moved closer. "You have a great attitude."

"I'm not ready yet," she added. "I want to grow Bellissima and make a name for myself. At some point, I'll be able to do both, have a career and children. At least, that's my plan."

"It's a good one."

Since they were on the subject, she said, "I'm not sure how my wants and needs fit in with your future plans."

"You're worth waiting for, Laurel."

"Dating me would not be easy."

He flashed that grin again. "Nothing worthwhile is easy. And nothing easy is interesting."

She laughed softly.

"What do you say to one date?" He narrowed the distance between them yet again, from the friendship to flirting zone. "Or we could just hang out. I can bring the girls if that makes you more comfortable."

"Like when we went fishing," she said.

"Exactly."

This was a big step and opposite of what she'd told him after their kiss. What if he got the wrong idea? What if she lost herself again?

What if Max was her person and pushing him away would be the biggest mistake of her life? "When?" she asked, warming to the idea.

"Whenever your schedule allows."

"These days, the only time I have free is breakfast. And that's if I miss meeting with Cash and Phoebe."

"Then, breakfast it is. Name the day."

Breakfast sounded casual and not too date-like. "You said Monday's your next wedding?"

"I need to be here by noon to get the carriage ready and the horses harnessed. We could have breakfast that morning." He raised his brows in a charming appeal.

"That would require you to make two trips here. And, besides, I have an appointment with a new notions supplier. What about Tuesday morning?"

"I have a ten o'clock meeting at Happy Trails with some of the city council members. If all goes well, I'll be added to the Payson website as a recommended local attraction."

"That's awesome, Max. Congrats."

"We can meet before then. Around eight? If that's not too early for you."

"It's not." She waited for the voice of reason to tell her she was making a gigantic mistake. It remained quiet. "Where?"

"Leave the details to me." The twinkle in his eyes returned. "I have an idea."

"Should I be worried?"

"Not at all." He pushed off the railing. "The girls and I will pick you up."

"Perfect." Everything had come together quickly and easily. Laurel didn't know whether to take that as a good sign or a reason to panic.

Addie and Daisy continued to play in the golf cart. Laurel watched them, which explained why she wasn't prepared when Max wrapped an arm around her waist and pulled her with him behind the column and out of sight. Her head shot up to meet his gaze, and she found herself captivated by the play of light and shadow on his handsome features.

"What are you doing?" she asked in a half whisper and pressed her hands to his chest. "You said the next move was mine to make."

"It is. Completely." He lowered his head until their cheeks grazed and spoke into her ear. "Should I stay or leave?"

This close, he was hard to resist, and Laurel wasn't convinced she wanted to. Max was so many things she wanted in a life partner. Good. Decent. Smart. Charming. Kind. A hard worker. Caring. And his pursuit of her was flattering.

"You're not playing fair," she said.

"My specialty."

She didn't push him away. Neither did she draw him closer. "Is this a mistake?"

"Doesn't feel like one to me."

Laurel raised her lips to his. She didn't surrender to him as much as embrace the inevitable.

Their kiss, while chaste, was potent enough to elicit a sigh and have her leaning into him. What would it be like between them when they were alone? That could happen. All Laurel had to do was say the word.

Jelly barked, the girls squealed and reality returned.

Laurel broke off the kiss. "Well. That happened again."

"Yeah. It did."

"You're going to be trouble for me, aren't you?" she asked, not entirely joking.

"The good kind, I hope."

She smiled and said nothing, keeping him guessing.

He chuckled as they emerged from behind the column. "Now who's being trouble?"

"Max. Are you sure about this?"

"I'm sure."

"But what if—"

"One day at a time, okay?"

She nodded and together they walked to the steps, close but not touching. She waited while he fetched the girls, the dog and their things.

"Thanks, Miss Laurel," Addie called as they walked to the truck.

"Bye." Daisy waved.

Max tipped his cowboy hat at Laurel and winked.

She waited until the truck disappeared down the driveway before going inside. She immediately ran into Phoebe who was on her way outside.

Her friend and sister-in-law stopped in her tracks, giving Laurel a lengthy once-over. "I'd ask how the costume fitting with Max and the girls went, but I can tell by the look on your face, it went well."

"It did," was all Laurel would admit to before turning toward Bellissima.

"Can't fool me," Phoebe called after her. "I see you floating on air."

She was right. And Laurel liked the feeling.

"DADDY, WHERE ARE we going?" Daisy asked.

"You'll see."

He shouldered the door open and ushered the girls into the bakery.

"Mmm. Smells good," Addie said.

Daisy ran ahead and pressed her nose to the glass display case. "Yummy."

She pointed to a huge assortment of sugary confections. There were so many, Max couldn't be sure which one had caught her fancy.

He got in line behind a young couple purchasing a pair of small cakes in the shape of cottages that looked too real to be food. Could they make cakes to resemble his tents?

"Addie, Daisy." He motioned to the girls. "Come back here and stand by me."

When his turn at the counter came, a middle-aged woman wearing a yellow polo shirt and chocolate brown apron offered him a friendly smile.

"Good morning. Welcome to Nothing Bundt the Best. What can I get for you?"

He almost asked her if she was the mother of the bride with the vintage wedding dress but thought better of it. That might be embarrassing if he was wrong and then he'd have to explain.

"Name's Max Maxwell. I have an order to pick up."

"Yes." She drew out the word as she examined a clipboard by the register. "I believe it's ready. Let me check in the back." Turning on her heel, she disappeared through a swinging door.

"Do you think Jelly's okay?" Daisy asked. Of his two girls, she was ever the worrywart.

"She'll be fine."

He glanced over his shoulder. Jelly's face appeared in the window, her ears pricked forward as she barked at him. He'd recruited the help of the boutique owner next door—someone he knew through PBP. She'd agreed to watch Jelly outside for the brief time it would require him to pick up his order. In exchange, he'd offered a discounted night at Happy Trails.

She'd earned every cent of the discount by the time they collected Jelly. The dog was now leaping at the window and straining on her leash in addition to barking. Max wouldn't have come into the bakery if he'd had a choice. But he wasn't much of a cook, and he'd wanted to surprise Laurel with a picnic breakfast rather than take her to a restaurant. Not to mention, a picnic would be easier with the girls and a rambunctious half-grown dog.

Max had brought along a thermos of coffee, powdered cream, sugar packets and individual bottles of orange juice, then stopped at the bakery for breakfast. Nothing Bundt the Best had a morning special: a selection of fresh-baked breakfast breads and croissants, various fruit and cheese spreads, yogurt cups and seasoned stuffed eggs.

"Here it is," chimed the woman as she re-appeared through the swinging door, carrying a large white bag.

Max inspected the bag's contents. "Looks great."

"Thank you," the woman said when he'd signed the tablet. "Come again."

"We will." Max nodded and left with the girls.

He had texted Laurel before starting out, advising her of their ETA. They'd spoken twice since their kiss on the porch. Brief check-ins that let her know, without coming right out and saying it, he'd been thinking of her. She'd let him know the same in return, also without coming right out and saying it.

Max didn't want to rush things or scare Laurel off by coming on too strong. And he wasn't ready to move quickly, either. Though she was on his mind constantly when he wasn't readying for Happy Trails' soft opening, his parents visit in two days and Sarah's wedding.

As of yesterday, his ex was still planning on arriving the day before the wedding, in time for the rehearsal that afternoon at five. The girls couldn't wait to see their mother, though that didn't guarantee Charlene wouldn't cancel last minute.

Laurel waited for them on the front porch. For a moment, Max simply stared at her, not believing his good fortune. She wore a flowered outfit that was part dress and part shorts. Her chestnut hair fell just past her chin and ruffled in the slight breeze. Glossy red lipstick accentuated her full mouth and had Max thinking about strawberries.

He put the truck in park and jumped out. "Morning."

She took the three steps down to the walkway, her small purse swinging at her side. "Morning to you."

Inside the truck, Jelly barked. Did that dog ever run out of energy?

Max went around to the passenger door and opened it for Laurel. "Hungry?"

"Getting there." She climbed in.

"Watch out for the bag." Max nodded at the food bag on the floor as he took her hand, helping her in. The task was by no means a hardship, and he was reluctant to let go.

He hurried around the truck and climbed in behind the wheel. By then, Laurel and the girls were chatting up a storm.

"We're not supposed to tell you," Addie was saying. "Daddy made us promise."

"Not even if I ask nicely?" Laurel implored.

"It's a secret," Daisy insisted and slapped her hands over her mouth.

Laurel pretended to be disappointed. "Your daughters refuse to tell me where we're going for breakfast."

"You won't have to wait long to find out," Max said. Rather than leave Wishing Well Springs, they stayed on the long winding drive.

"Wait. Are we going to the wedding barn? You know there are two weddings today."

Max grinned. "Not the barn."

"The Western town?"

"Guess again."

She crinkled her brow, her endearing expression causing Max's attention to wander from the road. He warned himself to slow down, both the speed of the truck and the rate he was succumbing to her charms.

He took the road that curved around the barn and headed up the hill into the woods. Though the day would warm up, it was still pleasantly cool. Thin clouds stretched across a vivid blue sky and added to the already incredible view from the top of the hill.

"This is where Cash proposed to Phoebe," Laurel said.

Max came to a stop and cut the engine. "He

mentioned that. Also, that it would be a great place for a picnic."

"Ah!" Her face brightened with understanding.

Okay. Step one accomplished.

"Ready, kiddos?" He turned and glanced into the back seat.

"I'm starving!" Addie said.

"Let's eat." Max got out and opened the back door on his side where Addie sat.

Without being asked, Laurel assisted Daisy from her car seat. When the little girl reached the ground, she threw her arms around Laurel's legs. What really got to Max was the tender, caring way Laurel stroked Daisy's hair.

Jelly bounded out of the truck, barking at the top of her lungs and chasing off every bird and small animal within a hundred-yard radius. So much for enjoying the sounds of nature.

"You got breakfast from Nothing Bundt the Best!" Laurel exclaimed when Max removed the bag from the floorboard.

"My first time there. I hope it's good."

"Their food is amazing. Prepare to stuff yourself."

As the girls explored the immediate area with Jelly hot on their heels, Laurel carried the bag to a shaded flat spot beneath a cluster of trees. Max fetched the blanket he'd brought from the truck bed—along with the thermos, bottled juice and condiments—and joined her. Together, they spread out the blanket and emptied the bag. The bakery had included paper plates, plastic cutlery and napkins.

"Coffee?" Max asked as they settled side by side on the blanket. He produced a small stack of plastic cups. "Or juice?"

She smiled. "Can I have both?"

"Whatever the lady wants is fine by me."

Max poured while Laurel set out the many containers. By now, the girls had wandered back and were inspecting the spread. Max snuck Jelly a piece of nut bread that had fallen to the bottom of the bag, a sucker for her soulful eyes.

"This looks fantastic," Laurel said and helped the girls fill their plates with croissants and thick slices of various breads.

Addie wanted a yogurt and declared she hated strawberry jam, which she didn't. Daisy inserted an entire stuffed egg into her mouth and made a comical face, earning laughs from the adults. Max waited until Laurel and the girls had chosen before making his own selections.

While they ate, Laurel engaged the girls in conversation about being flower girls in their aunt's wedding, the summer day camp Max had enrolled them in three mornings a week and their favorite animated movie, which turned out to be one they'd watched at least a dozen times about a baby panda bear. At Laurel's amused glance, Max gave his head a weary shake.

When they finished eating, the girls went off to play with Jelly. Max and Laurel relaxed over their coffee, with contented sighs and outstretched legs, their fingers occasionally grazing.

"My parents are arriving on Thursday," he said.

"I can't wait to meet them. I wish I had time before the rehearsal, but things are crazy. I'm down to the wire on my last three dresses. One of them is your former sister-in-law's. She's coming by tomorrow to pick it up."

"Don't worry. They're not getting in until the afternoon."

"Are they staying at Happy Trails?"

He laughed. "Are you kidding? The closest Mom gets to roughing it is sitting in a chaise longue by the pool. I offered them the sofa bed in my office, but they declined and got a room at the Old Town Luxury Inn."

"Ah. That's a quaint place."

Max worked up the nerve to suggest the

idea he'd been debating these last few days. Laurel might refuse, thinking they were moving too fast. "Would your mom like to come to the soft opening?"

Her face lit up. "I bet she would. I'll invite her. Thank you for thinking of her."

"She could meet my parents. And me."

"She'd love that."

"Have you told her? About us?"

"I might have mentioned you," she teased.

"Now she really needs to meet me. Just to learn all the stories aren't true."

She rested her head on his shoulder. "I told her nothing but good things because there are only good things to tell."

He could get very, very used to this.

"Have you rented all eight tents for the opening?" she asked, a lazy, relaxed quality to her voice.

"And pretty much for the rest of the summer. Reservations have been incredible. I expect things to taper off in the fall. Vacation season will be over. I should have the other tents ready by early spring." Max suddenly remembered. "How'd the photo shoot go with that magazine?"

"Oh!" Laurel beamed. "Great. Phoebe was an amazing model. I'm told we'll appear in the October issue."

"Prepare for an onslaught of phone calls and new clients."

"I hope so." She finished her croissant. "Are you ready for your meeting with the city council?"

"Ready as I'll ever be."

"Look at us." She sat up and smiled. "Two upwardly mobile business professionals."

He laughed. "Does anyone still say that?"

"No, and I'm not sure why I said it. Now you probably won't consider going out with me again."

He leaned in and kissed her cheek. "I'll consider it. And maybe more than once."

They were able to sneak in a quick couple of kisses before the girls' rowdy antics had them pulling apart. This time, when they sat back to enjoy the morning, they held hands.

When Laurel's phone rang, she extracted it from her pocket and asked, "Do you mind? This might be my client confirming our appointment."

"Go ahead." Max accepted that there would be compromises with Laurel.

It was clear that the caller wasn't her appointment. Laurel quickly went from professional to animated.

"Yes, yes." She pushed to her feet and began walking away from where the girls were playing loudly and Jelly barked, a finger pressed to one ear, her phone to the other. "I can absolutely do that. Thank you." She paused to listen. "I can't tell you how excited I am. I will. Of course." Another pause. "I'll clear my calendar. Is there anything you need from me?" She listened again. "Yes. See you then. Goodbye." She disconnected and spun to face Max, her expression radiating joy. "You won't guess what just happened. Nikolai will be in Payson on Thursday, and he wants to meet with me and tour Bellissima."

"Nikolai?" The name rang a bell.

"He's the designer I told you about. That was his personal assistant."

"Ah. The guy with one name." Max stood, as it seemed Laurel was too excited to resume sitting. "That's pretty cool."

"I had no idea he'd even heard of me."

Max went over and took her hand in his. "Congratulations. That's pretty exciting."

"I have a million things to do between now and then. Two million. Oh, my gosh." She looked around as if recognizing her surroundings, her hand slipping from his. "I have to get to work. I'm sorry. This is a once-in-a-lifetime opportunity. Nikolai is a trendsetter. Incomparable. I'm in shock."

"We can leave. Let me just pack up."

"I'll pack. You get the girls." She knelt on the blanket and began gathering the trash and leftovers at a furious rate.

Addie and Daisy didn't want to leave. They went from happily playing to throwing small tantrums. Embarrassed, Max summoned all his willpower to keep from raising his voice at them. Jelly made the situation worse by running off and refusing to come when Max called. By the time he'd wrangled her and the girls into the truck, his cowboy shirt collar was soaked with sweat.

Laurel had her phone out the entire short drive back to the main house, entering notes and texting people. She was fully engrossed. The entire world, including Max, had ceased to exist.

He understood meeting with this Nikolai was important to her. And he would never insist she stop focusing on the designer and, instead, pay attention to him—something her former boyfriend Jordan had done.

Yet, when she hurried toward the house after no more than a cursory goodbye, Max couldn't help the disappointment washing over him.

As he drove home, trying to ignore the girls bickering in the back seat, he told himself these were unusual circumstances. He should be supportive of Laurel. Not annoyed at her or needy. She'd assured him the meeting with Nikolai would be earlier in the day and wouldn't interfere with the wedding rehearsal or dinner with his parents.

That was enough. This relationship with Laurel wouldn't be like the ones either of them had experienced before, right? By the time he reached home, he'd almost convinced himself that they would successfully navigate whatever came their way.

Not entirely, but almost.

CHAPTER THIRTEEN

"Everything okay?"

Laurel turned at the sound of her seamstress Helena's voice, her stomach fluttering. "Not really. Frankly, I'm a wreck."

"Can I help?" The fifty-something woman produced one of her ready smiles.

She had the kind of open, friendly countenance that people immediately warmed to, and the personality to match. In addition, she'd quickly proved herself to be a valuable asset. After a short training period, she was already picking up Laurel's slack and working unsupervised. And despite having no formal design training, she frequently offered excellent suggestions and possessed a keen eye for editing looks.

Laurel leaned a hand on the worktable, as much to steady her quaking knees as to remind herself the last day had been real and not a dream. Helena sat across the room from her at one of the sewing machines, waiting expectantly for Laurel to answer her question.

"That was Nikolai's personal assistant on the phone. Nikolai." Laurel repeated the name with reverence. She still couldn't believe her good fortune. "She was confirming their arrival time tomorrow."

"It's really happening." Helena's smile widened.

"It's really happening," Laurel repeated. The one and only Nikolai, couture fashion designer to the stars, wanted to meet with her. Okay, she was being a tad dramatic, but Nikolai was soon to grace her little shop with his incredible presence.

Helena jumped out of her chair and ran across the room to pull Laurel into her arms. She was a hugger as well as a smiler.

"I'm so excited for you." She released Laurel and stepped back. "What do you need? Give me a list."

"I have to think."

In truth, Laurel had been thinking of little else since the picnic with Max and his daughters. Whenever she wasn't running around like crazy, that was.

Two more days remained in June, with four more weddings at Wishing Well Springs over the course of those two days. Laurel had designed gowns for all four brides, including

Max's former sister-in-law, as well as bridesmaid dresses for two of the weddings.

Charlene was arriving tomorrow, as well, for the late afternoon dress rehearsal, along with Max's parents. Laurel would be joining Max, the girls and his parents for dinner after the rehearsal. She'd also see them again at Charlene's sister's wedding. And then again at Happy Trails' soft opening where she'd have more time to get to know them in a less hectic environment. Her mom, too, would be meeting Max and his family for the first time.

On top of everything else, Laurel was preparing for Nikolai's visit. She'd spent every free moment yesterday tidying Bellissima and rearranging the shop displays, including the ready-made dresses. Now, according to Nikolai's personal assistant, he also wanted to tour her workroom. Everything had to be neat as a pin, no pun intended.

She could do this. She *had* to do this. Nikolai didn't visit just anyone.

"Did his assistant say why he chose you?" Helena asked. "Not that you aren't a fantastic designer."

"Only that he saw photos of some of my dresses and heard about me from a client." She pressed her hands to her cheeks. "I'm sure he's simply paying a courtesy call."

"Oh, sweetie. Nikolai doesn't pay courtesy calls. He's coming here for a reason." She gasped softly. "What if he wants to mentor you? He does that. Takes fledgling designers under his wing. I've read about him."

"You think?" Laurel struggled to keep her expectations reasonable. She didn't want to build her hopes only to have them crushed.

"I definitely think." Helena grabbed a pad and pen off the worktable. "Let's start with that list. First off, what time is he arriving tomorrow?"

"One o'clock."

"You'll need refreshments." The seamstress started jotting down notes. "Does he want to tour the wedding barn, too?"

"His personal assistant didn't say."

"I'll check with Phoebe just in case. Find out when we can sneak in for a quick peek."

"Good idea."

"If you're interested, my niece can come in for a couple of hours early morning. She's only sixteen, but she's a hard worker. She can vacuum and dust and wash windows."

"That would be fantastic. And I'll pay her, of course."

They spent the next twenty minutes prioritizing their to-do list, Helena once again proving herself indispensable. Laurel's phone rang several times, but she ignored every call, even the one from Max. She wanted to talk to him, but this visit from Nikolai was important, and Max would have to wait until she and Helena were done.

"I'll see if Joe's buddy can drive him to his chemo appointment tomorrow," Helena said when she and Laurel had finalized their list. "That way, I can oversee my niece."

"No," Laurel insisted. "I don't want to take you away from him. His treatments are too important."

"He'll be fine. The fact is, he'd rather I not be there. I mother him too much, or so he claims." She blinked back tears. "He's going to kick this cancer. We caught it early, and his prognosis is good. Better than good."

Laurel reached for her. "I'll keep him in my prayers."

"Thank you." Helena pulled herself together. "He'd much rather I be doing something productive and fun rather than sitting around watching the nurses pour poison into his veins. His words, not mine."

"Helena," she started and then faltered. In all the recent excitement, she'd forgotten about the older woman's difficulties.

"Don't you fret." Helena hugged her again.

"I need this as much as Joe needs me to get out of his hair every once in a while."

"Only if you're sure."

"You start on the list while I get back to that sewing machine and finish the trim."

Laurel left the workroom, confident matters were in capable hands. She went downstairs to the kitchen where she checked the refrigerator and the food supply. Deciding there was no way in the world she'd serve a store-bought cheese and fruit tray to Nikolai, she phoned their neighbor down the road, Joshua Tree Inn, and asked to speak to the catering manager. Wishing Well Springs did a lot of business with Joshua Tree Inn, who often supplied food for weddings and events at the barn and miniature town.

The catering manager was more than willing to send over a selection of elegant hors d'oeuvres and promised them by eleven the following morning. Laurel thanked the woman profusely and volunteered to return the favor at a future date. That handled, she tackled the beverages. There were plenty of supplies on hand. She could prepare a pitcher of iced tea, and another of fresh-squeezed lemonade. She could offer sparkling water and gourmet coffee, hot or iced.

Finally able to take a short breather, she sat at the table and returned Max's call.

"Hey," he answered, no rebuke in his voice for the delay in getting back to him.

Then again, they'd had several discussions on this subject. She couldn't always drop what she was doing and return his call. And vice versa.

See. Look at them. Being adults and all. Flexible. Compromising. Considerate of each other's needs.

"Hi," she said.

"I was just thinking of you." His friendly tone held a trace of intimacy.

"Me, too."

"I like hearing that."

What would he say if Nikolai offered her a mentorship? Now that she thought about it, Max had had an odd look on his face when she'd gotten the phone call. Had the situation struck a familiar chord? Or, rather, stirred a bad memory?

Laurel admitted her drive to succeed might remind him a little of Charlene. But there were some significant differences. Nikolai wouldn't be a financial investor in Bellissima. Max had no reason to worry on that front. Did he have reason to worry on any other front?

"Can't wait to see you tomorrow. My folks are excited about dinner. Mom must have asked a hundred questions about you."

"I'm excited, too."

"You hear from that designer guy? What's his name?"

"Nikolai. And his personal assistant called a while ago." Laurel told him the details of the visit and everything she was doing to prepare.

"Good luck," he said when she finished.

"All I'm hoping for is the chance to pick his brain and be inspired by him. With luck, he'll critique some of my gowns and give me useful feedback. That alone would be amazing."

"I'm proud of you."

"Thank you." She appreciated his praise. She only wished he sounded a little more enthused and not like he was saying what was expected of him.

Laurel instantly chided herself. She was reading too much into a perceived voice inflection.

"What about you?" she asked, checking the time. She needed to run, but hated cutting him off. "How's the soft opening coming?"

"I have to stop by the hardware store for some supplies and building material. Dad's helping me with a few things."

Laurel was suddenly curious. "Do your parents and Charlene get along?"

"Yeah. Or, I should say, they do their best to get along for the girls. Which is fine. My folks weren't happy when Charlene moved to Phoenix. They were understanding and non-judgmental of the divorce and of her wanting to grow her business. They were less understanding of her leaving her children behind."

"I can see why. Their first reaction is to protect their son and their grandchildren."

"They do a good job of keeping their opinions to themselves, which I appreciate."

Her phone vibrated, and she quickly read the text. "I'm sorry, Max. I need to go."

"Same here."

"Talk to you later."

"Bye, Laurel."

Hmm. His lackluster response bothered her.

Was he giving her space in order to prepare for Nikolai's visit? That had to be it. Just like she was giving him space to ready Happy Trails for the soft opening.

"Stop making mountains out of molehills," she told herself.

Standing, she headed upstairs to her workroom, her lengthy to-do list calling her name.

Her feet and hands, however, moved slower than she would have preferred.

What was wrong with her? Nikolai, *the* Nikolai, would be standing on this very spot tomorrow. She should be over the moon with joy, and she was. Only, as she organized the storage room with its many bolts of fabric, reels of lace and bins of accessories, she mentally dissected her conversation with Max to such an extent, she actually forgot about Nikolai.

No! Laurel wanted to kick herself. It was happening again. She was obsessing over a man and forgetting about everything else. With fresh determination, she pushed Max from her thoughts. She would be ready for Nikolai's visit and show him she was someone worthy of his notice.

"ARE YOU READY to see Bellissima?" Laurel asked, attempting to mask her nervousness by wringing her clasped hands.

Nikolai flashed a smile that must have paid for his dentist's new car. Laurel knew from reading his bio he was in his early fifties. He could, however, pass for late thirties. He had that kind of youthful appearance and, she was sure, a top-notch aesthetician on retainer. Impeccably groomed, he wore a custom summer suit that was understated and trendy and, at the same time, screamed elegance. "Absolutely. Lead the way."

He'd insisted that Bellissima be the final stop on their tour of Wishing Well Springs. They'd started with the barn and miniature Western town. He'd raved about both and complimented Laurel on using them as backgrounds for her recent photo shoot with *Fashion Forward Magazine*.

Then, she'd led him and his personal assistant through the main house lobby and up the stairs with its antique banister—another great location for a fashion shoot, he'd commented—to her workroom. There, they'd spent a full forty-five minutes. Nikolai had suggested she move her sewing machines to the opposite wall and the long worktables to the left of center.

"To create a more efficient flow of energy," he'd explained, demonstrating with his arms.

Laurel loved the idea.

He'd then examined several of her in-progress projects and made suggestions for changes in stitching, material selection, sleeve design and neckline trim. His eagle-eyed gaze missed nothing, not even the tiniest detail.

"Don't be afraid to take risks," he'd advised. "You have to find the balance between your aesthetic and what the client wants. Remember, it's your name on the gown. Never put anything out there that isn't one hundred percent you."

Laurel was marveling at her good fortune. Of all the wedding and formal gown designers out there, he'd noticed her and gone out of his way to meet in person.

"This way," Laurel said, escorting him and his assistant into Bellissima. She'd cleared her calendar for the afternoon and shut off her phone. There would be no interruptions.

While they'd been in the upstairs workroom, Helena had set out refreshments in the sitting area. Nikolai's assistant had requested champagne be ready for him, and a bottle was chilling in a bucket of ice next to the tray of hors d'oeuvres delivered from Joshua Tree Inn. The shop, cleaned and straightened, shone like a newly minted penny.

"Quite charming," Nikolai commented, noting their surroundings.

"Would you like some champagne?" Laurel asked.

He smiled, and a matching set of dimples appeared in his cheeks. If Laurel had expected him to be lost in the clouds or a condescending narcissist, like some other designers she'd met, she couldn't have been more wrong. Nikolai was genuine and down to earth and very, very savvy. He also possessed a delightful sense of humor. "Show me around first."

She started with the viewing area and its triple mirrors. From there, they examined the wedding gowns on display and then the stitch and fix area. He was very interested in her rack of original ready-to-wears—wedding gowns, bridesmaid and flower girl dresses, and mother of the bride and groom ensembles. Last, they peeked at the changing room, decorated with Phoebe's help.

"You have a real knack," he told Laurel while inspecting one of her ready-to-wear gowns, "for taking budget-priced fabric and turning it into an expensive looking garment. Well done, my dear. Well done."

She glowed at his compliment.

"But the real path to building your business is custom originals."

"I agree."

They continued chatting as they completed the tour of Bellissima. His assistant said nothing, simply trailed after them, either scrolling through her phone or speaking into it, fielding calls on Nikolai's behalf.

"How many fashion shows do you participate in during an average year?" he asked.

"Not many," Laurel admitted. "Two or three."

"Oh, my dear, you should have a showing at least every other month. And if you can't get away, have one here. You could use the stairs for an entrance and the lobby for your runway."

"That sounds…amazing."

"What about events like bridal expos? Don't tell me." He stopped her from answering with a raised hand, anticipating her answer. "One or two."

She shrugged with chagrin.

"Pop-up shops," he continued. "You absolutely must have them. Payson hosts events, and they attract tourists like bees to pollen."

"I have been wanting to put together a pop-up shop."

"Nothing's preventing you."

No, there wasn't. Now that June was almost over and she'd hired Helena, Laurel's schedule would hopefully ease.

"Thank you so much, Nikolai."

"Now." He grinned mischievously, his violet eyes, which could only result from colored contacts, twinkling. "About that champagne."

Laurel showed him and his assistant to the

sitting area where she poured champagne into three delicate crystal flutes and uncovered the hors d'oeuvres.

She and Nikolai occupied one couch while his assistant sat on the far end of the other. She was, Laurel realized, giving them a modicum of privacy.

Nikolai raised his glass of champagne. "Here's to your success, Laurel."

"Yes. And yours." They clinked glasses. She felt giddy inside, and not from the bubbly beverage.

"Speaking of success..." He leaned forward and snatched a delicate puff pastry filled with cranberries and brie cheese. "I have a proposition for you. One I think you'll find intriguing."

"Oh?" She tried to remain calm. Inside, her heart danced with excitement. "What's that?"

"A mentorship."

Was this really happening? Her wildest dream coming true?

"Tell me this isn't a joke."

"No, my dear." Nikolai smiled with amusement. "This is no joke."

Excitement and happiness mingled, nearly lifting Laurel from her seat on a wave of pure energy.

"Please don't take this the wrong way and

think I'm not interested, because I am. Extremely interested. But why me? I'm a mostly unknown designer from a town that's the furthest thing from a fashion hub."

"You're talented and innovative and have a strong point of view that impresses me. If someone showed me one of your dresses, I'd instantly know you designed it. You can't teach skill like that, only encourage those who already possess it."

"You're very kind, Nikolai."

"I'm speaking the truth."

"But…" She faltered. "I know what I'd get out of the mentorship. Experience I couldn't find anywhere else. My finger on the pulse of the industry. Invaluable contacts. Guidance on how to run my business. You'd challenge me. Inspire me. Push me."

"Indeed, I would."

"You'd also give me a new perspective and—" she smiled "—I won't lie, the ability to drop your name."

He chuckled.

"But what can I bring to the relationship?"

He snatched another hors d'oeuvre, this one a savory stuffed mushroom, and popped it in his mouth. When he'd finished chewing, he said, "I'd get the opportunity to collaborate. Everybody collaborates with *everybody* in this business. It's how we expand our client base and remain relevant. It's easy to become a has-been in our profession and wind up employed by some dreadful second-rate fashion house." He said the last part as if it were the worst fate imaginable.

"I'm not sure any of my clients can afford you."

"Not yet. Eventually you'll be attracting new clients, ones with more disposable income."

"Wouldn't that be great?"

"You're going places, Laurel, and I'd love to share some of the ride with someone who's unhardened by this cutthroat business. It's refreshing, and, dare I say, inspiring."

"Okay."

She wondered if he had a giant ego that he fed by helping fledgling designers. Her next thought was, did she care? Whatever his motives, she'd benefit.

"You have a clear vision," Nikolai continued, "and are your own designer, make no mistake. Yet, your aesthetic isn't entirely different from mine."

"That's quite a compliment."

"It's also necessary for any successful mentor/mentee relationship. We won't constantly clash. Though I do so enjoy a lively debate now and again." He patted her hand. "Who knows? If all goes well, it could turn into something more."

Laurel leaned closer. "Like what?"

"I'm glad you asked. Shows you have a good head on your shoulders and aren't just going to accept any old offer."

Something more with *the* Nikolai wouldn't be any old offer.

"Let me tell about how I've partnered with some of my former mentors."

"Yes, please," Laurel said, and proceeded to hang on his every word.

LAUREL AND NIKOLAI chatted for another twenty minutes. He was very clear about his future ambitions. Besides designing for his many celebrity clients, he had plans to start a ready-to-wear line for high-end department stores. He liked that Laurel could bring her ready-to-wear experience to the table.

"And accessories, of course. Jewelry, if I can find the perfect designer. Shoes and purses. My goal is to dress women from head to toe in the Nikolai look."

"Wedding dresses are my specialty," Laurel said. "I'm not sure how I fit in with your goal."

"The Nikolai woman will get married or

be in a wedding, yes? Plus, you design other gowns, as well, and flower girl dresses. Who knows, I might even venture into children's wear," he added with a broad gesture and grin that was anything but joking.

Only a fool wouldn't be interested, and Laurel was no fool. There were few in the business better to learn from than Nikolai. He was admired and respected. As much a star as the celebrities he designed for. Being mentored by him would not just give her career a boost, it would rocket her into the stratosphere.

"What would be required of me?" she asked.

He didn't miss a beat. "You'd have to come to LA."

"Move?"

"No, no. Twice a month should suffice. For the next year, if not longer. Three days each trip, minimum. Then there's New York and Paris Fashion Weeks, of course. You should plan a full week for those, at the very least."

"New York and Paris!" Attending those prestigious events were at the top of Laurel's list of ambitions.

"You'll be at my side the entire time."

"I can't even... Oh, wow." Think of all the

important people she'd get to rub elbows and maybe exchange a few sentences with.

"It's a commitment, I know," Nikolai continued. "A sacrifice. But you won't get another opportunity like this."

Meaning he wouldn't ask again.

"I'm very grateful, Nikolai," she said and then paused, choosing her words carefully. "Would it be rude of me to ask for a couple days to think about—" she started to say "it" and changed her mind "—how I can best make the necessary arrangements?"

There was a lot to consider and not just Bellissima, which demanded her constant attention. There was Wishing Well Springs. Laurel was part owner, involved in decision-making, and helped out when needed. And what if Phoebe had a baby? Laurel's help would be even more needed.

Frequent trips to LA and two long-distance trips would strain her personal life, as well. Her mom required periodic assistance, like when she'd sprained her ankle. Putting that entire responsibility on Cash wasn't fair. Then, there was her and Max. They were giving dating a try. Even if they kept things casual, her being frequently gone and then playing catch-up at work when she returned would leave little opportunity for them to see each other.

Not easy, but not impossible. Other couples managed. And a year wasn't forever.

Should she talk to Max about the mentorship before accepting it? Were they far enough along in their relationship for her to take him and their relationship into consideration? Jordan hadn't discussed his job offer with her before accepting it, and Laurel had felt shut out and disrespected.

Then again, she'd been in love with Jordan and had hoped to marry him. She and Max were at the beginning of their relationship. Though, she could picture a life with him, and the notion didn't scare her. Rather, it left her warm and tingly inside.

"Absolutely," Nikolai said. "Bellissima is your foundation. You must ensure it runs properly in your absence."

"I promise not to keep you waiting."

Though Helena was a wonderful seamstress, Laurel would need to hire a full-time assistant for this mentorship to work. One who was trustworthy. No way would she allow herself to end up in the same position as before, with an employee who stole from her because she wasn't there to supervise.

She smiled at Nikolai. "I'm very flattered and honored that you'd consider me."

"I hope you won't let me down."

Was that another subtle warning?

For the first time since their arrival, his personal assistant spoke. "Sorry to interrupt, Nikolai, but we need to leave for Phoenix or we'll be late for your next appointment."

"Yes, yes. Indeed." He stood, grabbed a puff pastry and popped it in his mouth. Dabbing his lips with a napkin, he said, "We'll be talking soon, my dear."

"I'm looking forward to it."

"Me, too." He pinched her chin before whirling on his polished boot heels.

Laurel escorted her guests outside, where a driver in a crisp white polo shirt waited by a luxury sedan parked in the shade. As they neared, he opened the rear passenger door.

Nikolai embraced Laurel with gusto. "I look forward to hearing from you soon."

"Thank you again, Nikolai."

She remained there, waving, until the sedan disappeared down the long driveway. Then she sprinted up the porch steps, inside the house and straight to the business offices.

"Phoebe. Cash. You won't believe it!"

"What?" Phoebe was instantly on her feet and scrambling out from behind her desk. "Did the meeting go well?"

"He offered me a mentorship."

"Of course he did." Phoebe hugged Laurel to her and then dragged her over to join Cash. "Sit." She pushed Laurel down into the empty chair next to him and perched on the edge of her desk. "Tell us everything. Leave nothing out."

"Congratulations, sis." Cash threw an arm over her shoulders and squeezed.

Gesturing animatedly, Laurel recounted the entire meeting with Nikolai from beginning to end. Finishing, she sat back with a lengthy exhale.

Phoebe asked the obvious question on everyone's minds. "Are you going to accept?"

"I don't know. It's a big decision. Leaving Bellissima every month. Leaving Wishing Well Springs. You both depend on me to help when you're shorthanded."

"Anything that's good for your career and Bellissima," Cash said, "is good for Wishing Well Springs. Your name linked with Nikolai's will bring in new business."

He was right.

"I'll help you hire a new assistant," Phoebe said.

Laurel looked from one to the other. "You think I should accept?"

"You'll regret it for the rest of your life if

you don't," Phoebe insisted. "New York Fashion Week. Paris."

Cash patted her knee. "I don't see how you can turn him down. And it's not forever."

"Both of you," Laurel's throat tightened with emotion. "Your support means the world to me."

"I'm sure Max will be excited for you, too." Phoebe's smile widened.

By comparison, Cash's smile dimmed.

Laurel started to ask him what was wrong only to bite her tongue. He wasn't the person she should be talking to.

"I'll tell Max once I've thought things through. Maybe at Sarah's dress rehearsal."

"Aren't you having dinner with his parents?" Phoebe asked.

"Yeah. After dinner might be better. Or tomorrow."

When he'd be in the middle of his parents' visit and getting ready for Happy Trails' soft opening. Maybe next week? Except Nikolai would never wait that long for her answer.

Cash must have sensed her indecision. "I have one thing to say, sis, which you can take or leave. If you're going to accept Nikolai's offer, then cut Max loose now. Before he's head over heels, and you crush his soul."

"That sounds extreme. You know I'm not cruel."

"Max is an all-in kind of guy. As it is, there's little room in your life for him. There'll be even less room for him after this. You don't want to treat him the way Jordan treated you. String you along and then toss you aside."

Laurel wished he didn't make such a good point. Max deserved, and wanted, someone who could give him more than a small part of themselves. If Laurel accepted Nikolai's offer, a small part of herself was all she could offer him.

"Nikolai mentoring you," Cash said, "is an incredible opportunity. As long as Max isn't a casualty. His daughters, too."

The elation Laurel had felt only a few minutes ago seeped out of her like a slow-leaking balloon. And all because what her brother had said made a great deal of sense.

A sharp pain struck her in the chest where her heart resided. She needed to decide soon and if the answer was yes, inform Max.

"I have to go," she said and hurried out of the office.

In the lobby, Laurel turned left and headed outside rather than to Bellissima. There, she hopped in the golf cart and drove up the hill to the spot where she, Max and the girls had breakfast the other morning. It was a good place to think, which she did at great length.

CHAPTER FOURTEEN

MAX LEANED AGAINST the wall at the back of the wedding barn. He and Laurel had stood in this same spot, watching the nuptials that first day he'd driven the carriage for Wishing Well Springs.

Only this time, his parents were with him. They'd arrived a few hours ago, and despite being tired from their two-day drive, refused to miss out on attending the wedding rehearsal. They hadn't seen the girls in forever, according to his mom, and didn't want to miss a single minute of being with them.

"Look at them. Two sweet angels," his mom crooned, an expression of pure love on her sweet face. She may have acquired a few more wrinkles in recent years, but, to him, she looked the same as always. Beautiful inside and out.

"They're Maxwells," his dad said, puffing up with grandfatherly pride. "No denying it."

"Oh, I can see a little of Charlene in them,

too," his mom added, never taking her eyes off Addie and Daisy.

"Maybe," his dad grudgingly agreed. "But the best parts they got from their father."

Max didn't comment. Rather, he watched the wedding rehearsal, all the while keeping a tight hold on Jelly's leash. The dog sat at his feet, wearing the dinosaur costume Laurel had altered for them and, for once, behaving. The same couldn't be said for Max's daughters.

He wondered if all wedding rehearsals were disasters. Phoebe, Wishing Well's wedding coordinator, tried to bring order to the confusion and was having no success. Her raised voice and pleas to follow instructions went unheeded.

No surprise. The overwhelmed bride appeared on the verge of a meltdown, and nothing the groom said helped. The groom's mother kept offering her unsolicited opinion. The youngest bridesmaid, a cousin of Charlene and the bride, was cranky because her latest romantic interest had canceled last minute, leaving her dateless for the wedding. One of the ushers, a goofy teenager, kept busting out moves to tunes he played on his phone. Lines were forgotten, cues missed and items had been forgotten at home.

Addie and Daisy contributed to the problems. They were too young to understand their duties as flower girls, throwing petals everywhere but on the carpet leading up the aisle. They refused to walk side by side, and then Addie pitched a fit when Daisy got to go first. They bickered, they whined and they refused to do as they were told.

Excitement at seeing their mom and both sets of grandparents and the attention lavished on them played a large part in encouraging their misbehavior. So did the sugary snacks Charlene had given them.

Not at all two little angels as Max's mom had described them.

Jelly let out a weary dog sigh and collapsed onto the ground, resting her head on her costume-covered front paws.

Max could relate. He'd let out a few sighs of his own.

"Where's Laurel?" his mom asked. "I thought she might be here by now."

"She's coming." Max checked his phone, rereading Laurel's last text. "As soon as she's done with work."

"I'd love to see her shop."

"I'm sure she'd love to show it to you."

"Maybe after the rehearsal and before dinner?"

"Tomorrow might be better. Our dinner reservation is at six."

Max smiled and patted his mom's arm. He'd ask Laurel, but he wasn't sure she could fit in a tour. This last frantic push to the end of the month had her stretched to her limits. That, and the unexpected visit from Nikolai today, which had sent her into a frenzy of activity. He hoped to hear all the details over dinner.

That was the reason they hadn't talked much these last few days. It couldn't be because she was having second thoughts about the two of them dating.

He ignored the uneasiness gnawing at him. Laurel was simply busy, and he should leave it at that.

"What's the plan for tomorrow, son?" his dad asked, breaking into Max's thoughts.

"I was hoping you'd help me dig and fill the horseshoe pits, and the picnic tables need a final coat of wood sealer."

"I'll make a big breakfast for everyone," his mom said. "Then, I thought I'd take the girls into town for some shopping and get them a few new outfits."

"Charlene's coming for them at ten, Mom."

"She is?" Her features fell. "I thought we'd have the whole morning together."

"There's a bunch of wedding stuff going on with her family." He didn't remind his mom that the girls' other grandparents seldom saw them, either. Another casualty of Charlene's choices.

"What time will they be home?" his mom asked.

"I'm supposed to pick them up around five."

"Then I'll make a big dinner. My special fried chicken. I can run to the grocery store while you and your dad are working."

"Sounds great, Mom."

Max had been torn. Part of him wanted the girls to spend as much time with Charlene as possible. Except she had ample opportunity while his parents didn't.

"We'll have the entire next day at Happy Trails' soft opening," he said. "Charlene's leaving right after the wedding."

His mom immediately brightened. "We'll have so much fun."

Max had initially worried the girls wouldn't remember his mom and dad and spent the last few days showing Addie and Daisy pictures of them with his parents and telling stories of their last visit. To his vast relief, the girls had been excited to see Nana and Pops walk into the wedding barn and had to be dragged away when the rehearsal started.

Charlene had gotten into town around noon

today, not late for once. She'd come right to Max's and retrieved the girls. After an elated reunion, they'd insisted on showing Charlene around Happy Trails, something she hadn't been able to squirm out of. She'd asked few questions and offered even fewer comments.

Max couldn't help but compare it to the time he'd shown Laurel around Happy Trails. She'd been enthusiastic, came up with the idea for the honeymoon tent and then offered to help decorate it, and complimented his work. A big and important difference.

Then again, he and Laurel didn't share an unpleasant history marked by her abandoning him in favor of pursuing her career.

Speaking of differences...

Charlene marched down the aisle, her destination clearly Max and his parents. Seeing the pronounced furrows creasing her brow, he pushed off the wall. This didn't bode well for him.

"Gary. Janice." She nodded at his parents. "Could you excuse Max and me for a second?"

"Um..." His mom wavered.

"It's okay. I'll be right back." Max passed Jelly's leash to her. "Do you mind, Mom?"

He went with Charlene. She led him to a spot several feet away. Anyone who cared to hear their conversation could. His mom tilted an ear in their direction as if attempting to do just that.

"Max," Charlene started in her I'm-being-reasonable tone, hands on her slim hips. "I need you to do something about the girls. They're, and I say this with love, being a couple of brats."

"It's a big day for them. You're here. My folks. Your folks. Their aunts and uncles and cousins. They're just excited."

"I understand. But we need them to behave and follow directions. My sister's wedding depends on it."

He doubted that. There were other, far more important, aspects to the wedding than whether or not the flower girls performed their duty correctly. He'd learned that much at least during his stint as carriage driver this past month. He didn't contradict Charlene, however, knowing how that would go.

"If they're not listening to you," he said, "discipline them."

"I don't believe in negative reinforcement."

"Then positively discipline them."

"Not funny, Max."

Charlene was on the tall side and stood nose to nose with him when she wore heels. She often used her height less to intimidate people as much as to emphasize her point. It worked. A lot. With anyone other than Max.

"You should have let them nap today," he said, feeling weary himself.

"We were busy. And aren't they too old for naps?"

"They're three."

"So? What's the cutoff age for naps?"

He resisted saying she'd know that if she spent more time with the girls. "Take them to a quiet spot away from everyone for ten minutes and let them unwind. No more sugary snacks or drinks. Offer them a small reward for cooperating and doing a good job. Not a toy or a prize. Say you'll read them a story at bedtime or play a game with them."

"Can't you do that?"

"I read them stories and play games with them every night."

"What if you take them to a quiet spot?" Her voice grew terser.

"No."

"I have a lot of responsibility. I'm the maid of honor."

"And your daughters are the flower girls."

"Come on, Max."

"You come on, Charlene. It's called parenting. You don't get to have only the good parts and dump the bad parts on me."

"I see where they get their stubbornness." She let out an angry huff and stormed off.

Hmm. That was the second time in the last fifteen minutes his daughters had been compared to him. Max stifled a smile.

He was about to return to his parents when he heard a welcome voice call his name. He turned toward the barn's wide entrance to see Laurel entering, the late afternoon sun lighting her face and giving her a golden glow. That, or maybe it was just how he felt about her.

"Hi. You're here." When she reached him, he pulled her to him for a quick hug, noticing a surge of tension coursing through her. "Everything all right?"

"Just hectic, like usual."

"It'll be better soon. Two more days left in June. After that, your life will return to normal."

"Right. Normal."

There was something off in the way she said the word, but he didn't question her. His mom had spotted them and was waving them over. Max didn't think he could put her off now that she'd spotted Laurel.

He took her by the arm and led her to where his parents stood. "Laurel, this is my mom, Janice, and my dad, Gary."

They shook hands, his mom clasping Laurel's in both of hers. "It's wonderful to finally meet you."

Jelly pestered Laurel and refused to leave her alone until she bent and gave the dog a pet.

"That pup of theirs likes you," Max's dad observed.

"She's not the only one," Max's mom added with a mischievous grin.

He'd told his parents about Laurel, of course, stating in no uncertain terms that their relationship was very new and tentative. Technically, they'd only been on one date, counting the picnic. His mom, naturally, had pounced on the prospect of her son finding someone special. Max had insisted he wasn't lonely, reminding her that he wasn't going to rush into a relationship because of the girls.

"You have a great place here." His dad made a sweeping gesture of the wedding barn. "I hear Wishing Well Springs was your brainchild."

"The initial idea was mine," Laurel admitted, "but my brother's an architect and the one who turned it into a reality."

Max remained quiet, content to watch Laurel and his folks, who appeared charmed with each other. While they chatted, he glanced around for Charlene and the girls. Charlene stood at the altar with the minister and the rest of the wedding party. The girls sat in the front pew with Charlene's parents. Apparently she'd delegated the parenting responsibilities to someone else.

Not a bad solution, Max conceded. Addie and Daisy were having fun getting to know their maternal grandparents, who were no doubt thrilled. And now that the girls weren't causing trouble, Charlene could concentrate on the wedding rehearsal. Hopefully, Addie and Daisy would do better tomorrow. How hard could it be, walking down the aisle, dropping rose petals from a basket?

Before long, the rehearsal ended, and people began to disperse. Addie and Daisy came bounding over, inciting Jelly to bark loudly.

"Miss Laurel!" Daisy threw her arms around Laurel.

Addie joined her sister in hugging Laurel. "We missed you."

"I missed you, too." Laurel stroked both their heads and gazed at them as if she wouldn't see them again for another month.

Max's parents looked pleased by this turn of events, not bothered that the girls were ignoring them in favor of Laurel. Max would have a hard time convincing his mom he and Laurel were going slow.

"I'm hungry," his dad announced and checked his watch. "Who's ready to eat?"

"Hey, kiddos." Max took each girl by the shoulder. "Say bye to your mom and Grammy and Gramps. You'll see them tomorrow morning."

When they resisted, Max's parents offered to take them over.

"We should say hello to Charlene and thank her sister for inviting us to the wedding," his mom pointed out.

Once he and Laurel were alone except for Jelly, an awkward silence fell over them. He longed to take her hand in his but wasn't sure he should with so many people around.

Would the girls mention him and Laurel to their mom? Had Charlene noticed the girls hugging Laurel? Maybe Max should have mentioned something to Charlene before today. She didn't always respond well when caught off guard.

When he saw Laurel staring off into space, he asked, "You sure you're all right?"

"Yeah." She shook herself back to the present. "I'm just…you know. There's a lot of stuff happening."

"How'd the meeting with Nikolai go? Is he as eccentric as they say?"

"Yes. But in a very endearing way."

"Everything went good, then?"

"It did. He had a lot to say. I'm still processing."

Max considered mentioning the mentorship but decided to wait. What if that was the cause of her obvious distraction?

"My folks really like you," he said instead.

"I like them, too. They're very nice."

"Thanks for coming to dinner with us tonight."

She nodded, and again a silence fell between them.

Max began to suspect the meeting with Nikolai had, in fact, gone poorly, and Laurel was upset because she hadn't been offered a mentorship. Before he could ask, his daughters came bounding over, followed by his parents. Jelly strained against the leash.

"All set?" his dad asked. "I guess we'll follow you to the restaurant."

They made their way toward the barn door and then outside. Though almost six, the summer sun still shone brightly as it sank toward the mountaintops. Max took hold of Laurel's arm and hitched his chin at the parking lot.

"My truck's over there."

"I'll drive myself. I can't stay late and don't want to inconvenience you by forcing you to leave early in order to drive me back here."

"I don't mind."

"You and the girls should spend as much time as possible with your parents. They're only here a few days."

She hurried toward her van, almost as if she wanted to escape him. Max didn't move, his worry building. He needed a moment alone with Laurel and soon—preferably tonight—to find out what was bothering her.

LAUREL FIDDLED WITH her napkin beneath the table. Dinner should have been a lovely affair. Max's parents were delightful, and the girls were cutie-pies, even when vying for attention. Max had been able to get a table on the edge of the Red Rock Grill's dog-friendly outdoor patio. He'd tied Jelly's leash to his chair. Luckily, their nearest neighbors on the patio didn't object to Jelly begging for food. Or barking at birds roosting on the patio's stucco wall.

But rather than lovely, dinner was a strained affair—at least for Laurel and Max. She did a good job of hiding her anxiousness from everyone except him, as evidenced by the concerned glances he constantly sent her way.

She'd chosen to wait to tell him about the mentorship offer. This was a conversation that needed more than a few minutes sandwiched between the wedding rehearsal and dinner with his parents.

She couldn't delay long, though. She'd promised to give Nikolai her answer soon. Laurel hadn't needed more than an hour sitting on the hill and contemplating her choices to reach a decision.

Eventually, the dinner came to an end after dessert and coffee, alleviating her slow torture.

"Will you be at the wedding?" Janice asked.

"Just at the beginning to guarantee all's well with the bride's dress. Then, I'll duck out."

"That's right. Max mentioned you made Sarah's dress. I can't wait to see it. I visited your webpage the other day. Impressive."

"Thank you." Laurel was pleased Janice had checked out her designs. It was flattering, of course. More than that, Janice cared about her granddaughters and son and took an interest in any woman he dated.

Laurel's mother was equally eager to meet Max and his family. She'd enthusiastically accepted his invitation to Happy Trails' soft opening—delivered through Laurel. Would she still attend if Laurel and Max's conversation later went poorly? Would Laurel? He may not want to see her again.

She refused to believe that. They'd shared their feelings for each other, and both wanted their relationship to succeed.

"She's very talented," Max said.

This time when his gaze found Laurel's, it softened, and her agitation eased.

"I'll say," his mom agreed. "The girls' dresses are darling. Max sent me pictures."

"I'm glad you like them."

Laurel checked her phone, more to vent her nervous energy than to check for any urgent messages or emails. Max had a full weekend. His parents' visit. The wedding. Happy Trails. What if the two of them talked and her news put a damper on his plans? She'd blame herself.

She had to stop overthinking and being her own worst enemy.

When the girls began to squabble, Max motioned for their server to bring the bill.

"We should probably head home. We have an early morning."

The server arrived tableside, and Max's dad insisted on paying. "My treat, son."

"What do you say, girls?" Max prompted.

"Thank you, Pops," they chimed together.

"Thank you, Gary," Laurel added. "My fish was delicious."

He grinned at her. "It's been a real pleasure getting to know you. I can see why Max is smitten."

"From what I hear," Janice said, "it goes both ways."

It did go both ways, which accounted for why Laurel's delicious meal sat like a lump in her stomach. She had to talk to Max about the mentorship tonight if possible. She owed him that much. And the tension was affecting them both.

In the parking lot, Max's parents found an excuse to take the girls and Jelly on a stroll along the sidewalk to window shop. Laurel recognized the ploy for what it was—an excuse to give Max and Laurel a few minutes alone for a private goodbye.

No sooner were they alone than Max reached for Laurel's hand. "I'm sorry, hon."

"I'm the one who should be apologizing. I wasn't myself at dinner."

They walked slowly toward her van.

"You said the meeting with Nikolai went well. Did something else happen?"

"No."

"What aren't you telling me?"

Here was her opportunity. She inhaled deeply, gathering her courage.

"The meeting went well. Incredible, really. Nikolai loved Wishing Well Springs and Bellissima and gave me a ton of advice, which I can't wait to implement."

He looked confused. "That's great. Isn't it?"

"Yes."

"Then what's wrong?"

She squeezed his fingers. This was way harder than she'd anticipated. Then again, it might go well. She shouldn't assume the worst. Max could be supportive, right?

"Nikolai offered me a mentorship."

"Congratulations." He kissed the top of her head.

"I'm still in a state of shock."

"There was no way he'd travel to Payson if he hadn't already decided to offer you a mentorship. He just needed to meet you first."

Feeling better, Laurel summarized Nikolai's plan. Only at the end did she mention her trips to LA.

"I suppose that's to be expected. He's based on the west coast."

"I have to go twice a month. Three to five days each trip. For a year."

Several beats passed before Max answered. "That's a lot of traveling."

"Then there's New York and Paris Fashion Weeks."

"New York and Paris," he repeated.

"I know it sounds like I'll be gone a lot."

"It does."

She tried to read his expression. The shadows from dusk falling made it difficult. Or was it the tight control he wielded on his emotions?

"I'm going to hire a full-time assistant," she said. "So I won't be stretched too thin."

He glanced away, his jaw tightening. "I didn't realize how demanding the mentorship would be when you first told me about it."

"Well, I didn't know. Not until Nikolai told me the details."

"Right."

She felt, as much as heard, the change in his manner. He was shutting down. No, shutting her out. Like a door slamming closed.

Panic hit her like an electrical shock. She'd considered the possibility of a negative reaction from him. She hadn't considered *her* reaction to it and the fear that suddenly seized her.

This wasn't new. She'd felt the same when Jordan told her about his job. And when she'd realized Bellissima was on the verge of financial collapse. And recently, to a smaller degree, when her previous assistant up and left.

Something she wanted was slipping away, and she was powerless to stop it.

"This is the chance of a lifetime," she said, desperate for him to understand.

"It is. You're right. You can't say no."

Why did she think this was the same thing he'd said to Charlene when the celebrity chose her as the winner on that TV show? And with the same clenched-jaw delivery?

"This doesn't change anything between us," Laurel insisted.

"But it will. It already has."

"Max. No. Cash told me I shouldn't let you and the girls become a casualty of my choices, but that won't happen."

"He's right."

That finality again. Was this the same man who'd professed to want a relationship with her only days ago?

"I care about you, Max. Truly. More than I imagined possible when we first met. We have something special." She clutched his arm. "Lots of couples manage relationships where one of them travels extensively for work. We can, too."

"I tried that before. It didn't go well."

"You said you wondered if Charlene had

already given up on your marriage and se-cretly wanted out. That's not how it is with me. With us."

"I'm just getting my life together after a long haul. Happy Trails. The girls. You. I thought. I'm not ready to throw a big obstacle in front of us that we might not overcome."

"We agreed to one day at a time. Can't we at least give that a try before calling it quits?" Her voice broke. "Nikolai's mentorship only lasts a year."

He nodded, and she thought she was get-ting through to him. She was mistaken.

"You're going to be busier than ever," he said. "The fashion shows and pop-up shops and events and new clients won't abruptly end just because your mentorship does."

"I can adjust my schedule."

"Like you've been adjusting it?"

"June is an unusually hectic month."

"You have lots of hectic months in your line of work," he said.

"You, too."

"Glamping is seasonal. Summers will be busier than winters. But even during peak tourist season, I won't work half the hours you do. I refuse. I've arranged my life so that I have time for my girls. You're arranging your life so that you'll be constantly busy for the foreseeable future."

"It's not like that."

"You told me you'd never let another man become the entire focus of your life again. You're making sure that doesn't happen by accepting Nikolai's offer."

"That's not true." She drew back to stare at him. "How could you think such a thing?"

"The girls are becoming attached to you. What happens when you miss a birthday party or a preschool play or Christmas dinner because of a wedding emergency?"

"You could just as easily have a Happy Trails emergency."

"I could. The difference is my business can almost run itself. And I'm not stretched paper thin to begin with."

Frustration at him and his obstinacy triggered a spark of anger. "It feels like you're using the girls as an excuse to break up with me."

"It feels like you're using the mentorship as an excuse to break up with me."

Laurel drew back. "I'm the one fighting for us."

"Are you? Are you sure you're not afraid of getting hurt again and are only willing to accept a relationship that's entirely on your terms?"

His remark made her angrier. "You're the one unwilling to bend."

"I have a ton at stake with my girls. And I've been burned before."

"As have I."

"Why didn't you talk to me before accepting Nikolai's offer?" he asked. "Were you afraid I'd convince you to turn him down?"

"Of course not! He…he needed an answer right away." It was an excuse. The same one Jordan had given her when he told her about the job offer. Nikolai would have waited until tomorrow. "I'm sorry, Max. In hindsight, I should have talked to you first. But you had the wedding rehearsal and your parents' arrival. Not to mention Happy Trails' opening. The timing wasn't good for a serious discussion that would distract you from all that."

His gaze traveled up the street. Laurel's, too. His parents and daughters were, at that moment, walking into a corner market. Perhaps Janice and Gary had noticed the intensity of her and Max's conversation and chosen to extend their stroll.

Laurel silently counted to ten before trying again to reason with Max. "I'm not using work as an excuse to break up with you or, like Cash told you, avoid getting hurt. The mentorship came out of the blue. It's not anything I purposefully sought."

"Regardless, your career will skyrocket. And I won't be the reason you turn Nikolai down and sacrifice a once-in-a-lifetime opportunity. Guilt will eat at me, and I'll blame you for that. You'll regret saying no and come to resent me. We'll have no chance after that."

"And if I accept the mentorship, you'll resent me."

"I won't," he stated earnestly. "I'll be happy for your success. You had Bellissima long before you met me, and becoming a prominent designer has been your lifelong dream. Just like you would never resent me for choosing my daughters and Happy Trails over you."

Sadness burned her throat, and tears pricked her eyes. "I'm not ready to say goodbye to you."

He pulled her close. A goodbye hug?

"You might have trouble believing it after tonight, but I admire your drive and ambition. I have my own ambitions. They just don't match up with yours."

Laurel couldn't help herself and stepped away from him. Against her better judgment, against Cash's advice, she'd put herself out there, only to have Max reject her. It stung.

More than that, it devastated her. Just like before. Was she always fated to have history repeat itself?

"Good night, Max." She started for her van. What else was there to do?

"Laurel. Please come back."

She turned. "You can't have it both ways. Deal me a blow and expect me to be okay afterward."

"Daddy! Daddy!"

The girls came bounding over, Max's parents a short distance behind them. Laurel saw them through the rush of tears blurring her vision.

"Nana and Pops bought us yo-yos." Daisy held hers up to show them. "She said you can teach us."

"I'm a little rusty."

Max tugged the girls to him for a hug. Laurel thought he might be using them as a distraction while he got his emotions under control. When his parents joined them, his mom put her hands on the girls' shoulders. Max's dad clapped him on the back.

They made a lovely family, one that didn't include Laurel—and never would.

She blinked back the tears. "Gary and Janice, it was great to meet you."

Without waiting for a response or a goodbye from Max and the girls, she opened her van door and climbed in. Max and his beautiful family that didn't include her moved out of the way. The girls waved. Laurel raised her hand, unable to smile.

She made it all the way home before breaking into wracking sobs. They didn't stop until she was home and hiding out in her workroom where, like always, she buried herself in her work.

CHAPTER FIFTEEN

"ENOUGH, ADDIE," MAX SNAPPED. "Stop feeding Jelly from the table. You know better."

"Sorry, Daddy." She slowly withdrew her arm from beneath the table and proceeded to sulk.

He rarely raised his voice at the girls. This was his second time in five minutes. He'd scolded Daisy rather sharply when she refused to even try one bite of the turkey sausage links his mom had cooked for their huge country breakfast.

Daisy pouted in solidarity with her sister. His parents gave him looks, his mom's reproachful and his dad's questioning. Even Jelly hung her head and gazed at Max with soulful eyes.

He folded under the pressure. "I didn't mean to yell at you, Addie. But I am tired of asking you not to sneak Jelly food. You're teaching her a bad habit."

"You didn't mean to make your dad mad." Max's mom patted Addie's hand, like she had

Daisy's when Max reprimanded her. "He has a lot going on and is stressed."

"What's stressed?" the little girl asked.

"It's another way of saying grumpy."

He wasn't thrilled that his mom minimized his disciplining of Addie and Daisy by indulging them and then making excuses for him. But he wouldn't argue with her. Not with the wedding this afternoon, and not in front of the girls.

A short while later, he told them to clean up their room and brush their teeth. "Your mom will be here in an hour."

His remark instantly changed the girls' mood. They brightened and scurried off, taking Jelly with them.

"Shouldn't you supervise the teeth brushing?" His mom rose from the table and carried a stack of dirty dishes to the sink.

His dad helped, removing the empty plate in front of Max. He left the half-filled coffee cup.

"I will," Max said, wondering if Charlene would be late as usual, and how soon he could get to work so that he wasn't constantly thinking about Laurel and their disastrous evening. "In a few minutes."

What had happened? Replaying events over and over in his mind gave him no clarity. They'd started out talking. She'd made her case for them to continue seeing each other despite the mentorship offer from Nikolai. He'd countered, stating why that wasn't a good idea, and they'd agreed to go their separate ways.

No, that wasn't exactly right. He'd insisted they put the brakes on their relationship. Why start something they couldn't finish?

Max needed another cup of coffee. Some aspirin. A good kick in the pants.

While his dad cleared the remaining dishes, his mom sat down in the vacant chair next to him. "When are you going to tell us why Laurel ran off after dinner, and you've been a grouch ever since?"

"I don't want to talk about it, Mom."

Rather than respect his privacy, she asked, "What did you say to hurt that poor girl?"

He drew back to stare at her. "Why do you assume I'm the one who said something hurtful?"

"You didn't?"

"Laurel made her choice." Without talking to him first.

"Did she? Or did you make her feel like she had no other choice?"

That sounded like a trick question to Max.

He turned to his dad, who was loading the dishwasher.

"You'll get no help from me, son." He held up a hand and shook his head.

Max's mom would pester him until he answered her. It was a technique she'd employed since he was three and lied to her about shattering her favorite glass figurine while playing ball in the house.

Grumbling, he drained the last of his coffee. Setting down the mug, he began his tale of woe. "She got a mentorship offer from a big-name designer out of LA."

"That's wonderful. She must be ecstatic."

"She is. It's an incredible opportunity." Max gave his parents the condensed version of Nikolai's offer.

"And you don't want her to take it?" she asked.

"I do. She'll probably never get another chance like it."

"Then what's the problem?" His mom's expression had changed. No longer reproachful, she studied him with concern and compassion. "Oh, I get it. Too much like what happened before."

"It's not that."

"Really?"

"Laurel isn't leaving Payson, though she'll

be gone a lot, dividing her time between here and LA. And she'll be very busy. It's a huge commitment."

"Well," his mom said, "whether or not it's identical to the past, some of the desertion you must be feeling is the same."

"She's not deserting me."

Yet, even as he said it, the word hit hard, like a fist to the solar plexus. His reaction to Laurel's news had been knee-jerk, and from that moment on, he'd grasped at every reason he could think of to stop seeing her out of fear he'd be dumped again.

Yeah, call it like it was. Dumped, not deserted. The latter was being left in the pursuit of something. Maybe something better. The former was being discarded, as though he was unneeded and worthless. And he realized with a start that that was how he'd felt for a long time.

Until the day he'd met Laurel in the miniature Western town. The way she'd looked at him had triggered a change for the better in him that grew each time they were together.

"You went through a lot when Charlene left," his mom continued. "I'm not sure you ever fully got over the rejection. Naturally, you wouldn't want to repeat the experience, or something that even remotely resembled it."

He had repeated it, though. He'd rejected Laurel.

"I have to consider the girls. They're fond of Laurel. I won't have them disappointed when she bails on them. They have enough of that in their lives already."

His mom leaned back in her chair and rubbed her chin thoughtfully. "You know, in hindsight, you were right to break things off with Laurel before you had too much invested in the relationship."

"I was?" That wasn't like his mom. She'd wanted him to stick it out with Charlene, at least at first, for the sake of their daughters.

His dad came over and refilled Max's mug with fresh coffee, for which he was grateful. "You mom has a point. Laurel's a terrific gal, but you don't need someone who's off gallivanting instead of staying at home all the time looking after you and the girls. You've been down that road before."

Max frowned. "I'm perfectly capable of looking after myself and the girls."

"Yes," his mom said. "But you're a traditional man. Old-fashioned. You'd be happier with a woman who doesn't work and puts you first."

"That's not true. And I think I'm offended."

His dad sat down beside him on the other

side. "Nothing wrong with that, son. A man needs to feel he's the breadwinner and the king of his castle."

Max looked from one to the other in shock. "Where did you get that idea? I'm not old-fashioned. I'm my children's primary care-giver. I fully support women with careers. I intend to raise my daughters to be completely independent and self-sufficient and the best in whatever occupation they choose."

His mom feigned bewilderment. "I guess I'm wrong then."

Realization dawned, and Max would have laughed if he wasn't annoyed. "You and Dad are playing me."

"Yes, and no," his mom admitted. "I'm sure when Laurel told you about this designer's offer, you had similar feelings as when Charlene announced she was moving her business to Phoenix. It's natural. You're only human. But the situation with Laurel isn't the same. And," she glanced at his dad, "we think you might have been a tad hasty. You said Laurel was willing to find common ground with you."

"Only you didn't budge," his dad added.

Max glanced toward the hall. Where were his daughters? He could usually count on them to interrupt his conversations. Except, apparently, when he was having an uncomfortable one that required him to dig deep and admit he might have made a mistake.

"It's too late," he said.

"Don't be ridiculous," his mom scoffed. "Talk to Laurel.

"I said some things."

"I imagine you did. But, if I'm right, she cares for you. She'll listen."

"As long as you don't blow it again," his dad cautioned.

Max swirled the coffee in his mug. "I have some thinking to do."

"Work's good for that." His dad pushed back from the table. "You can ponder while we put the finishing touches on this glamping place of yours."

Max didn't immediately move. "I meant what I said about sparing the girls any hurt. I'm tough, but they're vulnerable. They've gone through a lot with Charlene that no kids should have to endure."

"That's valid," his mom agreed. "But Laurel strikes me as the kind of person who would make the girls' emotional welfare a priority."

She would. Still, Max was hesitant. He had a lot to consider.

The interruption he'd been hoping for earlier arrived, only in the form of a ringing doorbell. Max glanced at the clock on the microwave as he stood. Was it possible? Could Charlene actually be early for once?

"Can you check on the girls, Mom? Make sure they've brushed their teeth and are ready to go?"

"Of course."

He braced himself. Encounters with Charlene were seldom pleasant. What would she find to complain about today?

Jelly came running from the hall to intercept Max, barking riotously. She headed straight for the front door, tail wagging. Max scooped her up, opening the door with his free hand.

Charlene stood on the front porch stoop. "Morning."

"Hi." He swung the door wide. By now, Jelly was a flailing, whining bundle of half-grown puppy excitement. "Come on in."

"Thanks for letting me take the girls early today. There's so much to do, getting ready for the wedding. Manicures. Hair styling. Makeup."

"Makeup, Charlene? They're three."

"Just a little blush and lip gloss. For the photos."

"Nothing else."

"Of course."

He decided to wait and see before battling her.

"Mommy, Mommy!" Addie and Daisy appeared and flew like small missiles directly for Charlene.

She stooped and gathered them close. "Hello, my sweet little sugar plums. Are you ready?"

Turned out, they weren't. After saying good morning to Max's parents and exchanging some pleasantries, Charlene went with the girls to their room to oversee the packing. Max helped carry out the dresses and tote bags filled with shoes, socks, accessories, a change of clothes and whatever else Charlene deemed necessary.

"I'll get the car seats from my truck," he said.

"Don't bother." She opened the back passenger door, showing him a pair of brand-new, state-of-the-art car seats. "I bought these last week."

"All righty." This was unexpected. She'd never bothered before, always borrowing Max's and offering some excuse about not having time to get to the store. "Climb in, girls."

Addie and Daisy giggled and squealed as

they each claimed a car seat. Charlene helped buckle them in and hung the dresses from a hook while Max loaded the totes in the trunk.

Leaning his head in the rear open door, he told his daughters, "Love you. Behave for your mom."

"Love you, Daddy," they chimed in unison.

"See you at the wedding," Max said to Charlene and turned to leave.

"Max. Wait. Do you have a second?"

He paused. "Something wrong?"

"No." Charlene pushed at her trendily styled hair. She'd changed her appearance since they'd split. The former jeans and boots cowgirl had been replaced by a well-dressed businesswoman. "I just wanted to tell you… I'm sorry."

"About what?"

"I wasn't fair to you. Leaving like I did. Sticking you with the girls."

Not the confession he'd anticipated. "You didn't stick me with Addie and Daisy. I love them and love being their dad."

"And you're good at it. They're terrific kids—thanks to you."

Terrific kids? Huh. What had she called them at the wedding rehearsal? A couple of brats?

"Thanks," he said. "That means a lot."

"I've let you down. I'm going to be better in the future."

He'd heard this before from her, but he didn't say it. She must have read his mind, however.

"I'm serious. I wasn't ready to be a mom and, to be honest, I hated staying at home. You were working long hours at the team penning facility. To have asked you to take on more responsibility for the girls just to free me up would have been unreasonable. I made matters worse by taking my unhappiness out on you. That was really wrong. But if I even hinted that being a mother didn't fulfill my every want and wish, people looked at me as if I was a monster or made me feel like there was something wrong with me."

"There's nothing wrong with you. The girls were unexpected. We were hardly married a year when they came along. That's a lot to handle all at once."

"You're kinder than I deserve, Max. I was a lousy wife, and I haven't been the best mother. I can admit it. But I want to do better."

"That's what counts."

"When did you…" She studied him, smiled and then said with a laugh, "Grow so much?"

"Believe it or not, the last couple of years have given me a different perspective."

"You were thinking about us in between potty training, running the house and starting a business?"

"In my few spare minutes." He laughed, as well, only to sober. "I wasn't entirely fair to you, either, Charlene. I expected you to hold down a job, raise two babies and take care of the house with little help from me."

"Are you kidding? You worked day and night so I could quit my job and start making my own hair products. You really tried."

"Not hard enough."

"That's not true," she said with heartfelt sincerity. "I've only recently come to realize how much effort you did put into the marriage and how often you put my desires and the girls' needs over yours. You're a good man, Max. We're not right for each other, but none of that is your fault and it isn't for lack of trying on your part."

"I appreciate that."

"And not being the best mom? That's entirely on me. I love what I do. Really love it. That's no excuse, however. Addie and Daisy deserve better."

"You're very talented, Charlene. And smart. I've always admired that about you."

She flashed a bright smile. "You've never said that before."

"I mean it. But. If I'm going to be honest, it was hard to say at the time when there were other things I didn't admire about you."

"Fair enough." Her smile waned, but she nodded in understanding.

"You weren't the only parent who made mistakes. Trust me. I share a lot of the responsibility for our marriage hitting the skids."

"You never said that before, either."

It was his turn to smile. "Time and distance have given me a different perspective. I'm still marveling at how you took an idea and turned it into a thriving, profitable enterprise. That requires determination and guts."

"Same can be said for you." She gestured to Happy Trails in the distance. "Mr. Businessman. Who'd have guessed?"

"I'm not profitable yet. I've barely opened. Talk to me again in a year."

"You'll do great," she insisted. "Maybe we're not so different after all."

"Maybe not," he conceded, but he was thinking of Laurel.

"I promise to see the girls more often. Spend quality time with them rather than spending money on them."

"I'm glad to hear it. They're getting old enough. You could take them for the weekend," he suggested. "I'd meet you halfway."

"I think that's doable. In fact, I'd really like it. What about next month? I'm not busy the weekend of the tenth."

He was pleased that she not only embraced his idea, she named a date.

"Sounds great."

"That'll free you up to spend time with your new girlfriend."

"I don't have a girlfriend," he answered quickly. Too quickly, judging by Charlene's knowing glance.

"No? I've heard all about Miss Laurel from the girls. And I saw the two of you together at the rehearsal."

"We're friends is all." Maybe if he said it enough, he'd start to believe it.

"Hmm. Friends who go fishing together and have breakfast together and make bride clothespin dolls with your daughters? That sounds like dating to me."

"We're not seeing each other," he said with that same gut-punched feeling. How long until that stopped?

"Well, perhaps you should start. She was very nice when I ordered the girls' dresses, and my sister thinks the world of her. And she lives here in Payson. No chance of her uprooting and moving away."

Not unless her career exploded, which it could.

"Mommy," Addie cried from inside the car. "Daisy sneezed on me."

"I'd better go." Charlene rolled her eyes. "It's going to be a long day." She surprised Max again by giving him a quick hug. "Thanks for taking such amazing care of our daughters. I'll call if I forgot something."

With that, she dashed around the front of the car to the driver's side.

Max watched them drive away, his mind replaying the earlier conversations with his parents and then Charlene.

He'd handled Laurel's announcement badly, and it had cost him a relationship he had very much wanted to explore. So what was he going to do about it—let the best, most incredible woman he'd ever met get away or fight to get her back?

CHAPTER SIXTEEN

"You look stunning!"

The compliment came from the bride's misty-eyed mother. She and Laurel, along with the bridesmaids, were crowded in the bride's dressing room at Wishing Well Springs' wedding barn.

She would not be making a grand entrance in the horse-drawn carriage. Rather, she would emerge from the dressing room in the back of the barn and walk down the aisle on her father's arm.

Laurel's duties here were officially done. The dress was a glorious creation of white silk with intricate beadwork and a spectacular mermaid tail. It fit to perfection. No last-minute wardrobe emergencies to detain her. The other ladies would see to the bride's needs.

Addie and Daisy were also ready and being watched over by their mother, just outside the barn entrance. They were beyond cute in their flower girl outfits and hair ornaments. No adjustments there for Laurel, either.

"Best wishes." She took hold of the bride's hands and squeezed tight. "I'm so happy for you."

Sarah pulled her into a hug, appreciation shining in her eyes. "Thank you for everything. You've helped make this wedding a dream come true."

"It was my pleasure and my privilege to design your dress."

"I bet you have something special in mind for your own wedding."

Laurel banished the stab of pain and forced a smile. "But of course."

She released Sarah and turned to go, her own tears threatening to fall. Laurel was frequently caught up in the moment at weddings. Today, her emotional display was for another reason—remnants from last night with Max. How she wished for a do-over.

Not that she'd change her mind and decline Nikolai's offer. But she wished she could change the way she'd sprung the news on Max and what she'd said afterward. Her timing had been terrible, too. She should have taken a few days to mull over her approach. Possibly waited until after Happy Trails' soft opening when they were both less overwhelmed. They might still be moving forward with their relationship.

Outside the bride's dressing room, she located Phoebe.

"You doing okay?" her friend asked. "You look tuckered out."

"I'm fine."

"Liar."

Laurel laughed weakly. "Okay. I've been better."

She'd told Phoebe about what had happened with Max. At the time, she'd been angry at him for giving up on them so easily. Phoebe had listened, held her when she cried and waited to offer advice until Laurel asked for it.

"Have you talked to Max yet?"

"I'm not sure he wants to hear from me." Just saying that triggered a fresh wave of misery.

"I don't believe that for a second. He's probably regretting how things turned out every bit as much as you and just as uncertain about calling."

"What's the point? Nothing's changed."

"You care for each other."

"That's not enough," Laurel said glumly. "Relationships require commitment. And commitments require sacrifices. How do I give up everything that I've worked so hard to achieve?"

"You don't. You find compromises. Look at your brother and me. I moved a little. He moved a little. The next thing you know, we found common ground."

"I suggested compromises."

"Seconds after you dropped a bombshell."

There was wisdom in what her friend said. Could Laurel move a little? Could Max?

"Phoebe," the mother of the bride called. "We need you."

"Be right there." To Laurel, she said, "I'm here for you."

"Thanks."

The two friends embraced. Laurel was glad Phoebe didn't offer any trite sayings like, "Someone new will come around," or, "It wasn't meant to be."

"If you don't need my help, I'm heading back to the house." It was only four. She could start on the preliminary designs she and Nikolai had discussed and review her most recent customer satisfaction surveys while forcing herself to eat something for dinner. Nothing appealed to her lately.

"See ya later," Phoebe said and dashed off to where the bride's mother waited anxiously.

Feet dragging, Laurel made her way toward the barn entrance, trying not to look around for Max. Seeing him would only cause the rift in her heart to widen further.

Outside, she spotted the girls hanging from the hitching rail where the horses and carriage were tied for post-wedding photo ops. Laurel hoped they weren't getting their white shoes and dresses dirty. Charlene was standing thirty feet away, talking on her phone. When she noticed Laurel's gaze, she glanced over at the girls and promptly covered the phone's mouthpiece. "Girls. Be careful. Please. Mommy will be right there."

Laurel approached, worried Addie and Daisy might already have grime on their hands and clothes. She automatically reached into her pocket for the travel packet of wet wipes she always carried on wedding days.

Motioning to Charlene, she pointed to herself and then the girls, indicating she'd take charge of the situation. Charlene nodded, smiled with relief and resumed her call.

"Miss Laurel." Daisy spied Laurel first. She and her sister ran over and hugged her legs.

"Hey, you two." Laurel bent and returned their hugs.

"We're waiting for Mommy," Addie said.

"She has work," Daisy added in a glum

tone that sounded to Laurel as if the little girl had heard this before, more than once.

She straightened and glanced again in Charlene's direction. The maid of honor dress she wore was the same off-the-shoulder, tea-length style as the others, only in dusty sage rather than daffodil. Tendrils were already falling loose from her hair, victims of the strong breeze.

Laurel's first impulse was to judge Charlene for putting work ahead of her daughters. But, then, wasn't Laurel also guilty of putting work ahead of others? Often?

Returning her attention to the girls, she held them at arm's length and gave them a thorough once-over. "Let me see. Did you ruin your pretty clothes?"

"We've been good." Addie spoke for them both.

Laurel used one of her wet wipes to clean a few smudges from their faces and hands and one from the hem of Daisy's dress. When she finished, she checked on Charlene, who was still on the phone but mouthed an exaggerated, "Thank you."

"Where's your dad?" Laurel asked the girls.

"Inside with Nana and Pops."

All right. So, he was here. "Maybe we should find them before you get dirty again."

Laurel motioned to Charlene, indicating she could take the girls inside. Even if facing Max wouldn't be easy.

Charlene shook her head, held up a finger signaling Laurel to wait and started walking toward them. As she neared, Laurel could hear parts of the conversation, which was indeed work related.

"Yeah, Martin," Charlene said into the phone, her previous smile fading. "Look, I have got to run. The wedding's about to start, and I don't know where the girls put their baskets of rose petals."

Rather than disconnect, Charlene continued talking for another two minutes, during which the girls pulled on her free hand and whined. Laurel could leave, she supposed. *Should* leave. Except she'd convinced herself the girls would get dirty without an adult to supervise them.

Finally, to Laurel's vast relief, Charlene ended her phone call.

"Sorry about that." Charlene released a long breath. "I had a fire to put out and got sidetracked. But I'm sure you understand how that goes, running your own business."

"Um, yes." Laurel had gotten sidetracked as recently as during the breakfast picnic with Max and when they went fishing.

"It's nice to meet you in person." Charlene shook Laurel's hand. "Thank you for all your hard work."

"Nice to meet you, too. I saw the girls and was afraid they'd, well—" Laurel stopped short, concerned her remark might be interpreted as criticism. Did Charlene know about her and Max? Then again, what was there to know, now that they were no longer seeing each other?

"I should have been watching them better," Charlene admitted. "This fire was more than my manager could handle. Distribution is difficult right now, what with the current trucking situation."

"We've had some problems, too," Laurel said. "Not getting supplies delivered on time."

"I need to find a solution soon. Not with the trucking situation. As if I could solve that." She let out a small laugh. "To better manage my time. I'll be taking Addie and Daisy more in the future."

"Really! That's great."

"Yeah. I'm looking forward to it. Now, if I can only get my act together."

"You will."

"I will," Charlene echoed and pulled the girls close. "I'm highly motivated."

Laurel didn't know what had prompted the

change in Charlene, but she was happy for all of them. Max included. He wanted Charlene to spend more time with the girls.

"I've heard so many nice things about you," Charlene said. "From my sister and the girls and Max."

Interesting. Laurel could see Sarah and the girls talking about her. But Max? That must have been awkward conversation between exes.

"Don't look so alarmed." Charlene winked. "It was all good. Nothing but praise."

"Miss Laurel sewed Jelly's dinosaur costume," Daisy said.

"She helped us with our bride dolls," Addie added.

Laurel averted her gaze. The last thing she wanted was for Charlene to feel like Laurel was attempting to one-up her or insert herself into the girls' lives. "You should be very proud of your daughters. They're sweet as can be and very smart."

"They are, on both counts." Charlene patted Laurel's arm. "And I'm glad you're their friend."

"Me, too."

"And I'm glad you're Max's friend."

"We, um…"

"Charlene!" her mother called from the barn entrance. "Hurry. We're ready."

"That's our cue, girls." Charlene took Addie and Daisy by the hands. "Let's find those baskets."

"I'm sure Phoebe can help you," Laurel said, thankful she'd been spared from having to respond to Charlene's comment about Max.

"No doubt. That wedding organizer of yours has accomplished more than one miracle today." Charlene started to walk away, then paused and looked back. "You coming, Laurel?"

"No. Actually, I'm heading to the house."

"Well, nice to encounter another kindred spirit."

"I beg your pardon?"

"Female entrepreneurs. One day we'll rule the world," Charlene added with a bright laugh before turning away.

Addie and Daisy glanced back at Laurel. "Bye, Miss Laurel," Daisy said while Addie waved.

Laurel raised a hand in return, an uncomfortable feeling landing like an anchor in her middle. She'd like nothing better than to deny any similarities between her and Charlene. They weren't kindred spirits. Except Laurel could see how someone, like Max, would note the similarities.

As she walked the quarter-mile dirt road back to the house, she thought about Charlene and Phoebe, and even Max. They were all committed, Charlene newly, to making room in their work life for their loved ones. If they could find a way, why couldn't Laurel? It didn't have to be all or nothing, did it?

Her success and being offered a mentorship by a top designer were points of immense pride for her and, in her opinion, well deserved. She worked tirelessly and had sacrificed much. She was a good role model for not just young girls such as Addie and Daisy but all children.

Only at what cost? Along the way, she'd lost the ability to balance her work and her personal life. How much of that had to do with her parents' bankruptcy, divorce, and her dad eventually leaving Arizona? In retrospect, Laurel might be constantly overcompensating for the giant hole her dad had left in her heart.

She tended to blame Jordan for her nearly losing Bellissima after their breakup, but the hard truth was Laurel, and Laurel alone, had made her choices in response to his abrupt departure. Just like she'd chosen how she responded to Max's reaction to Nikolai's offer. She'd panicked and tried desperately to hold on to him and what they had together. When that hadn't worked, she'd retreated into work.

Was Max right? Perhaps she hadn't talked to him before giving Nikolai her answer because she feared he'd convince her to refuse the mentorship. Was she—how had he said it?—arranging her life to be as busy as possible as an excuse to break up with him?

Max had uncomplicated his life. When his marriage fell apart, he made changes that not only allowed him to be the best dad possible to his daughters but gave him a job he enjoyed with a potential for future growth.

Could Laurel accomplish that, too? Make changes that freed up enough of her demanding schedule to pursue the things that mattered? Namely, a relationship with Max.

As the house came into view, quaintly framed on both sides by tall pine trees, Laurel made the decision to hit the reset button. Even if Max refused to give them a second try, she still needed to lighten her workload to make space for those she cared about.

Rather than go inside, she sat on the porch swing and, taking out her phone, placed a call to Nikolai. She reached his assistant, who immediately put her through.

"My darling," he gushed. "I didn't expect to hear from you again this soon. Don't tell me you've changed your mind."

"No. Of course not. But, I've been thinking about our agreement."

"And what have you been thinking?" Some of the sugar left his voice.

"I have a couple small requests." She paused.

"Such as?"

At least he didn't tell her no outright and hang up on her. Laurel relayed her requests, during which Nikolai remained mostly silent. Laurel faltered more than once, her nerves getting the best of her, only to plow on. At the end, she exhaled a long sigh.

"Is that all?"

She couldn't determine from his tone if he was amenable or about to tell her to take a hike.

"I realize I'm asking a lot," she said, "and please don't think I'm ungrateful. I am. Incredibly grateful. But I made the mistake once before of allowing one part of my life to consume my time and my energy, and I paid a hefty price. I won't let that happen again. Bellissima is too important to me to risk losing. As are the people I care about. I won't tromp on them while trying to climb to the top."

Nikolai made a noncommittal sound. "Are you done with your little speech?"

"Yes." Laurel winced. She'd gone too far.

She had to be the only person in the world to ever insist on contingencies before accepting a mentorship from the fabulous and famous Nikolai.

"All right. Now, my turn."

They spent the next ten minutes discussing her contingencies, with Nikolai doing most of the talking and Laurel chewing on a thumbnail. When they were done, they said their goodbyes, and Laurel disconnected. She gave herself a few minutes to regroup and clear her head. Had that really just happened? Rousing herself, she checked the time. The wedding should be ending soon. She knew from talking to Phoebe and Max that the reception at Joshua Tree Inn next door was starting at six.

Max would be busy with the girls. There would be a receiving line, photographs to take and old friends to greet. He wouldn't have time to talk with her. Not today. Maybe not tomorrow, either.

There was always the possibility he wouldn't want to talk to her again. Her chest constricted with acute pain. On second thought, maybe she shouldn't tell him about her call with Nikolai.

Yeah, and look where that had gotten her last time. She'd come this far, she'd see it

through to the end. Picking up her phone, she
sent Max a text message.

Sorry to interrupt. Whenever you have a few
minutes, can we chat? There's something I
want to tell you.

When he didn't immediately respond, she
tried not to let herself become disheartened.
He was at the wedding, for heaven's sake, and
likely had shut off his phone.

She went inside and had just entered Bellissima when her pocket buzzed. A text! She
grabbed her phone with fumbling fingers.

Charlene's taking the girls to the reception.
Meet you at the stables in 15? Told Cash I'd
feed the horses.

Laurel quickly combed her hair and applied some lipstick. Then, grabbing the same
floppy hat she'd been wearing the first day
she'd met Max, she raced outside and jumped
in the golf cart. She was at the stables and
waiting when Max's truck came bumping
down the dirt road.

MAX WOULDN'T LIE. Laurel's text had come as
a surprise. So was her standing by the pad-

dock gate, waiting for him. She was usually late, and he assumed he'd beat her there.

Otis and Elvis also waited, their big heads hanging over the paddock gate and their tails lazily swishing in the late afternoon sun. Elvis nuzzled Laurel's arm, and she absently stroked his nose with her other hand. Her gaze, however, remained riveted on Max as he parked.

Anticipation and excitement and worry jostled for first position as he got out and strode toward her. He wondered if this talk would bring them back together or drive the knife into his heart a little deeper.

He could have offered some excuse about the wedding and his parents' visit and Happy Trails. Except he wanted to apologize to her. In one short month she'd become a vital part of his life—one he wasn't ready to lose.

"Hey." He nodded as he neared.

"Hey," she said in return, her expression friendly but reserved. Boy, what he'd give to change that.

Otis and Elvis nickered. Otis pushed against the metal gate, causing it to creak worrisomely, and Elvis stomped his huge hoof, demanding supper.

"Let me get these guys fed first before we have a small disaster here."

Max hurried to the stables. There, he filled a bucket with grain and grabbed three thick flakes of hay from the stack.

This would likely be his last time feeding the old horses. His temporary stint as Wishing Well Springs' carriage driver was officially over. Their regular driver had returned this morning. For that reason and no other, Max took his time, stopping and giving each horse an extra petting.

"I'll be back to visit you, boys. Count on it."

Eager to eat, the elderly draft horses lumbered after him as he carried their dinner to the feed trough. He no sooner tossed in the sweet smelling hay and dumped the grain than they buried their faces with satisfied snorts.

Emerging from the paddock, he closed the gate and hung the bucket on a post.

"What's up?" he asked, falling into step beside her when she strolled leisurely toward his truck.

"It's been a wild month."

"You'll get no argument from me."

At the truck, he lowered the tailgate and gestured for her to sit. She struggled to hoist herself up, her efforts hampered by the floral sundress she wore. It, and her straw hat, reminded him of the first time they'd met.

Surrendering to impulse, he took hold of her by the waist and lifted her onto the tailgate.

Rather than object or get angry, Laurel laughed.

That was a good sign, he decided, and he swung up beside her, the tailgate dipping beneath his weight. "That's better. For talking," he clarified.

"Right." She smiled.

This was going well. She must still have feelings for him if he could get a laugh and a smile out of her.

"I met Charlene earlier today," she continued. "Before the wedding. You were inside the barn with your parents."

"Oh, yeah?" He waited, not sure where this line of conversation was headed.

"I can see the similarities between us. No wonder I scared you off."

"It's more like I scared myself off."

"I can relate." She nodded. "I'm guilty of that, too. Creating problems where there aren't any."

"Still scared?" he asked, liking where this was going.

Rather than answer him, Laurel continued.

"Charlene made a comment about women like us, female entrepreneurs, not needing a man."

"Ow. That's harsh. Is it true?"

Again, she didn't answer. Wait. Should he be concerned?

"I like being a business owner," she said. "Having a career gives me a lot of satisfaction and sense of accomplishment, which has nothing to do with me being a woman."

"It should give you satisfaction."

"But having a career and a…love interest shouldn't be mutually exclusive."

"Love interest?"

"Stay on topic, Max."

He grinned.

"Yet, I seem to have been operating under that assumption. Especially after Nikolai offered me the mentorship, and you pointed out that—"

"Stop right there. I was wrong."

"No. I was wrong."

"What are you trying to say, Laurel? Can I get my hopes up or are you just needing closure?"

"I called Nikolai right before I texted you and asked for some conditions."

Interesting. "Is this where I'm supposed to ask what conditions?"

"Nikolai, I'm sure, is used to his mentees

being at his beck and call. As he should be. What he offers is unique in the industry and of incredible worth. I'm sure I threw him for a loop when I explained that I had boundaries."

"And is he okay with that?"

Her mouth curved in an appealing smile. "Surprisingly, yes. He was very reasonable. I mean, reasonable for Nikolai."

"That's good. I think I'm starting to like him."

"I told him I'd travel to LA every month instead of every two weeks. We'll meet by video conference in between. The only exceptions are New York and Paris Fashion Weeks."

"Of course. Because, well, New York and Paris."

"That's not all." She leaned in closer to Max. He wasn't mistaken about that because his senses hummed like the air during a lightning storm. "I'm going to apply for a small business loan to cover the cost of hiring a full-time assistant *and* another seamstress. The assistant will be in charge of Bellissima's fashion shows, at Wishing Well Springs and pop-ups and any events. That will allow me to concentrate on designing and working with Nikolai. I hate the idea of borrowing money, but, if everything goes as planned, I'll repay the loan in a few years and double the size of

Bellissima. I may even open a second shop. I
have several clients in Palm Springs."

"Expanding." Max's rising spirits sank.
He'd gone and gotten ahead of himself again.
She was happy because of the strides she was
making in her career. Not about reconciling
with him.

"And delegating," she emphasized and
placed her hand atop his. "I'm giving up
my sixty- and seventy-hour workweeks. No
more killing myself. It's unhealthy physically,
mentally and emotionally. Work smarter, not
harder. That's my new motto."

His skepticism must have shown in his expression.

"I'm serious," she said.

"Okay."

"No. I am. I'm taking a lesson from this
guy I know. He's opening up a glampsite and
has figured out how to balance his personal
and work life."

"He sounds like a clever guy."

"He is." Her eyes shone with sincerity
and longing and, no denying it, affection. "I
know you have your doubts. You think I've
got these huge ambitions and that they'll consume me like before. But things are different.
I have a new priority."

"What's that?"

"Us," she said. "We're too good together to give up after one hiccup. We deserve a second chance. If you're open to the idea."

Max reached up and cradled her cheek. Here it was, the moment he hadn't believed possible. In no hurry, he savored it fully.

"I can assure you, I am. Very open to the idea. I've recently learned a few things myself, it seems."

"Mmm?" She melted into his touch. "Tell me."

"My mom thinks I acted hastily and ended things with you before you ended things with me."

"I was going to say the same thing about myself."

Max's thumb moved to her lower lip where he traced the outline. "We're quite the pair, aren't we?"

"We didn't give ourselves a fair shake," she said.

"No, we didn't. But if you give me another chance, I won't let it happen again."

Her expression softened. "I think that's possible."

Laurel had taken the first step by asking him to talk. The next step was his.

"I like you," he said. "I could easily fall in love with you." Who was he kidding? He was well on the way.

"I feel the same. Our past isn't a pattern for our future."

"Is that fashion design lingo?"

"You like it?" she asked coyly.

His answer was to lower his mouth to hers and brush his lips across hers. "Here's my promise to you, Laurel Montgomery. I'm going to make you fall so in love with me, leaving will never cross your mind."

"I like that." She kissed him back, lingering this time and letting him know in no uncertain terms giving them another try had been her plan all along when she'd texted him.

When they finally ended the kiss, she looked him directly in the eyes, her gaze steady. "And I promise you this, Max Maxwell. Except for when I'm in LA or during fashion weeks, we'll spend at least one afternoon together with the girls and at least one evening together just the two of us every week. Without fail. I have weddings most weekends—it's the nature of my job. But I'll try my hardest to carve out a Friday or Saturday night every month for date night. Is that enough to start?"

"More than enough."

They sealed their commitment to each other with a kiss. Then another. In between, they shared hopes and expectations and made plans for the following day when Laurel would attend the soft opening with her mom. The two of them would have lunch with Max's parents and the girls. His family would be thrilled to see her, and Laurel's presence would turn a good day into a stellar one.

They lost track of time as they lost themselves in the moment. Only his phone buzzing interrupted them.

"Duty calls," he said reluctantly after reading the text. "Dinner's starting, and the girls will be ready to go home right after that. My parents are already at the house waiting."

"Would you like some company?"

He grinned and tugged on the brim of her hat. "Look at you being impulsive. Better be careful, I could get used to it."

She grinned, too. "I'm turning over a new leaf."

He helped her down from the tailgate and continued holding her hand as he walked her to the passenger door.

Max also felt like he was turning over a new leaf—make that an entirely new life. One that included Laurel.

And tonight was just the beginning.

EPILOGUE

14 months later

LAUREL RODE IN the carriage on the drive from the house to Wishing Well Springs' wedding barn. She couldn't begin to count the number of times she'd been on the route or the number of brides she'd accompanied.

Today, her brother, Cash, drove Otis and Elvis. The old draft horses were officially retired last year and normally enjoyed a life of leisure, nursing their old bones and being the object of much adoration from Max's daughters. But, because today was an extra special wedding, they'd been harnessed one last time.

As usual, Phoebe sat with the photographer and videographer in the golf cart ahead, directing them on the best angles and shots and what to expect when the carriage arrived at the barn. She looked especially pretty in the yellow dress Laurel had designed for her. It flattered her eight-months-pregnant silhouette.

Laurel had learned a lot about maternity

clothes in recent months and intended to incorporate them in her new line of maternity bridesmaid and evening gowns. Her innovative designs had earned her a cover on *Southwest Bride Magazine*'s May issue, which was now framed and hanging at the entrance to Bellissima. She and Max had celebrated her reaching that coveted milestone with a romantic dinner.

During her year-long mentorship, Nikolai had taught her more than she'd ever thought possible. New York and Paris fashion weeks had been beyond her wildest dreams. While she'd been sad to see the mentorship end, she'd been eager to embark on the next stage of her career and put all she'd learned into practice.

Not everything she'd presented to Max on that day in June had gone as planned. She'd never been able to find a good assistant. Neither had she hosted as many fashion shows or participated in as many events as she'd planned. That would change soon. Helena's husband was in full remission and doing well, and, as of last winter, Laurel had begun training Helena to be her full-time assistant, a position she excelled at. She was as much a mother as a supervisor to the two new young seamstresses, and they adored her.

Other things had gone well for Laurel and Max. Happy Trails was an enormous success and had recently been named one of Payson's top places to stay. The two of them had overcome their challenges, kept their commitment to spend quality time together, individually and with the girls, and fallen so deeply in love, Laurel woke up every morning pinching herself.

A moment later, they crested the rise, and the wedding barn came into view. A large gathering of beaming guests stood outside to welcome them. Inside the barn, the groom waited, not allowed to see the bride until the start of the ceremony. He could watch the video of her grand arrival later at the reception.

Cash reined the old horses to a stop. "You ready, sis?" Cash glanced over his shoulder at Laurel, a huge smile on his face.

"Yes." She clutched the bouquet of yellow roses in one hand and gathered the folds of her dress—her most anticipated and cherished creation—in the other. Anticipation, the good kind, had her fumbling slightly. Luckily, her father was there. Opening the carriage door, he helped her down.

She'd finally reached out to him last Christmas after a long deliberation. Max had encouraged her, convinced the answers she sought would bring her comfort. To Laurel's great happiness, her father had responded positively. Since then, she and Cash had both taken steps to repair their relationship with their father and had made enough progress that Laurel asked him to walk her down the aisle.

"You're stunning," he said when she stood in front of him. Tears filled his eyes. "My baby girl's getting married."

"You're not so bad yourself." She brushed a tiny speck of white off the lapel of his dove-gray tux.

"Oh, sweetie." Laurel's mom materialized, looking striking in the ensemble Laurel had designed for her, a corsage pinned to her silk jacket and a tissue crumpled in her fist. "You are a vision." At that, her mom broke into soft sobs.

"Mom."

The two hugged. And then, in a moment that strummed Laurel's heartstrings, her mom hugged her dad. They, too, had been taking steps to get along and not just for the wedding. Laurel's mom wanted her dad to feel welcome when his new grandchild was born.

"You and I did good," she told him. "Raised two incredible children."

His expression turned tender. "That we did. Now, let's get this youngest one married."

When her mom stepped away, he presented his elbow for Laurel to take, which she did. Nearby, the photographer snapped pictures and the videographer filmed. The guests had filed into the barn to take their seats.

"Wait," Phoebe hurried over as fast as her pregnant state allowed. With Cash's help, she bent down, no small feat for her, and rearranged Laurel's long train. "There," she announced with satisfaction when she was done and straightened with some difficulty. "I love you." She kissed Laurel's cheek.

Cash did, too. "Max is a lucky guy."

"I love you both," Laurel said, emotion making speech difficult. "Everyone inside?"

"Everyone but the wedding party."

"Let's not keep them waiting."

Laurel and her dad followed her brother, best friend and mom to the barn entrance. At the door, they met up with the rest of the wedding party and Max's mom, who'd been keeping an eye on Addie and Daisy, absolutely precious in their flower girl dresses. Max's dad had been put in charge of Jelly, who wore a dog version of her young owners' dresses. Attached to her back was a satin pillow, and secured to the pillow with a ribbon were two gold bands, one for Laurel, the other for Max. The dog had barked happily upon seeing Laurel but otherwise sat still. A much better behaved adult than puppy, she'd been well trained for her part in the wedding.

Laurel's heart fluttered when she saw the rings. It was really happening. She was marrying Max, the love of her life.

Addie threw her arms around Laurel's waist. "Lulu, Lulu."

Daisy followed suit. "You're beautiful, Lulu."

Laurel had to smile at the nickname the girls had given her. Soon after she and Max started seriously dating, Miss Laurel became Laurel and then, shortened to Lulu. She never wanted to take the place of the girls' mother. But her role in their lives was large and becoming larger after today. Lulu sounded much more personal and affectionate.

"Now, girls," Max's mom admonished. "Don't get Laurel's dress wrinkled."

She didn't mind a few wrinkles given in love. Stroking the girls' heads, she was careful to avoid their flower crowns. "Are you ready? You two have the most important job."

The wedding party lined up. Addie and Daisy stood at the front, Jelly between them. The dog had been trained to heel, without a leash, and would walk alongside them. Laurel's cousin from Tucson was next, escorted by Max's brother, impressive in his full dress army uniform. Last came Phoebe, escorted by Cash.

Above them, the sun shone in a gloriously cloudless sky. Perfect weather for an outdoor reception. They would be taking over the entire patio at the Red Rock Grill and half the dining room.

Before Laurel could collect her wildly scattered emotions, the music she and Max had chosen began to play. Max's parents left to take their seats. After that, Laurel's cousin cued the girls to start. As far as Laurel was concerned, there were never any cuter flower girls or canine ring bearer.

"We're next," Laurel's dad said when their turn came and patted her hand resting on his elbow.

The photographer and videographer aimed their cameras at her. And then the music changed to "Here Comes the Bride."

As she entered the crowded barn, all eyes were on her. But the only person she saw was Max, standing at the altar, handsome beyond belief in his Western-cut tuxedo. Laurel teared up seeing him wearing her grandfather's bolo tie.

Cash had said Max was a lucky guy, but Laurel knew she was the lucky one. She had to stop herself from breaking her carefully practiced stride and running to him. That she'd almost once let him get away still astounded her.

Thank goodness she'd come to her senses. Max was going to be so much more than a good husband. He was a life partner in the truest sense of the word. They were each other's support system, personally and professionally. She loved Addie and Daisy to pieces and eagerly awaited the day she and Max would expand their family. Laurel now knew what was most important in life and that she could have the career she wanted along with a husband and family.

At the altar, the minister asked, "Who gives this woman to be married today?"

"Her mother and I do," her father answered.

And then, all at once, Laurel was facing Max, their hands clasped together.

"I love you," he mouthed.

"I love you, too," she mouthed back.

The rest of the ceremony was like a dream— her fondest dream come true. And, at the end, when the minister pronounced them husband and wife, Laurel had never heard any sweeter words.

Cheers and applause erupted, filling the barn. Max linked his arm with hers, grinning like the happiest man on the planet. He held Addie's hand while Laurel took hold of Daisy's. With Jelly following along behind, and the wedding recessional playing from the speakers, they started back down the aisle as a family—together forever and always.

* * * * *

Get 4 FREE REWARDS!

We'll send you 2 FREE Books plus 2 FREE Mystery Gifts.

FREE
Value Over
$20

Both the **Romance** and **Suspense** collections feature compelling novels written by many of today's bestselling authors.

YES! Please send me 2 FREE novels from the Essential Romance or Essential Suspense Collection and my 2 FREE gifts (gifts are worth about $10 retail). After receiving them, if I don't wish to receive any more books, I can return the shipping statement marked "cancel." If I don't cancel, I will receive 4 brand-new novels every month and be billed just $7.49 each in the U.S. or $7.74 each in Canada. That's a savings of at least 17% off the cover price. It's quite a bargain! Shipping and handling is just 50¢ per book in the U.S. and $1.25 per book in Canada.* I understand that accepting the 2 free books and gifts places me under no obligation to buy anything. I can always return a shipment and cancel at any time by calling the number below. The free books and gifts are mine to keep no matter what I decide.

Choose one: ☐ **Essential Romance**
(194/394 MDN GRHV)

☐ **Essential Suspense**
(191/391 MDN GRHV)

Name (please print)

Address   Apt. #

City   State/Province   Zip/Postal Code

Email: Please check this box ☐ if you would like to receive newsletters and promotional emails from Harlequin Enterprises ULC and its affiliates. You can unsubscribe anytime.

Mail to the Harlequin Reader Service:
IN U.S.A.: P.O. Box 1341, Buffalo, NY 14240-8531
IN CANADA: P.O. Box 603, Fort Erie, Ontario L2A 5X3

Want to try 2 free books from another series? Call 1-800-873-8635 or visit www.ReaderService.com.

*Terms and prices subject to change without notice. Prices do not include sales taxes, which will be charged (if applicable) based on your state or country of residence. Canadian residents will be charged applicable taxes. Offer not valid in Quebec. This offer is limited to one order per household. Books received may not be as shown. Not valid for current subscribers to the Essential Romance or Essential Suspense Collection. All orders subject to approval. Credit or debit balances in a customer's account(s) may be offset by any other outstanding balance owed by or to the customer. Please allow 4 to 6 weeks for delivery. Offer available while quantities last.

Your Privacy—Your information is being collected by Harlequin Enterprises ULC, operating as Harlequin Reader Service. For a complete summary of the information we collect, how we use this information and to whom it is disclosed, please visit our privacy notice located at corporate.harlequin.com/privacy-notice. From time to time we may also exchange your personal information with reputable third parties. If you wish to opt out of this sharing of your personal information, please visit readerservice.com/consumerschoice or call 1-800-873-8635. **Notice to California Residents**—Under California law, you have specific rights to control and access your data. For more information on these rights and how to exercise them, visit corporate.harlequin.com/california-privacy.

STRS22R3